A Million To Blow

A Million to Blow Series
Book 1

BLUE SAFFIRE

Perceptive Illusions Publishing, Inc.
Bay Shore, New York

Blue Saffire/Perceptive Illusions Publishing, Inc.
PO BOX 5253
Bay Shore, New York 11706
www.BlueSaffire.com

Publisher's Note: This is a work of fiction. Names, characters, places, and incidents are a product of the author's imagination. Locales and public names are sometimes used for atmospheric purposes. Any resemblance to actual people, living or dead, or to businesses, companies, events, institutions, or locales is completely coincidental.

Ordering Information:
Quantity sales. Special discounts are available on quantity purchases by corporations, associations, and others. For details, contact the "Special Sales Department" at the address above.

A Million To Blow/ Blue Saffire. – 2nd ed.
ISBN 978-1-941924-16-7

When the two become one, nothing is impossible. We complete each other. Two parts of the whole.

–Blue Saffire

First Sight

Clayton

I hate these events. My mother is the only reason I'm here. Only she can get me to New York for some bullshit like this.

This benefit isn't even one of the deserving ones. However, my mother doesn't know her best friend's son is an asshat who'd rather make up a fake charity to support his drug habit than actually find a legit source of income.

I grab a flute of champagne from a passing tray as I casually stroll the large ballroom. My uninterested expression wards off most conversations. I'm making my second pass around the room as a stunning woman in a purple gown catches my attention.

Unfortunately, Dexter Reed is breathing down her neck. I can't stand this prick. He thinks he's God's gift to the world. He doesn't even have the funds to back his arrogance, he's been coasting for years.

I move a little closer, wanting to learn more about the gorgeous woman. She has this vibe about her. Her long dark hair cascades like silk over her shoulder. When she turns her face my way, I'm blown away. Her face is as alluring as her body. Her brown skin has a glow about it.

She's stunning. Her lips, her eyes. I want to peel that dress from her body and devour every inch of her, but I'm Clayton Hennessy.

I learned a long time ago that I can't give in to every beauty I see. I need to learn more about her. I need to know if she'll be willing to enter my type of arrangement. Especially now.

I can't afford any more scandal. It's been years since the blackmail attempt, but it burned up the last of my trust. Relationships have to be my way or no way.

"Clayton." I turn to find my head of security with his eyes on me.

I point with my glass at the beauty in the purple dress. "Find out who she is."

"I believe that's Sidney James. At least from what I just overheard."

I move in even closer. David follows. However, I'm not paying him much attention, my focus is on Ms. James.

"Listen, I don't know who you think you are or who you think I am, but if you say one more inappropriate thing to me or try to touch me again, I'm going to throat punch you and step right over you like I have no idea what the hell happened," she hisses at Reed.

I purse my lips to keep from laughing. I like her. As a matter of fact, I want her.

"I need to know everything about her."

"I'll get right on it. Your mother is looking for you."

CHAPTER ONE

Problems

Clayton

I sip my drink as I look over my file on Sidney. I already have a plan working in my head. I'll be spending more time in New York, to keep a closer eye on her and her life.

Finding out my cousin was one of her potential clients has rubbed me the wrong way. Wade's an asshole. I don't like the idea of him being anywhere near Sidney.

"That will be all," I say to Levi, my assistant.

"Mr. Brick and Mr. Vault will be here to see you soon."

"Thanks. Send them in when they arrive." I stand and go to my office window, finishing my glass of brandy.

"Sidney, Sidney. I think we'd be great together. All I need is a little patience. I'll have you soon enough."

A knock comes at my office door. I turn in time to find Brick and Vault entering. Placing my glass on my desk as I walk by, I meet them to shake hands. They each tug me in for a one-armed hug.

Brick and I go way back. We actually own a few businesses together. I respect the Lost Souls. Their brotherhood reminds me of me and my brothers.

Gregor and Cane mean the world to me. I'd do anything for them. When I met Brick in college, he was a bit standoffish. I pulled him into the fold, and we became the best of friends.

If he needs a favor, I'm there for him and King—someone else I've grown to like. The Lost Souls pulled me in like a brother in my time of need, before I found my footing. King was the one to introduce me to the deal that set the first stepping-stones to my empire.

If King and Brick trust you, I trust you. That's how Valmik or Vault became my lawyer and ally. I guess you can say I'm an honorary Lost Soul in a sense. I offer information and places to bury the bones.

"To what do I owe this visit?" I say as I round my desk and retake my seat.

"You always have a word for us when the smoke rises. We thought we'd return the favor," Brick says.

"Oh?"

"Those stopped permits I've been having have one thing in common," he continues.

"What's that?"

"You. Every single one of them is a project I've entered with you. Took a minute to connect the dots, but now it all makes sense."

I sit up in my seat and fold my hands in front of me. "Did you find where the problem is coming from?"

"We have some thoughts. Your recent increase in investments through Burlington Roth Financial came up. You tripled your profile, and it's now a topic of discussion."

I bare my teeth. That has nothing to do with my real estate investments and I don't know why the two are coming up at all. Yes, I tripled my investments, but that's because I learned Sidney works for Steinway & Schwartz and she's great with money. I wanted to see what she could do.

"I've made some changes. I don't see what business that is of anyone's."

"Do you think this could be coming from your father?" Brick questions.

I fall back and think this through. My father loathes the fact that my brothers and I have made a way for ourselves but I don't think the old bastard would go this far.

"Listen, Vault. Sidney James is the name of the account manager I ran those funds through. She's in charge of my portfolio. If this is my father or someone wanting to fuck with me, I need you to keep an eye out for her name. You hear or see it, I want to be the first to know."

I get the feeling I may have just shined a light on Sidney, I wish I hadn't. However, if they go after her, it may be my way in. She'll need me and I'll be there waiting.

"Got it. Sidney James. I'll keep an eye out," Vault says.

CHAPTER TWO

Small Escape

Sidney

Three years later…

New York City summertime shopping on Madison Avenue —there's nothing like it. While I move between my favorite shops, the fumes coming from the big old city buses make me feel alive. From the reflection in the window, my oversized tan sun hat and huge black leather handbag speak of the mood I'm in, not just the need to block the sun from pounding down on me.

My cocoa-brown skin can't take all this heat. As I enter another shop, the arctic blast from the air conditioning hits me in the face. I sigh in relief. It's more than welcome. I think I've soaked right through my cotton blouse.

I've been in a mood to go on a shopping spree ever since the big event. That shit still has me in a fog, but oh well. I shove that thought right back where it belongs. The back of my mind.

I always take care of myself and come out on top. This time was no different, even though they intended to crush me. I smile because I got the last laugh.

The atmosphere in this store is like heaven on earth, it's exactly what I need. The fresh, welcoming scent, the music, the neat and inviting displays and shelves. I hate messy stores.

I remove my hat, holding it in my right hand with my bag. I look like I'm running from the paparazzi. Well, that may not be far from the truth, if things get any worse for me.

Stay positive, Sidney.

I want to escape from the last two weeks and finally find some peace. One of my favorite songs is playing through the speakers, drawing me further into the ambience of the store. I make my way to a rack of gorgeous stretch jeans. The black denim fabric has a shine that sets off the burgundy stitching.

"Yes, this is exactly what I needed for tonight," I murmur to myself.

I still have no clue where Chloe is taking me. Chloe is the only friend I have here in New York who I can count on. She understands me and doesn't judge.

As my thoughts turn from Chloe, I find myself lost in the world of shopping. It's exactly where I want to be. No distractions, just me and my power to purchase. It's a beautiful thing.

At least those are my thoughts, before being brought back to the real world. While browsing the store, I suddenly feel a small hand on my arm. I stop myself from hissing at the rude disruption.

"Hi, Sidney, how are you?"

I'd know that annoying ass voice anywhere. Oh, my God, I can't stand this chick. Of all the people to run into, why her?

"Hey, Amanda," I say her name with no excitement at all. She's a real dickhead.

As phony as they come. Always in someone's business with her mouth running to anyone ready to listen. I've found her gossiping about many since I've known her.

"How are you? Sorry to hear about you being let go by Steinway & Schwartz."

"It's okay, Amanda. It's been almost a year and six months, I'm fine."

"Oh, okay, because I couldn't believe *the* Sidney James was no longer running around the financial district."

I give her the look of death because this is one of the things I don't want to talk about. I'm free now. I'm ready to move on.

Amanda notices the look but keeps digging. This is why she's such an ass. She just doesn't know when to shut the fuck up.

"Sidney, people have been spreading horrible rumors about you being broke and depressed."

Bitch please, runs through my head as I purse my lips to convey the same sentiments. I lean on one hip and narrow my eyes. I start to count back from ten before I lose my last piece of good sense on this heifer, but she still continues.

"I couldn't stand by while they dragged your name in the mud."

Yeah, sure you didn't, Amanda. Who the fuck does she think she's fooling?

"How is the divorce going?"

My lips turn up into a smirk as she stops in her tracks. Her face looks like she's seen a ghost. *Gotcha.* Always ready to be in someone else's business, but not ready to have her own put out there.

Amanda has no idea. I still have eyes and ears in the district. This bit of information was sort of swept under the rug, something she's been keeping a tight rein on. The silence from her lips is priceless.

"Sidney, I have no idea what you're talking about. Patrick and I are better than ever. I'm meeting him for lunch in twenty minutes."

I want to laugh so hard. She didn't know that shit was coming. She has no clue, I'm not the one to be played with.

"Okay, Amanda, have a great day. I have some important people to talk to today. I have to run."

"Okay, talk to you later, doll. You be good, Sidney."

Underneath my breath, I let out a slight, ever so lovely, *shut the fuck up, Amanda.* It feels better than therapy, if you ask me.

I quickly go to pay for my jeans, then leave in a hurry. I still need shoes, but I need to know from Chloe if we'll be on our feet all night. As soon as I finish my thought, my phone starts to ring. She's always right on time.

"Hey, Sid. Where are you?" she says before I can even say hello.

"*Chloeeeee,*" I squeal into the phone. "I'm running errands in the city, looking for shoes for tonight. Hold on, Chlo." I reach to fix the bag my jeans are in because my phone is slipping out of my hand. "Okay, now I can hear you loud and clear. I was just about to call you and ask what kind of shoes I should wear tonight?"

"Sid, you can wear any type of shoes you want, just make sure they're superhot. Tonight, I'm getting you laid. You need some cheer-up, things-will-get-better dick."

Sometimes the things that come out of Chloe's mouth are just unreal. I stop in my tracks, my mouth falling open. A much-needed laugh slips free from my lips.

"No, Chloe, I don't need any cheer-up dick."

A man standing next to me overhears my words and starts to laugh. He damn near spits his coffee on a lady standing in front of us waiting for the red light to change. I roll my eyes and grin at my friend's bad influence.

"Say what you want, Sid. Honey, you need some dick. I can tell."

"Hey, if plans for tonight involve me getting drilled by some strange man, then I'm not going," I huff into the phone.

"No, no, no, Sid. I'm just joking. You have to come out. I have a surprise for you, nothing bad. I promise," she rushes out the plea.

"Okay, fine. I know I'm in good hands," I relent, rolling my eyes again.

"Come on, Sid. You have me sounding like I raise virgins on a farm."

You see? Comments like that are why I'm always laughing when Chloe is around. Who the hell thinks of stuff like that to say? When I need to escape and forget about my issues, I either talk to her, shop or write.

"I'm about to jump in a cab, you fool. I still have to get these shoes. I'll call you when I get home."

"Okay, talk to ya later, hun."

Clayton

"Have you and your brothers considered the terms of my agreement?" My father asks.

I puff on the cigar he gave me to go with this smooth brandy. When we're not at each other's throats, we've enjoyed this common bond.

It doesn't happen often because of this very conversation. He would love nothing more than for me and my brothers to marry one of the women he's tried to palm off on us. Like the rest of us Hennessy men, my father has control issues.

We've made our own way and come from under his thumb, but he's still found a way to wrangle us in. I actually have respect for the old bastard, he got this one by me. However, even if I didn't have such deep-seated trust issues, I wouldn't be interested in any of the women he has tried to saddle me with.

"Why is it so important to you for us to be married? Must you control everything? Let this go. We're paving our own lives."

"You and your brothers think I'm out to control you. At one time that may have been true. Now, I'm just a father who wants to see his sons happy, a man who wants to see his legacy live on. The Hennessy name can't end with me."

"Then back off. Stop trying to dictate our every move. It's not going to work. I'll find a way out, I always do. I'm not Brodi or Cane."

He scoffs. "*Clooney* and Cane are an entirely different story. You have your shit together. You should start a family. Stop looking at this as a trap."

I bare my teeth as he pointedly calls my older brother by his first name. He's the only one who does, and he knows how much Gregor hates it.

He continues when I remain silent. "You're thirty-eight, Clayton. How long do you expect your mother to wait before she becomes a grandmother?"

I stand, stub out my cigar, and button my suit jacket. I'm done here. This man knows damn well why I am the way I am. I'm so far from being able to marry anyone...I don't have it in me to have that type of relationship.

Sidney comes to mind. Little does he know, I plan to play my father's game. Although, I'm questioning myself when it comes to the one woman I want. I might be playing with fire, but I know how to get what I want. I grin and turn to leave.

"You never know, I might surprise you. You have a good day, Dad."

He sighs but says nothing more. I make my way out of the house, not even bothering to look for my mother. I need to check on my plans. I check my phone and see my assistant Levi has confirmed the delivery of the package I placed him in charge of.

"Where to?" David asks as I climb into my waiting car.

I smile. Tonight I have an important meeting. I'm going home to get ready for the meeting I've been waiting three years for.

"Take me home. Did you find Brodi? Does he know about tonight?"

"Check your texts. He had to leave, but he wants you to move forward as planned. I took care of the keys. They'll be waiting for you tonight."

"Thanks."

The invitations have been sent. All I have to do now is wait. It's been three long years. I've watched from afar, waiting for this day. Vault has come through on a number of occasions. Every time Sidney's name comes up, I know about it.

It's my only regret, bringing this shitstorm into her life. A storm I plan to fix. There's just one hole I need to figure out. For that to happen, I need to put my plan into play.

I need to connect the dots as to why our paths are crossing the way they are? I know her enemy is mine, but who the fuck do we have in common?

"Well, that's what we plan to find out," I murmur to myself.

Sidney needs to come to me. From there I have it covered.

CHAPTER THREE

The Invite

Sidney

After I finally found some heels for tonight, I made it home. Now that I'm in the apartment, I've kicked off my shoes and have myself a glass of wine. I've been in kind of a funk after seeing Amanda.

It's been almost a year and six months since I worked at Steinway & Schwartz, but I loved my job so much. Even to the last day, before the indictment. I was the manager of one of the biggest ETF funds in the world.

I helped many corporations and individuals invest their money and set up for retirement. The rush I would get to see ten percent returns in a quarter can never be replaced.

However, when the people upstairs were under investigation by the US Securities and Exchange Commission, it changed everything. My life was turned upside down because I was framed for skimming funds from the ETF account. None of it made sense. I worked at Steinway & Schwartz for ten years and I never had any problems.

While reading one of the monthly statements, I noticed a few things that seemed out of place. I took action and mentioned it, but I was ignored by Patrick Dupont. Yes, Amanda's Patrick, the very same husband.

He is the main account manager at Steinway & Schwartz. He always felt threatened by me for some reason. Like I was gunning for his spot or something.

I never paid him any mind, until those statements. I always felt like he knew something but wasn't talking. Once the Securities and Exchange Commission named me as a suspect in the fraud and embezzlement, I couldn't believe it.

I was in shock. They froze all of my accounts so they could trace my money. I kept telling them they had the wrong person.

I was on trial for a year and five months. I wouldn't wish this on my worst enemy. In the last two weeks, I've been so stressed out as I've been awaiting the verdict. I never felt as much joy in my life as I did when they said not guilty.

You start looking at life differently when you're facing twenty-five years to life, fed time. The one good thing that came out of me being cleared is that I won't lose my license. However, at this time, I have no desire to work in the district.

At thirty-two, I made a promise to myself to go and do what makes me happy and be my own boss. Although, I must say it felt good to see all of my clients vouching for me.

I didn't realize how many people I made rich. Just imagine if I would've put that same effort into me. Where would I be?

Should I go back to my old life? I thought about it plenty of times, but I can't. Not knowing how easy it was for them to throw me under the bus.

They held my money in my accounts all this time. I had big plans for that money. Do you know what effects that has had on a shopaholic like myself? That shit had me so mad, it was like they had me in prison without bars.

All in all, everything hasn't been so bad. I went back to my first love. I've had a love for writing ever since I was a kid. I used to write wonderful short stories with different characters. I started reading these erotic books and let me tell you—wow. I don't know what happened, but it woke up something inside of me.

After my life exploded, I needed an outlet for all my frustration. I started my very first blog, full of short stories and erotic tales. I knew I had a talent for writing, and it was time to let it be known. Although, I do use a pen name. Some of the stuff I write can be kind of crazy.

I couldn't believe the amount of money I made in the first three months. I sold short stories from my blog as well as creating a membership. In six months, I had a thousand subscribers. Nothing but loyal readers and good money. Who would've thought at thirty-two years old, my childhood dream would pay off after all?

"Big dreams, new things, Sid," I murmur to myself as I muse.

Chloe is the only person who knows the blog belongs to me. According to her, I have a lot of sexual tension. That's why it's so easy for me to write seven blog posts a day. I don't know, she might be right. I laugh to myself every time she says it.

As I walk into my bedroom, I noticed the time. I hurry up and jump in the shower before Chloe gets here. Despite all my shopping, I decide to wear a simple little black dress, nixing the whole jean ensemble. I've been dying to wear this dress. I might as well wear it tonight.

The shoes that I bought today are going to go perfectly with it. They're the hottest pair of six-inch spike heels. They're gold and strap around the ankle.

While admiring my shoes and looking myself over in the mirror, my mind drifts. I wonder what this surprise is that Chloe keeps talking about. For the first time in a long time, I'm so excited and can't even put my finger on why.

Just like clockwork, my doorbell rings. It has to be Chloe. As soon as I open the door, she whistles at me like a New York City construction worker.

"Wow, you looking good, miss," she catcalls in her best construction worker voice as I spin. "Look at that booty. Sid, I would love to have your shape, that dress is hot."

"Thanks, hon, you're looking great yourself. It looks like you're letting the girls hang loose tonight, huh?"

"I can't help it. These triple D's have a mind of their own," she sings, giving me a sly smile.

The blue-and-cream dress with its deep neckline fits her to a T. Her long legs are on display, looking amazing. I wish I was five-eleven like her, instead of five-two. She has on a bad pair of custom-made ankle boots that match her dress. This girl can dress her ass off. I always said she should've done something with fashion.

"Chloe, you look amazing. You look like a runway model," I compliment, waving her into the apartment.

We walk into my living room laughing, as Chloe sits down, while I finish getting ready. I need to know what the heck is going on and where we're going? What's the big secret?

"Hey, Sid, I heard you ran into Amanda today," she calls as I'm in my bathroom getting ready.

"Yes, I forgot to tell you about that wonderful encounter with that asshole. She had the nerve to say, *I can't believe they let the Sidney James go.* I was five seconds from punching her in her throat," I reply, tasting the bitter encounter as I speak the words.

"I can't with her," Chloe scoffs from the living area.

"Well, now I don't have to. She just gets under my skin," I hiss, feeling the tension coil within.

There's a pause in the other room. Chloe doesn't say anything for a few beats. I knit my brows, but then her words reach me.

"You see, that's why I don't bring up work stuff around you. You still sound so angry. Although, I can tell you this. Everyone at the office really misses you and it seems like you made some powerful friends."

There's regret and worry in her voice. Something about her words triggers my curiosity. I walk out of the bathroom, wondering what the heck she's talking about.

During the trial, I had a few hedge fund firms who wanted me to come and join them as a consultant, but I turned them down. What powerful friends could Chloe be referring to?

"I know that look, Sid. Please don't get in your head about this. It's a good thing and it's the reason we're going out tonight. We've been invited to Club Dream. It's an exclusive club that only the elites of the elites are invited to," she beams, bouncing in place.

"What the hell did you get yourself into, Chloe?" I narrow my eyes at her, placing my hands on my hips.

"I didn't do anything, you did it. During your trial, you had no idea that Burlington Roth Financial helped you get your not-guilty verdict. I didn't want to bring any of this stuff up because I knew it was weighing so heavily on you." Her eyes shift to true concern.

Chloe's right. I couldn't even think straight when I was in the middle of that mess. Right at this moment, I could be serving twenty-five years for something I didn't even do. Yet, her words aren't making any sense.

"Well, explain to me why Burlington Roth Financial was so concerned about me." I tilt my head with the question.

"Sid, do you realize how much money you've helped them make in the last seven years? The man, the myth, and the legend, Clayton Hennessey, himself sent his assistant to get to you. I was shocked when he handed me this letter for you," she replies, pulling a letter from her clutch and holding it out in my direction.

Chloe hands me a sleek black envelope with silver embossing on it. It's beautiful, it looks so rich and elegant. The writing on the front says, *To Sidney James from Clayton Hennessy.*

I opened the letter with shaking hands. As of late, I've only found trouble in the financial district. I fear the price my freedom has incurred without my knowledge. Just when I thought it was over, my gut tells me this mess has only begun. Yet, I read the letter anyway.

Dear Sidney,

I wanted to first say that you are a very brave woman. I know it was hard having the feds breathing down your neck. I admired your strength during your time of uncertainty. I was personally shocked to hear the news about you. I have heard nothing but good things from my staff and even my own clients.

You may not realize it, but you have helped us make well over 700 million dollars during your time with Steinway & Schwartz. I couldn't stand by and watch you get railroaded by your own firm. I made a few calls on your behalf to the judge who presided over your case. I want to personally thank you, as well as celebrate your victory.

I'm inviting you to my club, so we can finally get a chance to speak to each other. I would totally understand if you're not up to it, but if you are, the instructions and directions are in the other envelope.

Sincerely Yours,
Clayton Hennessey

After reading the letter, I look at Chloe to see if this is some sort of sick joke. Her face is serious as she looks back at me. I can't believe this.

"Chloe, is this real? You better stop playing with me." I narrow my eyes at her.

"I couldn't make this shit up. There was a letter for me as well. I didn't read yours. My letter just stated that we were invited to Club Dream and I was your guest."

"You said you had a surprise, but this...this is unreal. Clayton Hennessey is worth trillions of dollars."

"I know, Sid, and from what I heard, the man is drop-dead gorgeous. One of my friends from school works at Burlington Roth now." Chloe fans her face. "She said she saw him once and she couldn't even talk because all she could do was stare at him.

"She said she had to run to the bathroom to change her panties because he had her wet like an open umbrella. I never laughed so hard in my life."

I roll right over her crazy talk. "Chloe, I've never heard of Club Dream. Whoa, this is a little too much for me."

"Girl, this is a good thing. He just wants to meet you and thank you. How bad can this be? I say you go and say thank you. I don't know what you did, but whatever it was, it was good," she replies, with bright, almost pleading eyes.

All of a sudden, I'm so nervous and my stomach is in knots. I have no idea why. I rush to check my makeup and make sure my hair looks right.

As of a few months ago, I've been rocking a short lace front. I wanted to try out the short little bob before committing. Especially when it comes to the color, it's jet black with the tips dyed blue. I've been in an adventurous mood lately.

"Oh, my God, Chloe. The myth really wants to meet us?" I gush when I return to the living room.

"I know, right. I need to see if everything I've heard is all hype." She wiggles her brows.

I shake my head in wonder. "Are we overdressed for this club or underdressed?"

"Relax, you look great. That dress fits you like a glove, but I do have a question. How did you fit all that ass into that little black dress? You might give this man a heart attack," she teases.

"Stop it," I pout. "See, now I want to change or not even go at all."

"No, you're going. You need to go out and socialize with the opposite sex. You might have some juicy stuff to add to that sex blog you've been working on. I never knew there were so many horny women sitting around reading about cocks getting sucked.

"Who would have thought you would make way more money writing a sex blog? I tell you this, if I don't get my raise, I'll be right next to you writing…*as his cock grew in my hand, I knew it was time to plunge his man meat into my wet, hot mouth.*"

"Oh, shit, Chloe, that was good. Can I use that?" I chuckle.

"You gotta be fucking kidding me." Her mouth pops open in disbelief.

"I'm not kidding, but I'd tweak it a bit and can you please stop calling it a sex blog? It's erotic tales and short stories, it's not just hard-core sex," I sigh.

"Whatever, sex is sex. I don't care if you try to repackage it." She waves me off. "Let's get ready to go. I need a drink before we get there."

This is classic Chloe. She's always ready for a new adventure. I don't even know why I bother. She's always going to be Chloe, straight, no chaser. Someone has to reel this all in.

"What…a drink? No way, we don't even know where we're going. We need to be sober. Let me read these instructions and directions. Why would we need instructions to get into a club?"

"It's a secret club. Invite only, we might need a password or something," she says, with way too much excitement for me.

I shake my head, but give in. I know how annoying Chloe can get when she wants to have things go her way. From the look in her eyes, I know she's been looking forward to this.

"Okay, let's get going. This should be a very interesting night," I mumble the last part to myself.

CHAPTER FOUR

The Meet

Sidney

While driving to the club, I have all types of thoughts running through my mind. At this moment in my life, I don't trust anyone connected to Steinway & Schwartz. Should I even be going to talk to this man?

What does he really want? I hope he's not trying to get me back into hedging. *Nope, I'm not doing it.* I'm on my way to being in such a good space in my life. I don't need any distractions.

When we make it to the front door of the club, we follow the instructions sent. I knock three times on the inconspicuous black door. Waiting, I bite down on my lip nervously.

When the bouncer opens the door, I take a step back, bumping into Chloe. She wraps her arms around my waist as we both have to tip our heads back to look up at the bouncer. He's a big motherfucker.

I roam my gaze over him and start to have second thoughts about going into this place. The hell. My curiosity has burned out. I turn to leave, but that damn Chloe opens her big fat mouth.

"Roman gods roam the streets. Submission is required to have them revealed."

I come out of my shock and step on her foot, but I'm too late.

"Shut up," I hiss.

"Ow, what the hell did you do that for?" she whines.

"Do you not see this guy? I'm taking my ass home," I growl back.

"Mr. Hennessey has been waiting for your arrival. I have instructions to take you straight upstairs," the bouncer booms in a deep, throaty voice.

"Ah, Fuck," I groan.

Chloe rolls her eyes at me, turning me to face the entrance of the club once again. She has to shove me forward because I can't get my feet to respond to my commands. I stumble inside behind the bouncer as he leads the way.

This place is beautiful, everything about it screams opulence. I try hard not to trip while looking around and following the bouncer. The music is loud, but not unbearable. The dance floor is packed.

I relax a little. This place doesn't look as seedy as I had imagined it would. *I can handle this.* I nod to myself.

We walk up a gorgeous set of stairs onto a catwalk. The sparkling gold, translucent stairs and the black, iron and glass catwalk provide a breathtaking view over the entire club. You can see everything.

It also breaks off into four directions when you get to the center. The bouncer takes a left and we follow. As stunning as the view is, I start to pray that this catwalk doesn't start swinging, because I hate heights. We get to the door at the end and enter a huge room that has burgundy velvet walls and tables with gold-and-black tablecloths.

It's like we're in a skybox at a football game or something. There have to be at least twelve people in here with us. I take notice of a table set with platters of chocolate-covered strawberries and bottles of champagne chilling. A sign is in the center that reads, *Reserved for Sidney and Chloe.*

When I get closer, I can see there are six huge bottles of Armand de Brignac Brut Rose Champagne NV 6L Rated 91 W&S in the oval bucket anchoring the center of the table. I lift my brow. Nice, very nice.

We take a seat and I really have a look around us. It's a lot to take in at once. My mind has started to do the calculations on the offering before us.

That's sixty thousand dollars' worth of champagne, just for the two of us. I start to get nervous, but when I look at Chloe, I laugh at the smile on her face.

"Oh my God, this place is a dream for real. I didn't even know this place was in this building. I walk past here all the time."

"I'm speechless. Like, this isn't even real to me. We have a table reserved for us, with sixty thousand dollars' worth of champagne. I know how these guys from the district think, I'm not comfortable with this," I whisper nervously.

"Listen, just give me the word if you want to leave. We can go," she offers, but I can see the disappointment in her eyes.

As soon as Chloe finishes her statement, a gorgeous, huge, muscle-bound guy comes over to us. He has to be six-five, easy. He bends down and whispers in my ear.

"Mr. Hennessy would like for you both to join him." His voice rumbles low.

I nod my head as I pull Chloe away from those personal bottles. We had an agreement, no getting wasted tonight. I don't know what we're about to get into. We need to be levelheaded.

I think my grip on Chloe's arm is a little too tight. She confirms my thoughts when she turns to me, narrowing her gaze. She wiggles her arm in my hold.

"Relax," she hisses in my ear. "Stop holding my arm like we go together."

We enter another gorgeous room, but this one looks more like an office. There's a black leather couch with red pillows on it and matching accent chairs. The walls are black-and-red suede with gold stitching. A huge sparkling chandelier lights the entire room, it looks more like diamonds than crystals.

The music is no more once the door closes behind us. I can only feel a little bit of the bass in my feet as I stand surveying the room. Behind a huge desk is a door that draws my attention just as a voice comes from behind it.

"Have my guests arrived?" A rich, velvety voice fills the air.

Chloe leans over to me to whisper. "Wow, I need to find out who the interior designer was for this club. Why didn't I think of suede walls for my bedroom?"

We both laugh as the bouncer who followed us into the room offers us a seat. He opens the door that grabbed my attention, peeking his head in.

"Yes, sir, Mr. Hennessey. Ms. James and Ms. Sinclair are here," he replies, before moving back away from the door.

"Thank you," the owner of the sexy voice replies as he steps through the door.

When he enters the room, it's like time has stopped. I don't know if he notices, but at the sight of him, both Chloe's and my jaws drop. Oh, my God, the descriptions of this man were all wrong. He looks like he's been chiseled from Mount Hot Damn.

"Now that's my type," Chloe purrs. I turn to her and shoot daggers with my eyes.

His deep, dark, sexy chuckle draws my attention back to him before I can respond to Chloe. Man, on second glance he's hotter than I first thought. His dark-red hair and gray eyes match his perfect sharp face.

The light from the chandelier alludes to the red in his hair, otherwise, I would have thought it to be a dark brown. The man is just delicious in every way. It's like Michael Fassbender and Travis Kelce had a baby named Clayton.

You can tell he takes care of his body from the outline of his broad muscular shoulders beneath his suit jacket. He has to be six-five or more. He's almost as tall as the bouncer at the entrance door.

His suit fits him just right. I know tailor-made suits when I see them, and Clayton is wearing the fuck out of the fabric blessed just for his appetizing frame.

Clayton's skin looks so smooth, with a light tan, not that orange look I used to see in the office. In addition, even from this distance, he smells so good. I have to make sure I'm not drooling or making a fool of myself. I think my panties have become soaked in the five seconds since he appeared. No man has ever stopped me in my tracks like this.

"Hello, Ms. James and Ms. Sinclair. Thank you for coming this evening." His voice rumbles with his words.

I'm so busy checking out the myth, I forget Chloe is even with me. Her schoolgirl giggle breaks me out of my trance. I look to her and frown. *Someone needed to bring it down a notch.* Who am I kidding? This is Chloe.

"Thank you for having us as your guests, Mr. Hennessy. Chloe and I love what you've done with this club. It's very beautiful."

"Please, Ms. James. Call me Clayton," he replies in that voice that was meant for dirty talk and so much more.

He walks over to us and shakes both our hands. I've never seen hands so big in my life. He could cup my whole head or palm my ass with one. I would love to experience the latter.

"Did you guys have any of the champagne I had sent to your table? I had the chefs put together something sweet for you as well. I hope you had a chance to enjoy the spread." His words come out directed to us both, but those eyes remain on me.

"No, we were brought straight to you," Chloe says breathily, garnering my glance and an eye roll this time.

I have no idea why I'm hating. Chloe always turns it on thick when she sees someone she's down to fuck. Something in me just doesn't like the idea of her being in this man's bed. I shove that aside and turn my attention back to Clayton.

This man moves with so much confidence, like he knows he owns the world. I can't take my eyes off him as he hands us two champagne glasses. I'm so entranced, I take the glass without any further thought.

"Ms. James, I sent correspondence through your friend, Ms. Sinclair because I knew you were going through some serious matters. I hope I didn't offend you in any way. I just had to meet you," he says smoothly.

"No, I'm not offended. You can call me Sidney. I am a bit curious as to why you wanted to meet me. I was a regular fund manager in the district, going through the motions." I shrug.

"I beg to differ, Sidney. Nothing about you seems regular," he replies and licks his thick lips.

Did this man just make a pass at me? Oh, God, I can't believe I'm saying this, but I would take him right now on his desk. Damn, I need to get the hell out of here.

Clayton shifts his attention to Chloe, who's sitting in awe of him. I think I even notice him chuckle to himself. He turns toward her, an amused look in his eyes. I hadn't realized she had taken a seat.

"Excuse me, Ms. Sinclair, but are you okay?" His voice comes out like a caress each time he speaks. It's spellbinding.

It sure seems to have worked a spell on Chloe. I bite back a laugh. I don't know what is wrong with her. She's sitting there with her eyes all glazed over. I know something crazy is about to come out of her mouth.

"No, no, I'm fine. Just like you, Clayton," she says, fanning her face. "And please, call me Chloe. This might sound funny, but please don't laugh at what I'm about to say."

Oh, my goodness, here she goes. I brace myself for this. My girl is a nut and anything, and I mean anything, will come out of that mouth.

"We've always heard rumors about you and what you look like. You know the rumor mill can be all over the place. I thought you were some old guy with a hot wife, forty years your junior. One person said you were young and gorgeous. I think they were all dead wrong."

Clayton leans back on his heels and gives Chloe a real stern look as he goes to sip from his glass. That's when she blurted out. "You're angelic."

Clayton pulls his glass from his lips as he almost spits his drink across the room. We all roar with laughter, even the bouncers laugh from the corners of the room. Clayton can't stop laughing, he places his drink down.

"Well, Chloe, I have never been told I'm angelic," he says, with a wicked grin. "I guess you can thank my parents for that. My mother always said my brothers and I get it from her."

Chloe's eyes light up as her back shoots straight as a soldier standing at attention. I think I actually see saliva drop onto her breast. I want to cover my face in embarrassment for my crazy friend.

"Wait a minute, you have brothers? I need another drink. If you don't mind me asking, how many do you have?"

"I have two, I'm the second oldest."

Believe it or not, Chloe has broken the ice. The tension leaves the room as we converse. I feel less nervous. He seems like a great person, but I still have questions.

What does this man want with me? Is this a setup coming from Steinway & Schwartz? Hopefully, the questions I have will be answered.

I don't know, but I feel like I'm about to walk into something new and unexpected. Whenever I get focused on myself and my life, things get confusing and out of whack.

Chloe says it's because I'm always waiting for the other shoe to drop.

While we're talking, the bouncer who led us in here goes to whisper something into Clayton's ear. Clayton's face lights up like a kid on Christmas as he walks over to his desk. He logs into his computer as he calls out to us.

"Sidney and Chloe, I do apologize. I have to handle something quickly. Please make yourselves comfortable, I'll be back in five."

"Okay," Chloe and I say in perfect sync.

He exits the room with extra pep in his step. That man is wearing that suit, I can't lie. I check his butt out when he walks out. It's been seven years since I've had any type of relationship. I think my hormones are raging.

"Sid, I told you there was nothing to worry about. Clayton is a nice guy." Chloe breaks into my thoughts.

"Yes, he seems nice. Didn't you say this was an exclusive club?" I change the subject.

"It is, did you not see the *Mission Impossible* entrance and the walk through into this part of the club?" She purses her lips and lifts a brow at me.

"I know, but it seemed considerably crowded for a place only a few people know about. I thought it would be a small setting, sort of like a lounge," I muse.

"This place is huge. While we were walking, I noted that it looked as if there's a separate section of the club," she says thoughtfully.

"I noticed that too. I wonder what's on that side. Did you see the bouncers in front of those doors? They were huge." My eyes round as I look pointedly at Chloe.

"I caught a glimpse of the people going back there, showing some type of bracelets. Do you think that's some type of illuminati stuff?" Excitement fills my nutty friend's eyes.

I burst out laughing. "You need to stop watching all of them crazy YouTube videos. You said it yourself, this place is exclusive." I pause, lift a brow and shake my head. "What I want to know is, how did you notice all of that? Damn, you're nosy."

We both laugh, but truth be told, I'm even more curious about Club Dream and Clayton Hennessy. I like having Chloe with me because she sees things I don't see when we go out. I know later on, she'll remember something she saw and bring it up in a conversation.

Five minutes later, Clayton comes back with an even bigger smile on his face. There are two files in his hand that he throws on his desk. He pours himself a drink and asks if we want more champagne before turning back to us.

We take another drink, which he has one of his guys hand to us. I know I said no drinking but I'm still processing this night. This place, this man, can you really blame me—every bit helps at this point.

Clayton grabs the files he entered with before coming back to settle in the accent chair across from us. The wolfish grin on his face causes my mind to run off with questions all over again.

I shift in my seat while staring at this overly attractive man. I don't miss that his eyes seem to be devouring me as well, causing me to fidget in my seat some more. He smirks to himself.

"Okay, Chloe and Sidney," he purrs out my name as he locks eyes with me. "I want to share with you why I asked you to meet me tonight."

He hands over the files. One to Chloe and one to myself. Chloe opens hers first and her reaction causes me to pause.

"Oh, fuck yeah," she purrs.

I take in the mischievous look in her eyes and groan. I open my own file and scan the first page. My mouth hits the floor. My eyes snap up to Clayton's as I hiss.

"The fuck!"

Clayton

I lick my lips, as that fire blazes from every single one of her pores. I've wanted Sidney James for a very, very, long time. I've watched and waited. I've bided my time.

Then, when I was ready to stake my claim, that fucking case came out of nowhere. I don't like being blindsided. When Vault came to me with Sidney's name in his mouth, I was furious.

I knew they would come for her eventually. She's too good at what she does, but I didn't think they'd go that route. What happened to Sidney should've never happened on my watch.

After some digging, I found out Sidney and I may have some mutual enemies. Enemies, she's not even aware she has. As a matter of fact, I'm positive she has no clue she has this enemy I've homed in on.

This lack of knowledge is what's going to ensure I get what I want. Sidney and I need each other. She doesn't know it, but I'm the source of her problems. Or at least one of them.

I had planned to step in sooner, but this woman is very interesting to watch. I thought I would be able to swoop in as her knight in shining armor. Surely, she would need me.

However, she never did. Her assets were frozen, she lost her job and her stellar reputation, but she has moved around for a year and almost six months as if she hadn't had a care in the world. I found that fascinating, which led me to look even deeper into Ms. Sidney James, a.k.a. Azure Kiss.

Yes, Ms. Kiss has been writing her way to the security I thought I would be able to offer. She hasn't needed anyone because she's been exploring a whole new world. However, the cat is out of the bag.

They're coming for my naughty girl. Someone needs to cover their ass and they have a hard-on to do it with Sidney's pretty brown derriere on full display. That's a big mistake on their behalf. The only one who will have that ass on display will be me and not for the world to see.

Oh, the plans I have.

I want to know if my dear Sidney writes from experience or pure desire to experience the dirty things she dreams up. My lips curl into a smile. From the look on her face, I do believe it's the latter.

I settle back in my seat, resting one arm across the back of the chair while bringing my drink to my lips with the other hand. I'm in no rush to respond to Sidney's little outburst. I'm more than amused by Chloe's response.

I have my reasons for inviting Chloe along tonight. It was already my understanding that she would be the easier sell. I shouldn't have been surprised at the request for her presence.

My brother has a thing for redheads. Chloe will just be the first brown-skinned redhead I've ever seen him with. I run my hand through my own dark-amber locks.

When I speak, it's slow, drawing in my prey. "Is there a problem with the number?" I ask, lifting a brow.

My eyes travel down the length of Sidney's body. I can't wait to unwrap her with my hands. My eyes will do for now, just for now.

"Excuse me," she hisses.

"Is the number not to your liking? I thought it was a reasonable sum," I reply.

"Do I look like some type of fucking prostitute to you?" she says through tight lips.

"No, you do not. However, I will stop you right there." I slide forward in my seat and pin her with a glare. "Watch your mouth, Sidney. I will not tolerate disrespect. Talk to me, tell me what's wrong. How can I make this better for you?"

"*This*...what the hell is *this*?" She snarls and tosses the file onto the table before her.

She folds her arms across her chest, pushing those luscious breasts together in an appetizing way. My jaw tightens as she continues to use language I will not stand for. I already knew I would have some taming to do with this one.

It's the reason I chose her. It's how she came up on my radar. Sidney has this blatant disrespect for authority. It's what made her great at what she did for Steinway & Schwartz.

She made me millions with that *just don't give a fuck* attitude. She made those bastards even more before they tried to steamroll her. Her ability to dismiss those who would normally try to dismiss her is very entertaining.

When I first laid eyes on Sidney three years ago, at that benefit my mother asked me to support, I was blown away by her beauty, but the words I overheard her hiss at Reed tugged at something inside me. That was the beginning of my obsession.

I knew from that night I wanted Sidney and I would have her. It was all a matter of time and patience. I've been more than patient, but what I won't be, is disrespected.

I stand and squat before Sidney, coming eye to eye with her. I place my fingers under her chin and tip her head back. She glares back at me with surprise and defiance in her eyes.

"This pretty mouth will only talk dirty when I'm pleasing you to the point of insanity. Other than that, you will watch your mouth, I'm not above spanking that juicy ass of yours," I say huskily.

"Holy shit," Chloe breathes beside us.

Sidney tugs her chin from my fingers, but she doesn't move to get up from her seat. Instead, I notice that her thighs tighten together. I can't help the grin that tugs my lips up.

"I see we understand each other." I reach to brush a strand of hair behind her ear. She's cut off the longer locks she had when I first saw her. This bob will do, I can still grasp a handful. "Now, tell me the problem."

"You can't be serious," she replies, her words coming out husky, almost breathless.

Annoyance flashes in her eyes. Most likely, she's annoyed with her response to me. It's clear in her gaze and her body, she's curious about me. More than curious, I'd say. That's just what I want.

I tilt my head to the side and give her a crooked grin. "I'm as serious as it gets. Now, tell me, what's the problem?"

She snorts and moves back away from me, trying to give herself some space, I assume. I won't be making that so easy for her. I remain crouched in front of her.

"Let me get this straight," she begins, then pauses. Suddenly, it's as if I can see her thoughts shift. She turns to Chloe. "No, wait, let me see that file."

Chloe smirks, but she hands over the file without a word. Sidney licks her lips and eyes me while she opens the folder in her hands. Her gaze drops to the pages, I watch as she scans them. Her lips purse, her brows wrinkle, then those full lips part and fall open.

"The fuck," she repeats. "Are you out of your mind?" she says, looking up at me, then she turns to Chloe. "I already know you are. You don't see what's wrong with this?"

"Nope," Chloe says, popping the *p* and shrugging her shoulders. "Looks like what I need to kick-start my life in every way."

I give a short chuckle. "Tell me, what do you find wrong with it?" I say smoothly. "And watch your mouth."

"Mr. Hennessy, I am not desperate for money or attention. Neither am I a prostitute. I find your offer insulting and disrespectful," she sasses, with her eyes narrowed on me.

"Baby, when was the last time you looked into your bank accounts?" I question. "Not your Sidney Lena James accounts, the ones that were just about to be released. I'm talking about the Kiss, Inc. accounts. The ones you had your dear friend Chloe sign off on."

"How the—" she starts, but my look of warning halts her words. She shoves at my chest to be able to rise from her seat.

I lift to my full height with her, not giving her enough room to escape me. Yes, I'm patient, but I've waited long enough for this moment. Having Sidney this close, I know I'm not willing to let her walk away. I will accomplish what I set out to do this evening.

She reaches in her clutch and pulls out her phone. I watch her brows wrinkle as she checks her accounts. It takes a few minutes for her to look up at me, but when she does, I see the confusion and the tears that gather.

"What the fuck is going on? What have you done?" she says shakily.

I cup the back of her neck and draw her near, dipping my head to meet her eye to eye. My lips are just a breath away from hers. I can almost taste her.

"When I say watch your mouth, Sidney, I mean it." I crush my lips to hers and kiss her thoroughly. It's not what I'd intended to do, but I can't resist.

She moves her hands to grip the back of my hair as she tries to tug me away. It's a futile effort on her behalf. Her fingers go from tugging to tightening in my hair within seconds. I tighten my hold on her, devouring her sweetness.

My tongue dives into her mouth as she moans against me. I've never had a woman taste so good. I search her mouth with my tongue, seeking every delicious crevice of her warm, welcoming opening.

It's a battle, but I force myself to break the kiss before I lose sight of my plan. My goal isn't to have one night with Sidney James. No, that would be a travesty.

I know if I were to give her one night with the real me, I would lose her forever. No, I have to follow through with the plan. Only the plan will keep Sidney in my life long enough for me to savor her.

"This wasn't my doing. I'm not the cause of your problems, but I believe I know who is. This clusterfuck you've been dealing with isn't over," I breathe against her lips. "This is as much to help you as it is to benefit me."

"Wow," Chloe sighs from her seat.

However, I don't look away from Sidney. Instead, I patiently await her next reply. I watch as she blinks slowly a few times. She shakes her head slightly, reaching to touch her now swollen lips.

"Why is this helping me?"

"I have everything you need, even those things you have yet to become aware of," I reply.

Sidney stares at me for a long moment. Then she does something that makes my groin tighten, causing my need for her to surge through me. I don't even know if she knows how beautiful she is.

Her head is thrown back, exposing her throat. Her breasts jiggle with the motion. From this angle, being so much taller than she is, I can see the mirth in her eyes as she laughs from deep in her belly. It's sensual and sultry, without her even trying.

She wipes at the corners of her eyes. She looks at Chloe and laughs some more. My lips turn up into a smile when her words pour out.

"Chloe, you bitch. I knew you wanted to get me laid, but I didn't think you would go this far. You almost had me." She laughs.

This time I look to Chloe in my amusement. She shakes her head, looking between the two of us while fanning herself. She nods in my direction.

"First, I think you better actually watch your mouth. Secondly, girl, I had nothing to do with this. I promise you. This is all him." She shrugs. "I'm just as shocked as you are. I'm just not complaining."

Sidney whips her head back in my direction. "This isn't a joke?" she asks with wide eyes. "This has to be a joke."

"When it comes to you, I will not and do not joke," I say firmly.

Her mouth pops open, her eyes narrow, and her jaw twists. I know some more of that sass is coming my way. Just the thought sends my blood pumping.

No, I don't want to break that defiance out of Sidney. I want to tame it just for me. I want to harness that fire within her for my very own pleasure. When she burns with that aggression and fire, I want it to be beneath me as she writhes with pleasure unknown and unattainable from anyone else.

"Give me one reason I should even entertain you and this foolishness," she hisses at me.

I break into a full-on smile. "Just one?" I arch my brow. "I'll give you a few."

CHAPTER FIVE

The Offer

Sidney

To say I'm stunned is an understatement. A contract, this son of a bitch, this sexy as hell, son of a bitch has offered me a million-dollar contract. It looks like he offered Chloe the same, only her contract had someone else's name on it as I flipped through the pages.

I don't know what kind of kinky shit he's into, but I'm not about to play myself with this bullshit. My reputation has already been dragged through the mud after what Steinway & Schwartz has put me through. I don't even think I trust this man.

I will never place my future and life in the hands of other people, ever again. Suddenly, I feel like a hole has been punched through my chest. This all cannot be happening to me again.

How the fuck did they find out about Kiss?

I started the publishing company when I started to monetize my blog. Chloe is like a sister to me. I trusted her to open the accounts and place the company in her name until my shit was all cleared up.

Marnita Knight, a friend of mine from college, was able to get her brother to create some false IDs for me. That was how I was able to have access to the accounts, but for the most part, everything is in Chloe's name. It's how I was able to survive for the last year and a half.

This just can't be. Why are the Kiss accounts frozen? When did this happen? I just made a withdrawal to go shopping. I've been so careful. Paying Chloe a salary, which she has given back to me in cash, every single month.

Limiting my spending, I've purchased everything in cash, the only way I've been able to. None of this is making sense. Most of all, how does this man know my business before me?

If there was ever a time I wanted to throw the towel in and curl into the fetal position, right now would be it. However, that isn't who I was raised to be. I lift my chin and glare down this gorgeous man before me.

"Have a seat, Sidney. I will tell you all you want to know," he purrs in that rich, sexy voice.

I feel his words down between my thighs. The pulsing there tries to distract me from the fact that my world is trying to become unhinged once again. I hesitate for the briefest moment before I reclaim my seat.

I'm relieved when he doesn't crouch before me again. His presence is intoxicating. Those eyes are so penetrating.

Everything about him is demanding, even his kiss. I'm almost tempted to curse again, to see if he'll make good on that spanking or at least give me another of those addicting kisses.

He folds his tall body into the chair across from me again, his eyes drinking me in. I watch as his large hand moves slowly through his thick red hair. The move shows an immense amount of controlled power.

"You, Sidney, were the account manager for some very wealthy individuals. You had the best rate of return in your firm. However, when it came to light that you were a woman, and a Black woman at that, clients started to complain about the risks you were taking.

"Those bastards at Steinway & Schwartz weren't about to lose out on money. Not a chance in hell. Instead, they decided to make you a commodity at the firm. They made it look like your services were exclusive. Not just anyone could have access to you.

"Of course, you were unaware of this. You only did what you did best. However, you pissed someone off. No one expected you to be so good for so long. You improved in an arena that's all a gamble to begin with.

"Only you, sweetheart, seemed to have it down to a science. All the while Steinway & Schwartz was wading in shit. You triggered that investigation. Your numbers were adding up, but some others weren't.

"I knew it was only a matter of time before they targeted you. Although, I didn't think they had the balls to come after you the way they did. It's why I tripled down on my profile a second time. You were making me a very wealthy man on top of me already being a very, very wealthy man," he explains.

His words hit me like a punch. Realization forms in my mind as rapidly as the questions do. I remember when the request hit my desk, I was so proud of myself for securing such an increase in that account.

I gasp. "Right before the indictment—a few months before, Burlington Roth Financial tripled everything. I didn't question it. My numbers were so good, I figured your company saw a good thing and ran with it." My mouth runs dry and falls open. "Oh, my God, you knew...you knew then they were coming for me?"

"I had a hunch. What I didn't know was that my move would accelerate their bullshit and your indictment. It would seem you and I have a mutual enemy, gorgeous." He smiles, reaching for his brandy.

"Who?" I wrinkle my brows. My temper is simmering just beneath the surface.

"Umm, that I will tell you in time," he says, taking a slow sip of his drink. "I have an idea, but I need to prove it. I think you and I showing a united front will force their hand. I've proven that by asking you here.

"Your accounts were frozen the moment you walked into my club," he says pointedly.

I rub my temples. "How do they know about my company? Why can't you tell me now? Why would you bring me here knowing you'd be bringing me into the line of fire?"

I feel so tired all of a sudden. My head is starting to hum with a dull headache. Most of all, I'm frustrated as hell with his nonchalance about all of this.

"I needed to prove my point. Besides, you and I have unfinished business. Now that I'm certain, I want to move forward all the more." He shrugs.

I snort. "Move forward with a sex contract? You have to be kidding me."

"I think you should read it a little more closely." He sighs. "It's more than a sex contract. It actually has nothing to do with sex."

"So, I agree to be your companion and you'll fix my problems and give me a million dollars?" I say skeptically. I'm not buying this bullshit one bit.

He frowns. "Are you not going to read it?" He grunts when I budge no more than to fold my arms across my chest. "You will spend six months as my fiancée. Together, we'll fix your problem and, in the end, you will have a million to blow as you please," he says the last words with a seductive smile.

"That's it?"

"Oh, make no mistakes. You will be mine in every sense of the word. I will help you to enhance those scintillating stories you publish on your site," he purrs. "Read the contract, Sid. It will show you I have as much to lose as you do."

Sid, that's the first time he's used the nickname. The way it rolls off his tongue tugs at something inside me. It's like a slow stroke, licking up a fire. He makes it seem like something that should be said in private.

"I thought I was done with this," I mutter to myself.

"Oh, my God," Chloe gasps, beside me.

I groan and turn to look at her. "What, what now?"

Tears fill her eyes as she looks back at me. "My sister is texting me. They're trying to remove her from school. I paid her tuition, but they're telling her she owes. I checked my accounts. Sid, I think they've gone after my assets," she sobs.

No fucking way.

CHAPTER SIX

No Choice

Sidney

I think the room has started to spin. Tonight was supposed to be a way for me to release some steam. I was supposed to be celebrating my freedom. Now, it looks like things have just gotten worse. There goes that other shoe.

Chloe doesn't deserve this. She has been by my side the entire time, every step of the way, just like when we were kids.

I remember when I met her at school when I first moved to the neighborhood. Chloe and I had a bond that started from day one. We saw something in each other. We refused to be victims of our environments and fought our way out.

Chloe may not have made it to the top level of the firm the way I did, but she's still done a hell of a job building a great career for herself. We've always been fighters because we come from the bottom. We know how to hustle for more, for better.

I can't let my shit bring her down. When her mother died, she was left with the responsibility of her little sister. Chloe is all Ally has. We're so proud of her.

She wanted to play the flute professionally and that's what she's on the way to doing. I know in my heart that I'm not going to let Chloe and Ally go down with my mess. I reach for the file and start to scan through all the paperwork.

My fingers are shaking as I read. Chloe is beside me, freaking out, while she texts madly on her phone. I look up and Clayton is watching me closely.

"I'll do it, but Chloe doesn't need to be a part of this. There has to be a way to fix this for her," I say.

"That's not going to work." He shakes his head.

"Why not?"

"Well, to begin with, things have been set in motion that I cannot reverse just yet. Secondly, Chloe's presence has been requested. Unfortunately, Gregor couldn't be here.

"He was called away," he starts to explain, then he scoffs, grinning at his next words. "Brodi can be an ass when he doesn't get what he wants."

Chloe sits forward and gasps. "You've got to be fucking kidding me?" she hisses, snatching up the paperwork meant for her.

She flips through to the second page and reads. She then flips through to the last page. When I looked through her file there was a picture on the last page of a hot ass guy.

"Oh, hell no. See, I must be seeing things. This contract says Gregor Hennessy. I think that's a typo. Okay, now I'm with Sid.

This has to be a joke." She folds her arms over her chest and shakes her head.

Clayton tips his head to the side and examines my friend more closely. It's as if I can see the wheels turning in his head. I want to ask my own questions, but something tells me to wait.

Clayton narrows his eyes. "Something tells me you and my brother, Gregor, know one another very well already," he says suspiciously.

"Gregor," she scoffs. "What I know about Brodi is he shouldn't even be here. And he sure as hell shouldn't be trying this shit. How the hell didn't I see this coming? Nope, this is either a joke or that"—Chloe points to the file—"is one big ass typo, your brother hasn't lost that much of his damn mind."

"Chloe, what the hell is going on?" I snap.

She turns her head away from me, but not before I see the tears. I'm shocked. I've seen Chloe cry only a handful of times. When her mother died, once back in high school after a bad breakup with an older guy, and a while back, when she took off on some secret trip and returned a hot mess.

After that trip, she'd promised me she would tell me what happened when she was ready. I'm still waiting for her to be ready. My frustration grows as Chloe retreats into herself.

"My brother and I need both of your help," Clayton speaks up when Chloe won't answer me. Chloe scoffs, but it sounds more like a small sob.

"Wow, you have a great way of showing it. You're railroading me, no us into...I'm still not sure what," I huff, tossing the file back on the table.

My head hurts too much to focus on what I've read. I get the gist of it, I just can't believe the gall of this man to put this offer out there in the first place. I think his wealth and good looks have fried his damn brain.

"It's a proposal, Sidney. A proposal that will benefit both you and me, as well as Chloe and Gregor," he says smoothly.

I frown and shift in my seat. "I see the benefits to you, all right," I mutter.

"No, I don't think you do. I need you. My father is a powerful man. As such, he likes to be in control. Just when my brothers and I thought we outsmarted him, he pulled us right back in. Our empire rests in his palm if we don't make this happen.

"However, this is only until we can outmaneuver him. I, too, like to have control and I have my own level of power," he replies.

"So, what does that have to do with me?"

"I plan to kill two birds with one stone. Like I said, my family is full of powerful men. Once you are mine, my father will want to help you and I have the power to make things in your life much smoother. However, my father will block my involvement if you're simply some woman he thinks I'm lusting after.

"My father has been putting pressure on myself and my brothers to marry—Gregor and me being the oldest, he has started to apply a bit more. Clooney Hennessey is cunning. He managed to gain controlling interest of our businesses without our notice.

"He's now using that to force us into marrying and running our family's business. I need to get to the bottom of things with this enemy we share and keep my father from trying to mind my business. Gregor is pretty much in the same boat. We'd all be helping each other." He tips his glass toward me, then drains it.

At the same time, one of Clayton's men moves to his side, out of the shadows. He whispers something into Clayton's ear. Clayton's lips tighten, but other than that, he maintains his composure. I wouldn't have even noticed that slight change if I wasn't so focused on his mouth.

I can still feel his full lips on mine. I absentmindedly lick mine, tasting a hint of brandy. I think I've lost all my good sense. I'm sitting here ready to agree to this mess and I'm not even sure if it's all for Chloe and Ally anymore.

Clayton murmurs something into the guy's ear before he returns to the shadows. Clayton then turns his eyes back on me. The moment I look into them, I know I'm not going to like what I hear.

"The police are here. They have a warrant for both of your arrests," he says tightly. "The time is now, ladies. Are we going to help each other?"

I narrow my eyes in defiance. I feel like a trapped rat. I hate this feeling, but anytime my back is against the wall, I come out swinging—claws out and all.

Fuck it, I'm a boss and from what my gut tells me, so is Clayton Hennessy. At this moment, I do what feels like a boss move. After all, I understand a whole lot about mergers and acquisitions.

"I guess I have no choice," I say begrudgingly, reaching for the file on the table.

Clayton pulls a pen from his suit jacket and hands it over. "Wrong again. As mine, you will have plenty of choices," he croons smoothly.

CHAPTER SEVEN

Calling the Shots

Clayton

I nod at David, the head of my security and a longtime friend. I trust David like family. He nods back and delivers his instructions through his earpiece.

Turning back to my newly acquired treasure, I take her in fully. Her pretty eyes are narrowed on me, her delicate fingers hold my pen out in my direction. My lips turn up in the corners as I take the pen back, making sure to caress her mocha-brown fingers in the process.

My smile fully appears at the sight of her chest rising and falling. There's a commotion outside the door, prompting me to move to drop to my knee before her. Sidney's brows wrinkle.

I wink at her, reaching into my suit pocket for the box I have resting there.

I open the box right as the door flies open. Sidney covers her mouth with her hand as the huge engagement ring comes into view. The confusion on her face can pass just as well for surprise. It's a mix of both.

Just the reaction I was looking for, I think of my perfect timing.

Her reaction couldn't be faked, not for what I'm about to pull off. Her gaze jumps to mine, but I don't have the time I want to study her. I lose the smile on my face and turn to the disruption.

There are several officers standing inside my club office suite. I'm pissed at the nerve alone. This place is off-limits. Every cop in this city worth his salt knows this.

I look at the caramel, sour-faced brunette leading the entourage behind her. Her partner looks annoyed, as if he would love to be anywhere else. I can tell right away these two are going to make this interesting.

"What's the meaning of this?" I bellow, rising to my feet.

"Sorry, Mr. Hennessy. We have warrants for both Ms. James and Ms. Sinclair's arrest," the older, tall, blond male officer says.

His female partner turns to glare at him, her brown face tight with annoyance. The art of war, find the cop that's thirsty and use her ambition against her. It's clear which one of the two doesn't seem to understand the rules.

Bad move, I'll eat her and her partner alive before this is over. Two uniformed officers step forward, getting ready to cuff Sidney and Chloe. I step in front of Sidney just as my reinforcement enters the room.

I feel Sidney move to stand behind me, her hands resting on my back. I swear my chest inflates like a teenager defending his first girlfriend.

"I'm Ms. James's attorney. I'd like to see that warrant," Vault booms into the room. The female cop turns and frowns. "That better be one airtight warrant. We're all here to celebrate my friend's engagement that you just ruined."

"Fuck," the blond officer mutters. "I…we had no idea. Listen, we can take this down to the station and get it all straightened out."

"Sidney will not be going down to any station," I reply dryly. "I'll place a wager that your so-called warrant is bullshit."

Vault snorts as he looks the document over. "Let me place a call. This will be over in a sec," he mutters.

This is why I flew him in for tonight. This shit will be squashed in a moment. I watch as the eyes of the male officer widen and the female officer frowns. Her partner looks at her and scowls. The female officer starts to look a whole lot less confident.

"That warrant is legit," she hisses at Vault.

"Good evening, judge. This is Valmik Schultz." He takes a brief pause. "Yes, sorry to be calling so late. I have two warrants here in my hand this evening that say you signed off on them…Yes, concerning Clayton Hennessey's fiancée, Sidney James and the other for Gregor Hennessy's Betrothed as well, Ms. Chloe Sinclair."

Vault takes another pause, a smile crossing over his lips. "Yes, yes, of course. These things happen. Of course, just a mistake. No, no, I'll let you get down to your office to find the warrants you meant to sign," Vault purrs.

"No, Judge, you're not getting too old. Retirement is a long way off. This could happen to anyone. Thank you for clearing this up. No, I'm sure the officers here will be willing to comply. Yes, sir. You have a good evening as well."

Vault turns a hard glare on the female officer. His gaze goes to her badge. "Detective Garret, I'm afraid you're going to need to get in touch with Judge Harrison. There seems to be an issue with your paperwork," he says ever so smoothly.

"You son of a—" she begins to hiss back.

"Don't you dare finish that statement. You don't know my mother and you have no idea what I'll do to your career. I suggest that you wisely consider where you get your information from moving forward.

"Someone is out to ruin your career, as they are my clients'," Vault steps in closer to officer Garret. "You've been sent on a fool's errand, but you don't look like a fool to me."

"This isn't over, my source was solid," Detective Garret snarls.

The other detective snorts. "You've got so much to learn, kid," he sighs and turns to leave with the other officers.

"Oh, my God, this is bullshit," Detective Garret gasps as if in awe.

No one stops to pay her much attention. Vault is still hovering over her as she turns her fury on him. He remains unmoved by her glare.

"Whoever dumped this on your desk isn't a friend. Walk away," he warns.

Detective Garret looks toward Chloe, then to Sidney, standing behind me. She shakes her head, but clamps her mouth shut and turns to leave. I feel Sidney sag against my back.

When the door closes, I reach behind me and pull her in front of me. Her eyes look tired, I can see the worry in them. I caress her cheek.

"We'll always be a step ahead of them," I reassure her. I pull the ring from its box, reaching for her hand. I look into her eyes as I slip the gem in place. "Let's get to our engagement celebration."

Her eyes drop to the ring on her finger, she then looks up into my eyes. "I think I need another drink," she huffs and stumbles back over to take a seat on the sofa.

"That detective will be a problem," Vault says from behind me.

"Then fix it." I shrug, keeping my focus on Sidney.

"Already on it. Congratulations," he mutters before leaving the room.

"This just can't be real," Sidney says to herself.

"Doll, I'm looking at that ring. It's real. Your fiancé just saved our asses." Chloe shivers and takes a seat as well.

"It can't be that easy." Sidney shakes her head. "They're just going to walk away?"

"Oh, but it is. You will see. Things have just gotten a whole lot better for you, Sidney." I grin down at her.

"What the hell just happened?"

"I call the shots around here, sweetheart. That's what just happened," I reply.

"I need a minute. I just need a minute." She rubs her forehead.

I crouch before her. This time she scoots back away from me, trying to put space between us, but I'm not having it. Not now that she's mine.

I lock eyes with the gorgeous woman sitting before me. Sidney is so much more beautiful than I remember. Yet, I can see the wariness and hesitation. Placing my hands on her hips, I draw her back toward me.

I let my breath fan her lips while taking in the sweetness of her essence. Unable to help myself, I nip at her full lips. She shivers within my grasp.

"A lot has happened in a short period of time. I get that you may be overwhelmed. Join me to greet our guests. It's all for a reason. Once we've greeted everyone of importance, we'll go home," I say soothingly.

"Home, I need to go home," she says breathlessly and nods.

"I will take you home right after we're done. Promise." I nod.

"Okay." She nods back slowly. "Okay."

Sidney

Everything is happening in a daze. I don't know any of these people vying for my attention. All because they want to impress this man standing beside me with his large palm pressed against my back.

"Sid, baby."

I turn to look up at him. His intoxicating scent pulls me right in. He looks down at my lips and dips his head to kiss me. Cameras flash around us as he devours my mouth. I swear, I'm trapped in an out-of-body experience.

Clayton breaks the kiss and presses his lips to my forehead. I blink a few times, still not totally understanding how I got here. He slides his hand down to my ass and snaps me out of my fog for a sec.

I turn my attention to the man and woman who have been talking to us. I don't remember who they're supposed to be. I only return their smiles because it seems like the right thing to do.

"That ring is divine. You have great taste, Clayton," the woman purrs as she takes in my fake fiancé.

My jaw tics. I feel the twitch in my face. I know this isn't real, but it's the lack of respect for me. I look down at my finger. This ring is stunning. I've thought so a few times.

Clayton wraps his hand around my left one and gives a gentle squeeze. I look up at him and his reassuring smile. He winks at me and that does the trick.

I take a breath and relax, then look around for Chloe and find her with a drink in hand and a scowl on her face. I still haven't gotten down to what's going on between her and Clayton's brother.

I reach to rub my temple. *God, this has become a long night.*

CHAPTER EIGHT

Promises of Home

Sidney

I can't even remember all the people Clayton introduced me to. My head is still spinning from the fact that I'm engaged. Well, according to the contract I signed, I am—that contract and the amazing ring weighing my finger down.

You would think Clayton actually knows me. This ring is so me, on so many levels. It's classic but elegant, flashy but tasteful. I couldn't have picked a better ring myself.

I'm not the only one who's been admiring it since Clayton placed it on my finger. I caught the admiring and jealous looks from the women around the club. I can't say that I'm not happy to be away from that place.

The tension from being overwhelmed is knotted in my neck. I roll my head on my shoulders, but it does nothing to release the pressure. Suddenly, a warm, heavy hand begins to massage my neck.

I turn to find Clayton's eyes on me. The level of heat I find in his gray eyes is enough to sear me. Yet, I sag into his touch as if it's natural for me. I don't even want to ask myself why that is.

I turn away from him, feeling silly for blushing. I hope he didn't just notice the change to my cocoa-brown skin. I shift in my seat a bit as places other than the one his hand is connected to start to tingle.

The SUV stops, pulling my attention outside the window. We've stopped in front of a downtown luxury apartment building, not my uptown apartment. I turn back to Clayton.

"This isn't my home. You told me you would be taking me home," I say tiredly.

I just want to crawl into my bed. It has been a long and emotional night. I never want to see another pair of cuffs in my life.

I need answers. Tonight was only the beginning of round two. I need to find out what's really going on and why this keeps happening to me. Who has it out for me?

Clayton says he can help. Well, I plan to find out how, but I plan to do so tomorrow. Tonight, I need sleep.

"Yes, I did, and I have. Our New York home," Clayton says, with that wolfish smile of his.

"Wait, what?" I shake my head slowly.

He removes his distracting hand from my neck and tips my chin up with his fingertips. "I told you to read the contract, Sidney. If you would've read the contract in its entirety, you would have read that you'll be living with me," he replies, placing a soft kiss on the tip of my nose.

"Excuse me?" I breathe.

"Oh, this is priceless," Chloe huffs from the back seat, where she demanded to sit when we entered the SUV. "I'm guessing I signed up for the same crap."

Clayton chuckles and moves to get out of the car. Not answering me or Chloe. I look back at her, but she rolls her eyes and turns away from me.

We need to talk. I need to know what's going on with her. My head's pounding with the overload that it's on. Chloe starts to climb out of the car after Clayton. I sit for a moment, trying to find my bearings.

I wish I could rewind this evening or at least not go into it blindly. Resigning myself with the fact that at this point, I can't go back, only forward, I blow out a breath and slide to get out of the SUV. Clayton holds out his hand for me to take.

I wrap my fingers around his and regret it instantly. A charge zips through me. I shiver as I get to my feet outside the car. Without a thought, Clayton shrugs out of his suit jacket and wraps it around my shoulders.

As if the jacket isn't enough, he wraps his arm around my waist and tugs me into his side. His body is so warm, his heat is still inside of his jacket, and I can feel the heat coming off his body as it penetrates the garment.

My lids grow heavy just from being wrapped in his blanket of warmth. We all move into the lobby of the building quickly. The doorman greets Clayton by name and has a big smile for Chloe and me.

"George, this is my fiancée, Sidney, and this is my soon-to-be sister-in-law, Chloe," Clayton introduces.

"Yes, Sir, I was so pleased for you and your brother when I read the sheets this evening. I have your keys ready for you right here," he replies, handing over two key cards to Clayton.

"Thank you," Clayton nods.

"It's a pleasure to meet you, ladies." George nods his head to us both. "If you need anything, I'm here most evenings. The other boys are just as helpful."

"Thank you," Chloe and I say in unison.

Clayton ends the conversation by tugging me toward the elevators, Chloe following silently behind. When we get into the elevator, I turn to Chloe to see she's scowling at Clayton. I look to Clayton to find an amused look on his face.

"You don't like the way I introduced you?" He tilts his head.

"I don't know you, Clayton. So, I will save the words I have to say for your brother," Chloe clips.

"Well, you will need this." He holds out one of the key cards. "We live on the same floor. You can access all three levels from this elevator, but you will need that card. The main entrance is on the top floor. It's the one we prefer to use."

Chloe plucks the card from his fingers. "I think you should call your brother and warn him to stay away from me," she hisses.

Clayton tries uselessly to smother a smile, nodding his head. Chloe turns her back to us and fumes. I watch her shoulders sag as the elevator stops and the doors open.

Clayton leads me out of the elevator, kissing my temple. "Wait here, I want to get her settled in. It will only take me a moment," he says against my skin.

He moves toward Chloe and guides her over to the door on the far left. My feet hurt, so I shift from foot to foot. I eye the carpeted hallway, contemplating taking off my shoes.

Before I can make the decision to do so, a loud crash comes from inside the apartment Chloe and Clayton entered. I almost jump out of my skin, but my mind kicks into gear swiftly. I head toward the apartment.

"You motherfucker," Chloe screams before something crashes again. "How dare you?"

"Stop throwing shit at me and then we can talk," a man with a deep voice booms. It isn't Clayton, but it sounds a bit like him.

"Fuck you, Brodi, or Gregor or whoever the fuck you are," Chloe sobs.

"Go, Clay, I've got it," the guy commands. "Come here, baby. I know, I'm sorry."

My brows wrinkle as I hear the last words. I've just stepped into the apartment when Clayton appears and starts to walk me back out. I push at his chest to get to Chloe. His big frame blocks my view into the apartment.

"Let them handle their own shit. Trust me, we don't want to get in the middle of that if your friend is who I think she is," Clayton whispers.

"What does that mean?" I hiss up at him.

"Those two have history. An ugly one at that," Clayton murmurs.

"How do you know?" I follow him as he leads me away, but I can't help looking over my shoulder, back at the apartment door.

"I knew it. It makes sense now. Chloe is Cee," Clayton says as if talking to himself. He shakes his head and keeps moving.

When we arrive at the door on the right side of the hall, Clayton opens the door with the key card in his hand. I follow him into the apartment and stop in my tracks. The place is amazing. Frosted glass provides the illusion of a front room.

It's decorated with a small table that holds a glass vase full of white roses. Black-and-white paintings hang on the bright-red accent wall. It's bold, but I like it.

Clayton removes his jacket from my shoulders, and I bend to unfasten my shoes. I step out of them and kick them aside by the door. Cool marble greets the soles of my feet. I wiggle my toes and make a small sighing sound.

Clayton grabs my shoes and steps behind me, placing a kiss on my neck. "You look exhausted. I can show you around in the morning," he says in my ear.

"I'll be going home in the morning," I yawn in protest.

"No, you won't." He chuckles. "We have things to do. I've set up a few meetings and we meet with the wedding planner."

I spin in his arms. My brows drawn. "Wedding planner?" I choke. "I thought we were just pretending to be engaged?"

"Planning a wedding is all part of the pretending." He smiles down at me.

He begins to roam down my back toward my ass with his hand. I grab his wrist. "I'd like for you to show me where *I'll* be sleeping for the night," I say pointedly.

He kisses my forehead, that smile on his full lips again. Yet, he begins to lead me through the apartment. I take in the expensive, spotless hardwoods. The contemporary and masculine decor, all within an open floor plan.

The living space is open to the kitchen. It's very spacious and has divine views from the large glass wall of windows. It's all stunning.

We get down the hall and walk up a staircase to a partially open loft space. At the top of the stairs is a frosted glass door. Clayton opens it and leads me inside. It's a vast bedroom space with a large king-size bed. It's a gorgeous design, very unusual.

"I have a partner who's an architect. He comes up with the craziest ideas and makes them happen. This place was nothing like this when I purchased it," Clayton says, looking around.

"It's very nice. Okay, good night." I turn to him expectantly.

His smile grows as he begins to remove his cuff links while stepping out of his shoes. I lift a brow, my eyes glued to him. Removing his socks first, he then moves farther into the room and flicks on a switch. The wall behind the bed illuminates.

"Our closets are behind that wall. Your things are on the left side," he says. "The bathroom is in the center. You can walk through either closet to get to it."

"I'm not sleeping with you...wait, what things?" My tired brain kicks into gear. "Hold on, you had keys waiting for us and the doorman already had instructions. You were pretty sure of yourself tonight."

"I told you, I'm always a step ahead. Sidney, you're tired. Don't fight with me about this. Go freshen up and come to bed. I assure you. I want you rested and firing on all cylinders when I take you. That's not tonight," he says seductively, his eyes traveling over my body.

I fold my arms over my chest. I may have signed that contract, but it was to save my ass, not to give it up to some stranger. A sexy as hell stranger, but stranger, nonetheless.

He only proves my point about him being sexy when he begins to unbutton his dress shirt and shrugs it off. I wouldn't have pegged Clayton to be one for so many tats. However, that ink on his ripped body is purely impressive, even from this distance.

I lick my lips before I can catch myself. Clayton's right pec flexes and I feel my chest expand as I inhale deeply. *What was I going to say?* I need my own room. Yup, I sure do.

I shake my head, forcing my eyes up to his. There's mirth in his gaze. I frown, placing my hands on my hips.

"Can you please show me to another bedroom," I say through tight lips.

Clayton lifts a brow at me. His gaze rolling over me again. I can almost see him thinking while he looks at me. A perplexed expression crosses his face for a moment. Then it's like a light bulb goes off.

"We can do this the easy way, or the hard way, but I will have you in my arms tonight," he finally says. "I want that sexy body next to me when I wake. So, what's it going to be?"

"I'm not—" Before I can finish my sentence, he moves across the room and tosses me over his shoulder.

I yelp in surprise, wrapping my arms around his waist. He gives my ass a swat but keeps moving fluidly with me in his grasp. I'm too stunned to do more than hold on.

"Bath or shower, baby?"

"What?" I say breathlessly.

"Are we taking a bath or shower?" he clarifies.

"We're not taking anything," I hiss.

"Shower it is." He laughs.

He walks into the spacious bathroom, from the closet he just walked us through. Even from this angle, the view is impressive, both of our surroundings and Clayton's ass. When I get his full attention, I yelp and start to wiggle on his shoulder.

"Don't you dare," I scream.

He completely ignores me, stepping into the large glass-encased shower, with me fully clothed and him still in his dress slacks. I grab a handful of his pants, not sure what I think that will do for me. My back arches the moment I feel the cold water soak through my dress.

Clayton roars with laughter as I squeal and slide down his front. He crowds my space, backing me against the shower wall. I watch as his strong body towers over me.

The water is ice cold, but steam seems to be coming off this man. Pure fire, that's what I see in his eyes as he looks back at me. He dips his head so that our lips are only inches apart.

"Do I have your cooperation yet?" he breathes against my lips as I shiver in front of him.

I have no words. Instead, I growl back at him. He laughs, shaking his head while reaching behind me. The water begins to warm up, taking the chill with it.

Clayton uses one hand to flatten me against his front, and the other to unzip my dress. His eyes remain locked on mine. The hand pressing me to him roams slowly up my back, to my shoulder, where he peels my dress from my skin.

The intensity flowing between us is so strong, I can't help staring up into his eyes. Somewhere in my brain, I'm aware of the fact that he's removing my dress and my panties along with it. I just don't know how to call my brain into action at the moment.

"You feel it too?" he says softly, looking up at me from his kneeling position before me. He leans forward and inhales. "Yes, you feel it."

My chest rises and falls of its own accord. I'm sure it's giving me away, even if I try to remain impassive. He tilts his head to the side, observing me, yet I still give nothing away.

However, my lips do part when he leans in, placing his nose to my mound. He inhales deeply, causing me to remain stock-still. I can't move a muscle; I don't even try.

Clayton does though. Slowly, he drags his nose up my center. From my mound to my belly button, from my belly button to between my breasts, from the center of my breasts over my throat, he leaves a path of scorching heat. By the time he reaches my lips, hovering just a breath away from me, I feel light-headed.

I don't even remember when I stopped breathing. Clayton darts his tongue out and licks my lower lip, commanding my breathing to restart. He nips the same lip before taking my mouth in one of the hottest kisses I've ever had in my life.

Mindlessly, I put my arms around his neck. In the next motion, my legs are wrapped tightly around his waist as his hands palm my ass in his firm grasp. I don't have the good sense not to grind on the massive erection, still covered by his slacks.

It's been so long since I've had sex. Oh, and good sex, I don't remember the last time I could claim that amazing pleasure. The way Clayton kisses me and from the bulge in his pants, I have a feeling he will deliver the package I've been missing.

He breaks the seal of our kiss. "You have exceeded all of my expectations. This is going to kill me," he groans.

I wrinkle my brows at his words, but it all becomes clear when he peels my body from his and takes a few steps back. His scorching eyes roam my body. The gray in his orbs is so dark in this moment.

My gaze falls to his strained pants. I bite my lip at the sight of his impressive offering. I have to fight back a real pout when he shakes his head and backs out of the shower.

"Shower and come to bed, Sidney," he says hoarsely.

My mouth pops open. I know I said I wasn't sleeping with him, but you don't just kiss someone like that and leave them hanging. I feel my cheeks heat as I get pissed off all over again.

Then it hits me, my hair is soaked. It will be a mess in the morning. I grit my teeth, now beyond pissed.

Although, I'm not too pissed to watch through the shower glass as he strips out of his slacks. Clayton has an amazing round, tight ass. His back is just as chiseled as his front, with more tattoos decorating his smooth-looking skin.

I try to get a peek at his front through the mirror, but I don't have the right angle to get a good view. I fume in frustration. Clayton, on the other hand, seems to be unbothered. He walks out of the bathroom, without even a backward glance.

"Un-fucking-believable," I mutter to myself. "Just priceless."

CHAPTER NINE

I'll Wait

Clayton

I knew my first real taste of Sidney would be unforgettable. I could tell from the look in her eyes, she would leave me wanting more and more of her. Yet, I've now had more than one taste and I burn for the entire entrée.

This is beyond the original desire I had for her. This isn't even what I had planned. Sidney was to take my room while I slept in one of the guest rooms.

Yet, I'm not warring with myself nearly as much as I thought I would. I glance at the bedroom door I've left open. I think of Sidney and the impulse to close and lock it doesn't come.

Sidney has burned herself into my soul with just a kiss. The way she yields to me when she's not giving me that sassy mouth has my groin so tight, I'm in pain. Yet, sex has never caused me to ignore the panic or need to control my environment. I'm stunned I'm not freaking out from having her in my space.

It's the reason I know I will wait. Tonight isn't the night for me to take her. Sidney doesn't trust me the way I need her to, and I don't yet understand this trust I have for her.

She's right not to trust me. I haven't earned it. I plan to, I will have all of Sidney's trust when it's said and done. It's a necessity for me, almost as much as my need for respect.

I frown as I think of the lack of respect shown tonight at my club. I'm almost sure I've figured out where this shit is all coming from. There are only two people who would have the balls to lead a thirsty cop into my club.

I lift my phone to my ear as I listen to the water run. It took everything in me not to take Sidney in that shower. Her smooth sexy skin felt like heaven beneath my fingertips.

Watching the water cascade over her cocoa-brown skin was mesmerizing. Her mouth tasted of the champagne and strawberries from the club. I ache to have her suck my cock tonight, knowing she'll remember the taste of fine champagne, fresh fruit, and my throbbing rod in her mouth.

"Clay, you there?" David's voice comes through the line, dragging me from my thoughts.

"Fuck," I mutter under my breath, shaking my head clear. "Yeah, did you look into what I asked you to?" I ask, forcing myself to focus on my call.

"Just finishing up. Her place was definitely bugged. If she talked about coming to the club, they heard her," he replies.

"I want all of her electrics replaced. See what you can do about transferring her stories to a new laptop, without transferring any corrupt files. Her writing is important to her. Don't fuck this up," I grunt.

"I got it, Clay. I'll handle the laptop myself. We still have a few problems. The sister was still thrown out of school. She'll be here on a flight in the morning. You're not going to like the shit she's gotten herself into. I need to talk to her sister, but she isn't answering her phone," David says, sounding annoyed.

"Gregor came back earlier than expected. He was in the apartment when we arrived. She may not answer for a while." I grin to myself.

I saw the looks that passed between those two. I'm steering clear of that apartment. If I didn't know my brother so well, I just might fear for him.

"That's not the only problem. Sidney's friend, Marnita, she's having a bit of trouble. What do you want me to do?" he asks.

I throw my head back and blow out a breath. "We need to put an end to this shit," I growl.

"I'm just about sure the bugs in Sidney's apartment have given all of this ammunition. She's better off there with you," he sighs back.

"Yes, but the ball has already started rolling down the hill," I huff. "Look into the friend, see if this indeed will snowball. If she needs us to step in, you get your ass on a plane and go help her."

"Got it," he responds.

"And David, for now, I want this contained. If she needs help, give her a reason to come see her friend. The wedding or I'm sure one of the rooms around here needs to be remodeled."

"Understood," he says before hanging up.

The shower cuts off just as the call ends. I settle my back against the headboard and wait. My eyes are closed as I wait to feel her presence.

Sidney has this energy that courses through her straight to me. I feel it each time I'm near her. I've felt it throughout the night. It's even stronger when she's in my arms.

Perhaps that's the reason I'm choosing to stay the night in the same room as her. I try not to dwell on that thought.

It takes longer than I expect for her to come out. When I hear the blow-dryer running, I remember my mistake. I knew as soon as I turned on the shower, I fucked up. It was a miracle Sidney didn't go off on me.

A smile tugs at my lips when I feel her enter the room. I turn my head and open my eyes to see her standing at the side of the bed, staring at me. She's draped in one of the silk gowns I had placed in the closet for her.

It clings to her chocolate skin perfectly. The peach color does amazing things to her complexion. My cock twitches beneath the covers, just from taking her in.

Her hair looks cute. It's not pin straight like it was earlier this evening. It's now in a crown of short wavy curls. I think I like it better than the straight hairstyle.

There is a better man inside of me than I thought. My first mind is telling me to drag her into this bed and stake my claim. The other part of me calls for calm, clarity, and patience.

I peel the covers back in a silent command for her to join me in bed. She shifts from foot to foot before slowly climbing in. Her eyes never leaving my face, even though they're narrowed at me.

I lean over and kiss the tip of her nose. I won't dare sample those lips again tonight. I don't own that much restraint. I know I don't.

"I'll take care of it," I murmur, twirling a lock of hair around my finger.

"You better," she snaps.

I grin but hold myself back from kissing the sass from her lips. "Let's get some sleep. We have a long day ahead of us tomorrow," I mumble, pulling her into my chest and settling down into the bed.

It takes a few minutes before Sidney relaxes against me. So long, at first, I don't think it will happen. When she finally does relax, she places her hand on my ribs and runs it up to my chest.

I reach for her fingers and kiss the tips. "Sleep, Sid," I yawn.

"I'm halfway there. You're the one that wanted to hold me. I get touchy when I'm this close to someone in my sleep," she yawns back.

I chuckle. "Is that right?"

"Mmm-umm," she murmurs sleepily.

I smile, my lids too heavy to lift, my mouth too lax to respond. I haven't been this comfortable in years. Just think, this is the first woman I've allowed to sleep in my bed…ever.

I didn't think it would be this easy to allow someone this close to my space. I had been prepared to give her this room if this felt wrong to me.

You, Sidney James, are the exception. I just might not let go.

I don't know who I think I'm kidding. I don't think I ever had the intention of letting go. Not too quickly, anyhow.

Maybe, not at all.

CHAPTER TEN

Morning Rush

Sidney

When I wake, I feel like something is missing. I roll onto my back and find cold sheets beside me. When I blink open my eyes, it all comes back to me. I lift my hand to stare at the engagement ring and my mind fills with a million thoughts.

I shiver a little and it hits me. I'm missing his warmth. I spent the night wrapped in his strong arms. I haven't had that kind of peace in years. My last few boyfriends were assholes. I could never do enough for them.

Eventually, I gave up trying. I had to find Sidney before I allowed another man to tell me who Sidney should be. I like to think I know myself now, which is why this all shocks the hell

out of me. In my mind, I would've demanded my own room or
to be taken to my own home in the first place.

Something about Clayton Hennessey makes me second-
guess myself and want to explore option *B*. I can't help asking
myself, why him? It's not just his handsome face or his well-
sculpted body. It's *him*, his presence, the way he takes charge
and seems to be in control of everything around him.

I don't give over control of my life to anyone. Yet, with
Clayton, I feel like I can give him my trust. I frown at my
thoughts and shake my head. The movement reminds me of my
ruined hairstyle.

One thing I love about this wig, when it's wet, its curl
returns. Unfortunately, I'm just not the greatest at taming it
back into the straight style it had been in. I tried last night, but
I was too tired to make a real effort.

I smile when I think of Clayton's offer to fix it. I doubt he
even knows it's not my real hair. Besides, I'd like to know what
his version of fixing this will be.

"I might as well get up. I'll need time to work this out," I
murmur to myself.

After a quick shower, I enter the side of the closet Clayton
referred to as mine. Last night, I was shocked to find it full of
items in my size. Everything from lingerie to shoes and a
designer wardrobe. I ignored the glass display, filled with
designer bags. I refuse to get sucked in by my weakness.
However, I did note the Hermes bag, which nearly had me
swallowing my tongue.

This morning, as I stand here, you would think I shopped
for every item in this closet. It's my style to a *T*. I don't want to
think too hard about what this says about Clayton.

I think about the meetings he mentioned we're supposed to be having today, feeling my defiant streak rear its head, my lips lift into a mischievous grin. Clayton looks like a man who likes to set a certain impression for the world. I plan to test that theory.

"Wedding planner," I mutter and snort.

Let's see if he's ready to go through with what he's asking for. I'm not some trophy wife who will sit pretty and perfect. Men like Clayton like to have women like me seen but not heard. I've worked around his type enough to know.

I've never been willing to bend to their rules, and I don't plan to start now. I move past the designer dresses and pantsuits neatly hung before me. I pluck the first pair of jeans I find from the hanger, wiggling my thick hips into the dark-blue denim.

"Oh, wow, these fit like a glove," I muse to myself, spinning to look in the mirror. I turn from side to side.

I'm truly impressed. It's not easy for me to find such a perfect fit. Pleased with my new find, I turn for the drawers I went through last night. I grab a black tank top, tugging it on. With a cheeky smile on my lips. I walk across the bathroom to Clayton's closet.

Reaching out, I run my hand over the collection of suits, followed by dress shirts. I stop when my fingers run over the soft fabric of a navy-blue shirt. Pulling the shirt from its hanger, I slip it on. The shirt swallows me, but it smells so good. I fasten most of the buttons, tucking the front into my jeans.

I turn for the mirror and watch my eyes sparkle with mischief. The shirt hangs off one shoulder and hangs loose in the back like a dress over my jeans. It's a cute look. I head back over to my side of the closet, rolling my eyes at myself for thinking of it as that—*my side.*

I grab a pair of black peep-toe platform heels. Stepping into them, I take another look in the mirror. I sigh at my hair. Shrugging, I reach up to peel the unit off, revealing my braided, natural hair beneath.

I blow out a breath, letting my lips flap in exasperation. I may have been better off trying to tame the wig. I toss the wig aside on the vanity in the closet before reaching for the pins to release my hair.

"Excuse me, hello, Ms. James." Comes from the bedroom.

My brows furrow as I move toward the sound of the voice. When I get into the main area of the bedroom, a thin chocolate girl stands nervously in the entryway. She gives me a small wave and matching smile.

"Hello, Mr. Hennessy was on a call. He told me to come up and find you." She holds up a case. "I'm your hairstylist."

"Oh," I say, surprised. I lift a brow as I think of Clayton's promise last night.

A man of his word.

I don't allow myself time to get too deep into that thought. I eye the girl, wondering if I trust her enough to tame my hair or if I should turn for my wig to let her fix it. I grin internally as I imagine the look on Clayton's face when I show my face wearing this outfit and my natural wild hair.

I look over the girl's long sleek waves and shrug, deciding to take a chance. *Big hair, don't care* floats through my head. Sidney from the district was always polished and dressed to the nines for the workplace.

This new Sid, the one who doesn't have to cater to anyone, will show up anyway she pleases. Still flawless but doing things by my standards. If Clayton wants to play, then he has to learn my ground rules.

"I had my hair washed and braided yesterday morning. You can just work with it," I say, watching for her reaction.

I breathe in relief when her eyes light up. I take another look at her trendy-looking outfit of brown ankle boots, black jeans, a black tank top, with a yellow duster sweater. Her makeup is flawless. The yellow eyeshadow makes her brown skin glow and her eyes pop.

Yes, honey can do some hair.

An hour later, Ashley and I are giggling like longtime friends. She has freed my hair of the braids, straightened the edges, and used a crimper to add volume to my long thick waves. I've never seen my hair look more healthy, thick, and flowing.

The large wavy mass looks like a halo on top of my head, pulling my entire ensemble together perfectly. There's no cookie-cutter fiancée here. Clayton may be able to help me out, but I'm not just going to roll over and play nice when I don't have the details.

Besides, he has been in control from the moment we stepped into his club last night. I need to assert myself and show I will not be taken advantage of, no matter how small this gesture may be in making that assertion.

"You look great. I love your hair. It's a pleasure to work with," Ashley says, as she swipes lip gloss onto my lips.

I wasn't expecting her to do my makeup, but the girl has skills. I'll have to get her card before she leaves. I may not go to client parties and fundraisers anymore, but you never know when a stylist may come in handy.

"You did an amazing job," I praise, fluffing my waves. "I just hope it holds a bit before it becomes unruly and looks like a cotton ball on top of my head."

I laugh because I'm expecting it to be a cotton ball by the time I get downstairs. It's gorgeous, but I'll sweat it out in five minutes. It's one of the reasons I wear it under my wigs.

"Oh, you're talking to the best. You will be able to rock this for at least a week, two if you twist it and tie it down at night." She winks at me.

I narrow my eyes skeptically, causing us both to burst into laughter. Ashley shakes her head as she starts to place her things back into her case. I realize that this has been the most relaxed I've been in months.

"I'll take that unit with me and get her as good as new for you," Ashley says, pointing to my discarded wig on the vanity.

"Girl, please, you don't have to worry about that. I'm sure he's only paid you for your services today." I wave her off.

Ashley's skin forms a little crease between her perfectly drawn brows. "I was hired as your personal stylist this morning. I'll be here every morning unless you would like me to come in later. Mr. Hennessy also gave me a list of events that I'll be needed for in the coming weeks. I'll be back this evening, actually," she replies.

I snap my head back a little. I wasn't expecting that. I don't know how to feel about this revelation. Does Clayton have a problem with the way my hair looks?

I tell myself to ease my ruffled feathers. This could just be his way of attending to my needs. After all, the man has stocked an entire closet for me.

"Oh," I say simply.

"Sid, are you guys almost finished? The wedding planner will be here in ten and you haven't had breakfast. I need to run a few things by you and get you up to speed," Clayton rumbles before he appears in the entryway of the closet.

His head is down, focused on his phone, as his big body moves with that sexy swagger. *Damn.* I wasn't expecting to see him in jeans and a white T-shirt. The way his muscles stretch the fabric has my nipples straining against my bra. The ink on his arms stands out against his tanned skin.

His hair isn't as neatly combed as last night. It looks more like he's been running his fingers through it. It's sexy, just calling my fingers to take a pass through.

Even the tight knit of his brows as he looks down at his phone has me biting my lip, while trying to force myself to tear my eyes away. This man is hot as sin.

I shake my head, finally tearing my gaze away to peek over at Ashley. She's looking at Clayton with awe written all over her face. My lips twist as a possessiveness I don't like rises. Yet, the ring on my finger tries to tell me I have every right.

"Baby?" Clayton's voice pulls me from my mental rant, I slide my eyes back to him.

His eyes are still on his phone as he texts furiously. I blink a few times, registering the fact that his endearment was aimed at me. When I still don't answer, he lifts his head, his eyes finding me.

I watch as it happens. His eyes roll over me from head to toe, then back up again. Those gray eyes turn so dark, my panties flood at the sight. He reaches behind him, pulls out an envelope, and holds it in Ashley's direction.

"This is for making yourself available at the last minute," he says huskily, not taking his eyes off me. "I'll place another grand in your account this afternoon."

"Thank you," Ashley gasps, moving forward to take the offering.

"No, thank you," he replies. "You can help yourself to breakfast on your way out."

I snort to myself. He has effectively dismissed her. Ashley hurries to grab her things and leaves the closet. I fold my arms across my chest. Clayton's eyes still haven't released me and I'm starting to feel naked standing before him.

Once Ashley is out of sight, he stalks toward me, eating up the small distance between us with his long legs. My heart is pounding as his delicious scent grabs me, arresting me in my spot. I have to tilt my head back to look up at him.

His penetrating eyes search my face before looking over my hair. I can see the questions in his eyes, then a smirk reaches his lips. He lifts his large hand, easing his fingers into the nape of my hair.

"I thought you cut all of your hair off," he murmurs. "This…it's gorgeous on you. I love you in my shirt."

His other hand falls onto my hip and starts a slow slide to my ass. I grab his wrist, lifting a brow at him. He grins back, tugging me into his body. Then dips his head. Before I know it, his lips are taking mine.

I whimper, my body having a mind of its own. I melt into him, releasing my hold on his wrist to wrap my arms around his neck. His hand in my hair tightens and the one that was traveling to my ass, completes the trip, grasping a handful over my jeans.

The man literally swallows my face with the most passionate and aggressive kiss I've ever had. It's the perfect amount of everything. I open to him, allowing him to taste me fully. I can taste something sweet on his lips and tongue.

I moan when he starts to knead my ass with his large hand. It feels so good, mixed with the bite of his grasp on my hair. The sensation fires off all over me. My toes curl in my shoes.

Clayton releases a loud groan when I lace my fingers in his hair. I tighten my hold as he tilts my head back. His lips graze my chin, then his teeth nip at the same place. I quiver in his hold.

"You." He pulls away, shaking his head. Placing his forehead to mine, he inhales deeply. "You're like a drug, the more I have, the more I want. We need to get you fed and we need to talk."

"I'm not hungry," I say breathlessly, only to have my stomach rat me out.

My cheeks heat, while Clayton kisses my temple, chuckling at me. I miss his heat, as soon as he releases me, taking a step back. I want to reach out and pull him back into me. Instead, I reach for the fabric of his shirt I'm wearing, pulling it up onto my shoulder.

It only slips back down, causing Clayton to step forward once more. He bends his head down, kissing the exposed skin of my shoulder. He peeks his tongue out for a taste, but before I can reach for him to draw him in, he's gone.

"Come, we have a long day. You need to eat something before we get tied up," he commands.

I'm pissed that my body obeys him before I have a chance to tell my feet to stay put. Clayton wraps my hand in his long fingers, leading me out of the room. His hand is so warm, I relax in his hold without a thought.

"How far do you plan to take this wedding thing?" I blurt out, trying to find a distraction from the current buzzing up my arm.

Clayton looks over his shoulder at me as he leads me down the stairs. His eyes search mine before he turns to focus on descending the rest of the steps. I can't help allowing my eyes to travel over his body. I watch his broad back as it stretches his T-shirt, then my eyes fall to the jeans hugging his ass.

I suddenly feel like I need a glass of water. Phew, a sister is parched, staring at this man. I lick my lips, remembering the taste of his lips. I'm so focused on him, I stumble on the last step.

With lightning-fast reflexes, Clayton turns, catching me in his strong arms. My face burns with embarrassment. I look up through my lashes to find him staring down at me.

Those gray eyes stare back at my browns. My thoughts and questions are completely forgotten. A smile tugs his full lips in one corner.

He lifts a brow, mirth written in his orbs. I try to step back out of his embrace, but he's not having it. He tugs me closer, his hands taking that familiar trip of his. This time I don't try to stop him.

His warm palms on my ass are more comforting than I want to admit. A war is happening behind the amusement in his stare. I can also feel him growing hard against me.

I see the moment he makes a decision. His focus drops to my lips, his hold tightens—biting into my curves, and his head begins to descend. I don't realize I'm holding my breath until his phone starts to ring at the very same time the doorbell chimes. He looks at his watch while placing his phone to his ear.

"Go eat," he says to me, holding the phone away from his mouth, leaning in to place a kiss on my temple.

He moves toward the front of the apartment, affording me another look at his spectacular ass. I blow out a breath, shaking my head and move over to the kitchen. There's food on the countertop, but a table comes into view, revealing two place settings with covered plates.

I move to those, figuring Clayton had them placed there for us. I lift one of the lids to find what looks like turkey bacon, an omelet, and grapes. The aromas captivate me, causing my mouth to water. My stomach makes a low growl. I roll my eyes. A smile touches my lips.

I take a seat and get comfortable before digging in. My eyes close instantly, a moan moves from my lips. I look down at my plate in awe.

This is the best omelet I've ever had. So good. I reach for a piece of bacon and bite into it. It's delicious as well. Not salty or soggy.

I really tuck into the plate, saving the fruit for last. As I eat, Clayton's voice rumbles in the nearby distance. A lithe middle-aged blonde makes her way into the dining area with a big smile on her face. I place my fork down and wipe my hands on the napkin I placed on my lap.

"Oh, please continue," the blonde chimes as she places a binder on the table. "Clayton said you were having breakfast. I'm just going to grab a cup of coffee. I'm Delta, by the way. I'll be helping you plan the wedding of your dreams."

"Nice to meet you, I'm Sidney." I take the hand she offers, shaking it.

"Let's see the ring," she says, with a twinkle in her eyes.

I lift my left hand up for her to see. Her eyes nearly pop from her head, but she recovers nicely. I almost laugh out loud at her.

"It's lovely, might I add, not as lovely as the bride-to-be," she sings.

"Thank you," I reply, feeling a little self-conscious.

Delta beams at me before moving to the coffee maker. "Would you like a cup?" she offers.

"No, thank you."

"She doesn't drink coffee," Clayton says as he appears, once again focused on his phone.

I'm stunned at his knowledge of this fact, but I hold my tongue. My fiancé should know something like that about me. I don't know if Delta is in on this hoax. I don't want to say anything that could prove a problem.

Clayton strolls my way with that swagger rolling off him. He looks up from his phone long enough to dip his head and kiss the side of my temple, his lips lingering longer this time. I hear when he inhales me.

Before he pulls away, he tips my head up and plants a soft kiss on my lips. He pulls away with a grin. I clear my throat, turning back to my plate. I refuse to get lost in his eyes.

I continue to eat, feeling his gaze on me. When I look up, he's tucking into his plate while watching me. His phone is forgotten on the table beside him, despite it buzzing.

"You two are adorable," Delta says. "I can see the love."

I almost snort but catch myself. Clayton raises a brow at me while he chews. His eyes turn to Delta once he swallows.

"I'm a very lucky man," he replies, then turns back to me to wink.

Again, I remain silent, moving on to my grapes. I've polished off the omelet and bacon. I would love to meet Clayton's chef. I need to know what was used in that omelet.

"Everything smells delicious, I bet Clayton's cooking helped to win you over," Delta coos.

I'm caught off guard, but I don't let it show. I look to Clayton, and he gives me a small nod as if reading the question in my mind. I wipe at my mouth to buy me time, as I process this new information.

"Maybe." He shrugs. "Among some of my other talents," he says and licks his lips.

I squeeze my thighs beneath the table, shifting in my seat. The heat in his eyes is enough to melt me right where I am. I'm grateful for Delta's presence because I think I would opt to be this man's breakfast if she weren't here. I mean, how do you make chewing sexy?

"Do you have a venue in mind?" Delta inquires, saving me from Clayton's stare.

"We'll be using the Egyptian Room at the MET. My assistant has secured the location. You'll be receiving an email with all the needed contacts in a few moments. Sorry for the delay, we had a few things come up this morning," Clayton says, wiping his mouth.

"Oh, what a divine location," she says, as her eyes light up.

I'm stunned once again. The MET's Egyptian Room is absolutely breathtaking. I've only dreamed about getting married in such a beautiful location. I have to chide myself and remember this wedding won't actually be happening. It will remain a dream.

"Do I have a budget?" Delta asks as she begins to take notes.

"No," Clayton says firmly. "Whatever she wants, she gets. I don't want her stressed with the numbers. Find what she wants and send the logistics to me. Sid may try to be modest. I'll need you to ensure she has the best of the best."

"I don't think we have to go crazy," I interrupt.

"Are you seeing my point?" He chuckles.

"Oh, Sidney, what bride doesn't want the world when her prince is handing it over to her? It's not often I'm given free rein to make a dream wedding come to life. Enjoy the blessing, dear." She reaches over to pat my hand.

I feel so uncomfortable wasting his money, but if this is what he wants. I relent as Delta pulls out a tablet and we jump headfirst into planning a fairy-tale wedding. Clayton remains with us the entire time, occasionally glancing at his phone or sending a text.

He watches me closely. So closely, I think about every decision and detail twice before I answer. I feel like he has undressed me in his mind by the time we're done.

Clayton shows Delta out around one o'clock in the afternoon. My head is spinning. We just went through planning an entire wedding, minus me looking for a dress. No detail was left out. I rub my temples as I pace in the living area.

I'm so lost in thought, I don't even hear Clayton as he walks up behind me. He puts his arms around my waist, pulling me back against him. It feels so natural and comforting. I try not to analyze that too much.

"I'll get our lunch ready and then we can talk a bit before we need to get ready for this evening," he says into my hair.

"This evening," I say, turning in his embrace.

"My parents are expecting us for dinner."

I knit my brows and gasp. "You can't be serious?"

"Why not?"

"I just became your fiancée last night. I'm not ready to meet your parents," I say incredulously.

"You'll be fine."

My face heats as my temper starts to rise. I'm getting a little annoyed with his high-handedness. He brings his large hand up to cup my face, then runs his thumb over my lip.

"Trust me," he breathes.

"How are we going to fix my life?" I demand, instead of offering my trust.

"Trust me," he repeats.

I narrow my eyes at him, searching his face. I want to protest, but for some reason, I decide to trust him. I nod my assent, just as he leans in to commandeer my lips. I find myself clinging to his T-shirt. I call on my good sense to stay grounded and not wrap my body around him.

His tongue flicks my lower lip as he ends the kiss. I feel thoroughly devoured. Any reservations I had moments ago float away. I stumble to the couch when he releases me.

He chuckles as he disappears into the kitchen to prepare our lunch. I'm grateful for the space. My nerve endings are sizzling.

What are you doing, Sid? You need to get your life back, not fall for this man. Get focused.

CHAPTER ELEVEN

Meet the Family

Clayton

I enjoyed my day with Sidney. Surprisingly, I like having her in my space. I also enjoyed watching her savor my cooking. I made us a light lunch of grilled chicken and salad. Nothing fancy, but you would have thought I made her a steak dinner. I'm still chuckling to myself about her comment.

"You season the hell out of your food. This is great," she said with wide eyes.

She was so sexy and gorgeous while sitting in my home, eating my food, and sharing my space. I watched her during the wedding planning, taking mental notes. There were things she wanted that she didn't ask for. I typed them all into my phone and sent them to Delta to make the appropriate changes.

Little does Sidney know, if I can help it, she will have the wedding of her dreams. I'll move heaven and earth to get her whatever she desires. She will learn this soon enough. When she acknowledges that she's mine, the world will be at her fingertips.

As I fix my tie, I grin into the mirror hanging beside the front door. I'm not surprised that Gregor texted me to say he won't be attending tonight's dinner. However, that means all the attention will be on me and Sid.

I'm not concerned. Tonight has a purpose and I will get the results necessary for me to move forward. That is a guarantee. I've dotted all my i's and crossed each one of my t's. I'm a meticulous man. When I go after something, I always have a plan.

"You two look amazing," Ashley gushes, causing me to turn.

For the second time today, Sidney has rendered me speechless. I thought she was gorgeous when I walked into the closet this morning to find her hair wild and her body covered in one of my shirts. Now, I have no words for her beauty.

Sidney's hair is still wild, with the right side brushed back away from her face, a red rose looks as if it's holding the mass back. Her sexy body is draped in an off-the-shoulder silver evening gown. The gown has a split on the right side, her thick thigh is peaking through. I lick my lips and groan. The red heel wrapping her ankle shows off her cute toes. It's the sexiest sight I've ever seen.

I'll be sending Ashley another thousand-dollar bonus. Sidney looks fabulous. I know it's not all Ashley's work, but she's done well with the magnificence given to her.

I hold my hand out for Sidney to come to me. I'm more than pleased when she takes my hand, moving into me without a thought. I love that she's becoming more and more responsive to me.

I don't hold back the smile of satisfaction that creases my lips. I peck her red lips, needing just a taste to hold me over for now. When I look into her eyes, I can see how affected she is. She dips her beautiful browns away from me, but I'm not allowing it.

I pinch her chin, lifting her head. Our gazes lock and I hold her stare. I love her defiance that sets in. I lean in, only inches from her lips.

"Relax, kitten. You can put the claws away," I say, not able to hide the humor in my voice.

"Don't we have someplace to be?" she says breathlessly.

"That, we do," I reply, pecking her lips once more.

The evening has become chilly, so I turn for her cape and help her into it, then throw on my lightweight coat before leading both ladies out of the apartment onto the elevator. Placing Sidney in front of me, I wrap my arms around her for the ride down. Again, she melts into me, comfort radiating from her.

She smells delicious, I can't wait to devour her. We're in our own car as soon as I ensure Ashley is in a car to take her home. As Sidney and I ride in the back of the Phantom, I fill her in on small details I believe she should know for this evening.

I watch through her eyes as her brain absorbs and turns over details. I'm confident she's ready by the time we pull up to my parents' estate.

My jaw tightens. In college, I used the connections I gained to build my future. I got to know all the right people for the time when I planned to make my own way in the world. Some think my father's money is what afforded me my reach. I beg to differ. I made my name and reputation on my own merit and relentlessness.

The men who have chosen to deal with me do so out of respect for me. Not their ties with my father. I know that rides his nerves. I had my claws in too deep by the time he noticed what I'd done and planned to do.

I became my own man without his dictatorship. I learned a long time ago, my father does what's best for what he wants. He would leave me out to dry if it meant getting what he wanted. I'll never be put in that position again. Which is why I need Sidney and this engagement to buy me some time to get back from underneath him.

Sidney's small hand on my thigh calms me, bringing me back from my dark thoughts. I turn to find her watching me. Seeing her concern, something tugs in my chest. Her beauty draws me in.

I reach to cup her small face, capturing her lush lips. As if she knows how much I need her in this moment, she reaches to lace her fingers in the back of my hair. I devour her for a few more moments before I have to force myself to release her. I place my forehead to hers, collecting myself.

"They can't be that bad." Her sweet voice fills my ears.

I scoff. "You're a guest. They'll behave for you, but I'll be in for it every time you disappear from my side."

Sidney pulls her head back to look up at me. "Am I not the kind of woman your parents would approve of?"

I can hear the accusation and wariness in her voice. I shake my head, pecking her forehead. My father is an asshole at times, but I could never call him a bigot. I smirk as I reveal a little-known fact.

"My great-great-grandmother passed the entire time she was married to my Scottish great-great-grandfather. She only hid her race because my grandfather feared for her safety when he would have to travel. It was at the very end of their lives, after her husband passed that she revealed to their circle the truth," I say.

Sidney lifts a brow. "Um," she murmurs.

"Let's go, Love. I have a fiancée to show off." I lift her finger to my lips, kissing the ring I placed there.

I can feel the nerves running through her as we enter the house. I squeeze her hand in my grasp to remind her I'm here with her. She has nothing to be concerned about.

We'll have dinner, play nice and return to our home. *Our home.* I like the sound of that.

Again, I question releasing Sidney ever. Watching her plan our wedding, something inside me rose, wanting to complete the process and see to it she remains in my life.

Initially, I hadn't planned to pursue the wedding entirely. Somewhere along the line, as I planned and lined things up, I changed my mind. Yet, I considered only remaining married until I've had my fill.

Not now. Now, I don't know if I'll actually have enough of Sidney, even after I have my first full taste.

I give our coats to Mark, my parents' Butler. Sidney looks around the foyer, taking it all in. I grew up in this house, but I try to see it from her view.

"Clayton, what's the meaning of this?" my father bellows the moment he enters the foyer, surprising me.

"What would you be talking about?" I reply, completely unfazed.

"The embarrassment of it all," my father huffs in indignation.

Sidney stiffens at my side. I give her fingers a gentle squeeze before releasing her hand to wrap my arm around her waist. I pull her to my side and watch my father's expression the entire time.

He eyes Sidney with those sharp blue eyes. My father has aged well. If he would stop stressing about what my brothers and I are doing with our lives, he may fare even better.

Yet, he's still a handsome man. My brothers and I look like a mix of him and our mother. I get my eyes from my mother, my hair from my father's side.

At the moment, the frown marring his face isn't complementing his good looks. He looks pissed as fuck. The longer I remain silent, the more pissed off he seems to become. I'm nearly amused.

"What exactly are you embarrassed about?" I sigh.

"I have to agree with your father for once," my mother miffs as she joins my father's side.

I lift a brow and tilt my head at her. She looks as pissed as my father does. I'm curious as to how this is going to play out at this point.

"Mother," I croon, giving her a smile, revealing my teeth.

"Don't you mother me," she snaps. "I would expect this from Cane. Gregor, maybe, but not you. Why would you announce to the world you're engaged without saying a word to me and your father? Do you know how embarrassed I was to be at tea, only to find out that those hags were gossiping about my own sons' engagements?"

"It wasn't my intention for you to be embarrassed," I say in exasperation. "Things leaked faster than I intended."

"Leaked," my mother shrills, placing her hands on her hips. "You had an engagement party at that club of yours. I know you too darn well, Clay. You knew what would happen."

My mother pauses, rolls her lips, and places a hand on her forehead. She shakes her head, then looks at Sidney. Her eyes widen in horror as if just realizing Sidney is with me.

"Oh, my. This isn't how I would have liked to meet you. You must be Sidney," my mother says, her tone changing completely. "This is my husband, Clooney and I'm Eileen. It's so nice to meet you."

I love my mother. She can go from zero to a thousand at the drop of a dime. Not many outside of our home know of the fierce force she can be. Watching her genuinely welcome Sidney brings a smile to my face.

I rub my hand up and down Sidney's ribs to relax her. I'm sure her reaction is because of the shrewd look my father is still giving her. He's accessing his new competition. Oh, yes, Sidney is competition all right. I know the man and I know how his mind works.

"It's nice to meet you," Sidney directs her words toward my mother.

Mom lifts her gown and comes closer. She looks lovely tonight in her black dress. Her hair pulled back in her signature updo. My mother's makeup is always flawless.

"Wow, just look at you. You're simply stunning," she coos, cupping the sides of Sidney's face. "Seeing you makes me very happy. It gives me hope to someday have grandchildren."

Sidney goes ramrod straight once again. When my mother releases her face, Sid looks up at me with panic in her eyes. I smile down at her. Dipping my head to kiss her lips softly.

"I can't say I haven't had the same thought a few times today, Mother." I chuckle.

"We haven't even finished planning the wedding," Sidney says, while eyeing me warily.

"Oh, Dear. I think Gregor was conceived the night of our engagement," my mother says, her cheeks turning a rosy pink. "The men in this family go after what they want."

I clear my throat in unison with my father. I can see the embarrassment in his cheeks as well, but he plays it off. I can tell he's still pissed, but he finally offers Sidney a greeting.

"I guess you're officially family now, with those intimate details," he rumbles. "It's a pleasure to meet you. I would've liked to meet you a long time ago, but it's still my pleasure."

"Things have been interesting in my...our lives. The engagement was very surprising for me as well," Sidney offers.

"Yes, you have been through quite an ordeal. I have to say, a day ago, this would have been a conflict of interest for me. Now that you're engaged to my son, I'll be making sure to engage that conflict," my father says firmly.

"I have it handled," I say, sharper than I intend.

My father waves me off. "You have a wedding to plan. I'll ensure things are restored," he says boastfully.

I bite my tongue; otherwise, this will turn into a battle of wills this evening. I'm not here for that. Well, technically, I am, but I'll be steering this ship.

"I'm sure whatever you two are talking about can wait. Sidney, I think you and I should make our way to the dining room. If we stand here with these two, there's no telling what kind of mess will splatter our fine gowns," my mother teases, wrapping her arm with Sidney's and pulling her away from me.

I'm bereft the moment she's no longer at my side. I literally ache with the absence. It's the strangest feeling.

"I questioned this sudden engagement when your mother dropped the bomb on me. Then I picked up the paper to find more evidence of her sobbing words," my father murmurs beside me. I turn to find him watching me.

"Dad—" I go to interrupt, but he lifts his hand to halt me.

"I can see in the way you look at her this isn't just another of your attempts to rebel against me. She's not on my list of wives for you, but I see the fire in your eyes, she's something special." His words stun me into silence.

I stare at him. I expected all-out war when he got me alone. I'm thrown for a moment as my brain tries to figure out if this is one of his tactics to derail my plans. Only, I see the sincerity in his eyes as he looks back at me.

"She is special."

My father's face softens, he reaches to pat my cheek. I watch as his anger defuses completely. My hackles are up. My father never relents. However, before I can assess the situation any further, my youngest brother strolls in, throwing an arm around my shoulders.

"Hope I'm not late," Cane croons lazily.

"Right on time as always," I mutter, sarcastically.

"Always. Where are the sisters-in-law?"

"So you haven't met either of them either?" my father asks with narrowed eyes.

"Sorry, Dad, I have a life. I don't run behind my big brothers and their conquests." Cane shrugs nonchalantly.

"Where's Clooney?" My father inquires sternly.

As always he's the only person who calls Gregor, Clooney. I've called my big brother Brodi for as long as I can remember.

It has only been recently that I've started to call him Gregor, due to business dealings. Gregor hates being called Clooney. It drives him insane.

"*Gregor* couldn't make it." I frown. "Got a text, he's on his way to Dubai."

I don't like prying into my brothers' lives, but Gregor has been keeping secrets. Something is going on in Dubai and I don't think it has anything to do with business. When I tried to dig, I hit a wall. A sure sign my brother is hiding something big. I know he would never shit on me in business, so I let it go, for the time being.

I have this feeling that when the curtain is pulled back, something ugly will be lurking. I'm ready. I will always be there to cover for my brothers. I will do whatever's necessary to make sure they're okay.

"Um," my father replies.

I can see the gears turning in his head. Brodi cutting out may not have been the greatest idea. My father will be watching these engagements closely.

My brother should tread lightly. I don't know his endgame with Chloe. I have a feeling there's so much more there, but I'm not going to stick my nose in that one. If Chloe is who I believe she is to my brother, things are bound to get very interesting.

"I'm starving." Cane pats my stomach instead of his own. "Let's get to the meat."

I chuckle at my little brother, always the one to sense tension and just as quick to defuse it. I love that about him. He's a good kid. His demons just ride him closely. I keep an eye on him.

I'm not willing to allow him to self-destruct. Although, lately, I have a feeling I need to watch him through a finer lens. It's on my list of things to make right.

He knows it. It's why he's been avoiding me. I'm the problem solver in the family. I get to the root of the problem and then I make it go away. I get the feeling Cane has some things he doesn't want me getting to the bottom of.

"You and your brother will have a proper engagement party. I will not hear of anything less," my father grumbles beside me as we head to the dining room.

"Ah, there's the old man," I mutter under my breath.

"I have your fucking old man. I'm wiser than I look. You boys keep trying me, I will have the last laugh," he says with an eerie gloat in his voice.

A chill runs through me, his words have omissions, I feel. I halt my steps, watching my father as he swaggers his old ass into the dining room. I narrow my eyes at him.

"I never underestimate you, old man," I mutter to myself.

CHAPTER TWELVE

Houseguests

Sidney

"It was lovely to meet you, Dear. You have to come by so we can have tea soon," Eileen says as she kisses my cheek while Clayton helps me into my cape.

"It was a pleasure to meet you. Thank you for having me."

"Anytime. I haven't seen Clayton smile so much in a very long time. I think you're good for him."

I look up at Clayton and find him smiling down at me. I can't help but return the smile. I drop my gaze to his lips. My body has been on fire all night as he's been stealing kisses and subtle touches.

"I look forward to getting to know you more," Clayton's father says.

Before I can reply, Clayton wraps his arm around my waist. He pecks my lips, then guides me out the door. He calls over his shoulder as we go.

"It was a lovely evening, thanks for having us. We'll talk, Dad."

I frown. That was kind of rude. Clayton's parents turned out to be quite pleasant after all. His mother is a sweetheart, I felt bad when she looked so disappointed about not being in on the wedding planning.

I told myself that she was better off not having the experience than to be let down when the plans are all for nothing. Clayton's father even warmed up to me as the night moved on. That man scares me a little.

He's just as intense as his son, if not more so. It's like I could see his mind calculating the entire night. He never missed a thing.

However, it's Cane who I'm not too sure about. Clayton's little brother watched me throughout the night. I felt like he was trying to look through me. I'm not sure what's up with him, but it started to get on my nerves after a while.

"We're riding with Cane," Clayton says as he leads me to the running SUV.

"What happened to our car?"

After his behavior all night, I don't want to ride with Cane.

"I sent the Phantom to pick up a friend. I need to talk to Cane, so it made sense to ride with him." He kisses my temple and then helps me into the car.

I'm more annoyed as I climb into the back of Cane's SUV. I've had my fill of this dude for one night. As Clayton settles in his seat, he reaches over to place his hand on my thigh, rubbing his thumb back and forth against my skin.

I relax and close my eyes. The warm murmur of the two brothers' voices helps to lull me into a light sleep. I can still hear them but I'm drifting right outside the reach of consciousness.

I can tell the brothers are close. Although, I also noticed Clayton keeping a close eye on Cane during dinner. Again, I will say I have reservations about Cane. He seems a bit nervous or something.

I can hear it even more now as I near unconsciousness. There's something in his tone that reveals he has something he's trying to hide. I open my eyes as it stands out and grabs my attention.

I can't put my finger on it. I've seen the behavior before, but it hasn't clicked in my head where yet. During dinner, I tried to place the behavior as I homed in on it. However, the way he watched me unnerved me and I gave up.

Like now, I can feel those gray eyes locked on the side of my face. I thought he and Clayton would have their conversation as we ride back to the penthouse, but they have both fallen silent.

Actually, Clayton has become a little tense. His hold on my leg has tightened and when I turn to look at him, his lips are pursed tightly. I'm not sure what happened. Did I drift off deeper than I thought and miss something?

I remain silent and turn to look out the window. The tension within this car is enough to cut through. The ride seems to be taking forever.

"Can my brother trust you?"

It's the first words spoken in the last thirty minutes. I turn to look into the gray eyes staring back at me. They're not as welcoming as his brother's. His eyes are narrowed at me, his lips thinned in a tight line.

Cane is as handsome as his brother, with a younger version of Clayton's face. He has that dark-red hair I noticed they get from their father. I also noticed as the men entered the dining room earlier this evening, Cane is a little taller than Clayton, if possible.

Both Clooney and Eileen are on the tall side, so I'm not too surprised by their giant offspring. More so in awe of their extremely good looks.

I go to reply to Cane, but Clayton beats me to the punch. I'm stunned and turned on all at once. I've never needed a knight in shining armor, but phew. However, to watch one come to my rescue is the hottest thing I've ever seen.

"You don't want to do that," Clayton warns, with a deep rumble in his voice. "My woman is my business, not yours. You have any questions, you come to me. Whatever's been going on in your head tonight, squash that shit and move on. Sidney is mine, I don't play that shit, Cane, and you know it."

My panties are soaked. Cane is forgotten as I stare at the side of Clayton's face. He has nearly turned completely in his seat, as if ready to lunge at his brother. His jaw is tight, and his fists are clenched.

"Fine," Cane huffs.

Clayton turns his eyes on me, revealing that fire in his fierce gray gaze. The car comes to a halt, bringing my attention to our arrival at the penthouse building. Clayton's jaw flexes a few times before he speaks.

"Go on inside. I need to speak with my brother. I'll be right in, don't go up, just move out of the cold." He leans over, capturing my lips in a kiss that should most definitely be private.

I try not to whimper into his mouth and fail. I can taste the bourbon he shared with his father and brother before we left his parents' home. I feel like I'm withering in my seat.

When Clayton releases me, he licks his lips, still giving me a heated stare. He nods for me to step out of the door the driver is holding open. I collect my senses and slide out from the seat.

When my feet touch the pavement, I feel like I have baby deer legs. I wobble on my heels like it's my first time in them. His kiss has literally left my knees weak.

I stagger to the building, and it has nothing to do with the wine and champagne I had this evening. I'm kiss drunk. I haven't been this dazed by a kiss in…hold on, that would be never. I have never been kissed so thoroughly or been so turned on by a man.

I'll need to find my own bed tonight. I'll admit. Clayton is more than I'm willing to or ready to handle at this point in my life.

A man like that is the type of man you need time to evaluate and assess. Meaning, after he knocks the dust off my pussy, I would need to sit and seriously think about my life before I offer him my right arm, a few babies, and access to my bank accounts.

Not that Clayton would need access to my bank accounts. I learned a lot at the Hennessy estate. Not that his parents were boastful or flashy. Wealth was just evident at every turn. I knew Clayton had money, but I witnessed the depth of his family's money while sitting and observing.

I have to say, I'm a little more uncomfortable with this arrangement as well as the planning of the wedding. Eileen is so sweet. I hate what I know all of this is going to do to her. I almost spilled the beans and told her the truth when she pulled out baby pictures of Clayton and started talking about how gorgeous our babies will be.

"Are you okay?"

I jump, startled, when Clayton's warm hand lands on my hip. I'd been so lost in my rambling thoughts, I didn't realize he and Cane had entered the lobby. When I look up at Clayton, his gaze searches my face with concern.

"Yes, I'm fine." I nod.

"Come, we're needed upstairs." He nods toward the elevator, guiding me forward.

My heart races and my mind goes into overdrive. I haven't heard from Chloe since last night. I've texted her, but I haven't received a reply.

Clayton assured me that she's fine. She and his older brother are traveling. I'm not too sure how much I trust that. Yet, hearing the words from him did put me at ease.

A million scenarios run through my head as we ride upstairs. I feel like a terrible friend for not going to the apartment to check on Chloe. I'm in the middle of berating myself when Clayton leans into my ear.

"Chloe's fine. That's not the issue. My brother would never hurt her," he whispers, while rubbing a calming hand up and down my arm.

I nod. Not wanting to speak. I can feel Cane watching me again and the attitude rolling off him. It's stronger than before but I ignore him, willing the elevator to hurry up and get to the top floor.

When we arrive, everyone steps off the elevator. My heart pounds harder when we turn for the apartment Chloe entered last night. Only, we make a right as another hallway comes into view. Cane frowns as he pulls a key card to open the door.

My mind is spinning and whirling, it dawns on me how little I know about those men. I step inside hesitantly, but as I'm becoming used to, Clayton places a reassuring hand on the small of my back. I follow his lead but stop short when a welcome sight comes into view.

"Ally," I squeal, causing her to stop midpace.

Ally whips around, her big bright eyes go wide. It only takes a moment for her to run right into my arms. We're hugging each other to the point I don't think either of us is breathing.

"I don't know what's going on. Where's Chloe?" Ally says into my shoulder.

Ally is a tiny little thing, no taller than five feet. Anyone who can make me feel tall is a shorty. She's a darker version of Chloe, more mocha chocolate skinned, with brownish-red hair. Ally has hazel eyes like her sister, but they darken when she's afraid, nervous, or worried.

Just like now. I look into her eyes as I go to reassure her. This girl has become such a big part of my life. When Chloe and Ally's mother died, I never thought twice about helping Chloe out. We became a team. They're my sisters.

When Ally was selected to go to Europe this summer, I was so proud of her. She works so hard to be the best flutist she can be and it's paying off big time. Yet, she's here. The realization of what that means slams into me. This has all hit home like a ton of bricks.

"They sent you home," I gasp, my brows drawing in.

It's more of a statement, not a question. The trip was through her school. No enrollment, no school, no trip. My heart hurts, and I stagger back, but Clayton's big body appears behind me before my legs can give.

I turn in his arms and look up at him. I feel like I've been duped. He promised to take care of this. I narrow my eyes up at him.

"I know what you're thinking. That's not why she's here. I've taken care of the situation with her school as promised," Clayton explains calmly.

"Then, why is she here?" I snap.

Clayton smirks, looking over my head. "It seems Ally has some other things we need to take care of," he replies and winks at her over my head.

I spin to face Ally. She's biting her lip as something at her feet has become very, very interesting. I go into mom mode. Ally has put me and Chloe through some shit a time or two. This is no band geek standing before me.

There was a time I wasn't sure if Ally was a Blood, Crip, Latin Queen, or a Netã. We moved away from the old neighborhood to get her away from all the gangs before she fell into them for sure, but that didn't keep her away from her friends. I'm surprised Chloe and I don't have heads full of gray hair.

If it weren't for her music, I don't know if we would have kept her on track at all. Ally tends to make friends with trouble.

"Ally, what the hell is going on?" I fold my arms over my chest.

"Something came up." She sighs, still avoiding eye contact.

"Yeah, I think I got that from Clayton. I'm asking you what?"

Just then, Ally's stomach growls so loud, I lift a brow. She finally looks up at me through her lashes. A little smile is on her lips.

"I'm sort of starving," she says sheepishly.

"I'll take you out for food." The last person I thought would offer speaks up.

I whip my head toward Cane. His eyes are locked on Ally. There's something in his eyes I can't put my finger on.

"You've got to be fucking kidding me," Ally hisses.

I turn to look at her, then back at Cane. He now has a cocky grin on his lips. My patience is fried. I want to know what the hell is going on with Ally.

"You know him?" I ask, turning back to Ally and thumbing over my shoulder at Cane.

"No," she grumbles.

"Yes," Cane purrs at the exact same time.

Ally makes a sour face and narrows her eyes at him. If I were Cane, I'd run in the other direction. She gives him such a death glare I think she's going to lunge at him.

"Well, which is it?" I huff in impatience.

"It seems it's a small world. We do know each other," Cane croons.

"You don't know me," Ally says in a deadly calm that has my mouth falling open.

"You two can go do whatever you were going to do. My little friend and I will grab a bite and catch up," Cane says silkily.

I keep my eyes on Ally. She tilts her head to the side, studying Cane like he's her prey. She looks coiled for a fight. I shake my head, not having any of this.

"No, I don't think so." I turn and snap at Cane.

He waves me off, not even bothering to look away from Ally. The sly smile on his face says he doesn't have the good sense to know Ally is set to rip him apart. I should let her. His arrogant butt is starting to piss me off as well.

"David will go with them. Ally has been with him all day," Clayton breaks into the exchange.

I turn to face him, placing my hands on my hips. I go to open my mouth, but a loud slap sounds across the room. I turn to look for Ally, but she's no longer standing where I left her. I turn to where Cane was. He's now rubbing his cheek while Ally stands in front of him with her fists balled.

"What's with the women in that family?" Clayton chuckles. "Let's go."

I turn to him to find him shaking his head at Ally and Cane, amusement lighting his gray eyes. I don't find anything funny about this situation and I'm not leaving Ally here with Cane. Nope, not happening, not a chance.

"I'm not leaving." I shift my weight to one hip.

Clayton lifts a brow. "My pretty little one, have you not learned your lesson?" he purrs down at me.

I narrow my eyes at him, both hating the way he's peering down at me from all the way up there, but also thinking he's sexy as hell as he does it. His sensual lips are taunting me, while I should be telling him off for trying to leave Ally here with his little nutjob of a brother. I purse my lips and twist them up at him.

"What the heck is that supposed to mean?"

"Let me remind you," he says, just before scooping me up and over his shoulder.

"Clayton," I gasp. "Put me the f—"

He squeezes a tight hold of one of my globes, then slaps the cheek he's squeezed. I yelp, clinging to his coat.

"I told you about that mouth, Sid. Cane's not going to hurt her, and David will make sure she's fine. We're leaving," he says firmly.

I clench my teeth to keep from saying the words on the tip of my tongue. I notice David move into the foyer as Clayton makes his way to the front door, with me balancing on his shoulder. David shakes his head, amusement written all over his face.

I'm completely mortified, but I'm also turned on. Yet, I'm still plotting to kick his ass when he puts me down. Enough is enough, Clayton will not continue to manhandle me whenever he feels like it.

I'm in a full rant in my head by the time he opens the door to the apartment, walks us inside and marches us to the master bedroom. My thoughts of handing him his ass turn to dust when he deliberately slides my body slowly down the front of his.

I feel him hard against me. When my eyes lock on his, all the air whooshes from my lungs. I've never, and I mean never, seen so much intensity in a man's eyes.

"It's that same fight and fire that draws me to you," he says huskily.

Before I can reply, he captures my lips in a searing kiss that melts my bones and every single thought I have right along with it. I wrap my arms around his waist to anchor myself. My only thought is, *how does a man devour you so completely while giving you life?*

CHAPTER THIRTEEN

I want to Know...

Clayton

I intended to kiss the fight right out of her, but I might have just set myself up for failure. I only meant to kiss her senseless. Yet now, I can't think of anything other than savoring her lips.

I deepen the kiss, groaning into her mouth when she releases the sweetest moan I've ever heard. The warm skin of her back feels like silk beneath my palms. Her soft breasts are pressed against me in the most tempting way. I'm growing harder by the second.

Having her little curvy body next to mine, as I tower over her, fills me with a need I can't even describe. I want to protect what's mine while also wanting to claim her. I haven't felt this way in years. Actually, I've never felt this way.

It's the exact reason why I release my hold on her. I want too much and taking Sidney tonight wasn't a part of my plan. I break the kiss and inhale deeply while staring down into her dazed gaze. Sidney looks punch drunk. I love that look on her face after I've kissed her thoroughly.

"Tonight, I want to get to know you and I want you to get to know me," I breathe when my head clears.

Reaching to cup her face, I brush my thumb across her kiss-swollen lips. She's so gorgeous. When the time comes, I'm going to cherish the sight of those lips wrapped around me.

I chuckle when she only stares back at me as if she's lost. Removing my coat and suit jacket, I toss them toward the accent chair. I remove her cape as well, throwing it over my things.

Sidney watches my every move, her ample breasts heaving. "Come, baby." I reach for her hand and walk her into the bathroom.

Before turning my attention back to her, I turn on the water in the bathtub. It seems she's beginning to come out of her kiss-induced fog. I grin as her arms cross over her chest and that sass sparks in her eyes.

"How is this bathtub supposed to help you get to know me?" she says, lifting a brow at me.

I reach out to tug her toward me, sitting on the edge of the tub. I don't say a word as I look up at her and unzip her gown. I watch as the fabric falls to the floor at her feet, revealing a strapless lace bra, sexy lace panties, and the most beautiful brown skin I've ever seen.

I dip my head and kiss her belly. I like that it's not completely flat, but it's perfect for her curvy body. Before I get lost in her scent or the softness of her skin, I pull back.

Standing, I move her back a bit with my palms on her waist. She eyes me warily as I move deliberately slow. I remove my dress shirt, then my shoes, socks, and slacks. When we're both standing before each other in our underwear, I turn to shut off the water.

Turning back to face Sidney, I wrap my arms around her waist and draw her closer. Palming her ass, I dip in to peck her lips. Her soft hands land on my chest, causing my cock to twitch against her stomach.

"We're going to get into that bathtub, and we're going to relax and talk. Because you're so damn tempting, I'm going to sit on one side and you're going to sit on the other," I finally answer her question.

I've unclasped her bra with one hand while answering her without her even noticing until it falls to the floor. I laugh when she looks down in surprise as her lush breasts bounce free. Smoothing my hands down her sides, my fingers enter the waistband of her panties, pushing them from her hips. They, too, land at her feet.

She looks up at me with her pleading brown eyes, nearly breaking my restraint. I call on the power of three hundred men to stay the course. Squatting before her, I reach to unfasten the strap of her shoe on one ankle, then the other.

I run my palms up the backs of her legs, then back down again. I can feel the goose bumps rise. I lick my lips at the sight of her mound in my face, but I don't dare lean forward for a taste. I'm not a fool, I know what that taste will do.

Instead, I allow my fingertips to travel up her calves again. This time rising to my full height as I do so. I take the course slow and steady, enjoying the feel of her.

"Clayton," she yelps, when in a swift move, I wrap her waist with one arm and lift her from her shoes.

Her fingers go into my hair, my free hand goes to her delicious ass. Sidney wraps her legs around my waist as if they were meant to be there. I shove down my underwear with one hand, then step into the bathtub, slowly lowering into the water. Our eyes remain on each other as we descend. I lean forward to deposit her on the far side of the tub before retreating to the other side.

Sitting my back against the tub, I move my legs on the sides of Sidney's body, caging her in. I reach for her small feet, bringing them to rest against my stomach. I watch her face as I take her right foot and begin to massage it.

"Tell me about your family and childhood." I give the soft command.

I watch as she leans back, allowing herself to relax under my watchful gaze and the feel of my touch. She bites her lip, and her head falls back. I wait patiently for my answer.

These are things I read about her in reports, but that doesn't compare to her memories and real-life experience. I want to know her, what makes her tick and feel.

"My dad wasn't around for long," she begins, looking up at the ceiling. "I vaguely remember him. Not that he was a bad dad, he was a soldier. He was gone so much I don't remember him. He went MIA when I was about four. They never recovered his body or any of his team.

"I do remember the day my mom was told. I was playing in the backyard of my grandmother's house with my little friend, the neighbor. We lived with grandma then. Mommy had been hanging clothes on the line to dry. Grandma called her inside.

"Suddenly, I could hear the piercing wails of my mom. It stopped me in my tracks. Somehow, even at such a young age I knew that sound would change our lives forever…" Her words trail off.

There's sadness on her face as tears gather in her eyes. I wait patiently for what I know is coming next. It pained me when I read it in her file. Sidney is a remarkable woman. Her strength to persevere is astounding.

"My mother was never the same after that. She and grandma fought a lot until one day, we moved out and into the projects. Everything changed from there. My mother started to lose more and more of herself.

"Chloe and her mom were my saving grace. Ms. Sinclair made sure I was okay. She became like a second mother to me. She made sure I had school clothes and that I wasn't dirty. She fed me and took care of me when I was sick.

"I don't know what I would have done without her. I think my love of numbers and learning came from Chloe's mom. We never had much, but she made it her business to show us it didn't have to stay that way.

"To this day, I don't speak to my mom much. Her devastation ate her alive. I've always hoped that someday she'd come back, and I would have my mom again. Especially in the past year." She falls silent, still staring up at the ceiling.

I don't say a word. I'm lost in my own thoughts. My own problems seem to pale next to the life Sidney has been through. Yet, I feel the need to share.

"Everyone has always seen my family as picture perfect." I frown, placing her right foot back down on my stomach, switching to her left. "The money, the connections. My parents come from deep pockets and old money.

"If you talk about money, yes, we had the perfect life, but emotionally, not so much. My father is a hard man to love. It's his way or no way. My brothers and I never really got to be children. We had to be responsible for all our actions.

"There wasn't room for mistakes, flaws, or failure. For as long as I can remember, I've known to be accountable for my actions. I've never run free and gotten dirty like most little boys.

"Running could cause wrinkles or sweaty clothes, or God forbid a scrape from a fall. We never knew when our father would need us picture perfect, so we never did a thing to force a hair out of place. I hated it, I wanted to break free.

"Then, as a teenager, I let my guard down for just a moment." I pause to get my anger in check. "My father used my most vulnerable moment to teach me the greatest lesson of my life. I was left to become my own man, so I did. I haven't let my guard down since."

This time I'm the one who falls silent, lost in my thoughts of the past. I still hold so much resentment from that time in my life. It shaped me to be the man I am today.

Water splashing brings me back to the present. When I focus, I see Sidney has pulled her foot free from my hold and now both of her knees are pulled into her chest. She's watching me, assessing me.

I'm not ready for her to see into my darkness. I close the shutters, making my face impassive. I take control of the moment, steering the conversation back to her.

"You say you have a love for numbers. What made you get into the finance world?" I question.

Her eyes light up and her shoulders relax. I reach out for her legs, pulling them to drape over mine. I need the connection. I can't help stroking her soft skin.

"Sometimes, I just didn't want to go home. Ms. Sinclair worked so hard, I didn't want to be in her house all the time, though she didn't mind. I did, though, so I'd spend a lot of time in the center. Old Man Petey used to play chess with some of the older kids. One day I asked could I play.

"Now, if you played with Petey, you had to be ready to talk and learn. He expected you to hold a real conversation. He would talk about the stock market with me. I had to research whatever we talked about and come back with updates for our next game. If you tried to bullshit him, he'd tell you to get up from his table.

"I loved to play, and I loved to talk to him about stocks. I soaked it all up. By the time Chloe and I were in high school, I had a thing for flipping money. I would take the little money Chloe's mom would give us as an allowance and I'd turn it into two to three times the amount we started with." Her eyes sparkle with this memory.

Loving the way she speaks of learning to play chess, I venture further into the path. I continue to release the cool water and add warm, until our pruney skin forces us from the comfort of the tub. I learn about Sidney from every word spoken, every gesture made, and every single emotion her expressive eyes reveal.

By the time I dry her off with a towel—before wrapping her in it and carrying her to bed—I know one thing for certain. I'm beyond captivated by this woman. Her mind and her big heart are a dangerous combination. Yet, I don't think I want to stop the collision that's on course to happen.

CHAPTER FOURTEEN

No Worries

Sidney

"Good morning," Clayton croons as he leans in and pecks my lips.

He smells great and so does this kitchen. He's cooking again. I can't help the smile that comes to my face. He's shirtless and has on gray sweatpants. Gray sweatpants that come with a nice view from either side.

"Good morning. You're cooking breakfast again?"

He looks at me through his lashes. "I got the impression you were a fan of my cooking."

"I am."

"But?" He lifts a brow.

"I don't know. You're worth trillions. I didn't expect you to cook for me."

He snorts. "I'm a big man. I get hungry at all types of hours. I'm not waking staff in the middle of the night because I want a steak or some pasta. I'm quite capable of feeding myself. My chef leaves things for me to heat up, but I'm not always in the mood for that. I actually enjoy cooking for myself. Besides, Carlos is on vacation, so I get to show off." He winks.

I nod. "That makes sense."

He places eggs on a plate, then moves to reach for me. He plants his hands on my waist and dips his head to kiss me. My toes curl in my shoes as I open to him, and he consumes every corner of my mouth.

When he breaks the kiss, he presses his lips to my forehead. "I also enjoy watching you eat. I want to hear you moan over my food."

He steps back and grabs the two plates from the island before he heads for the table, gesturing with his head for me to follow. I drop my gaze to his ass.

Get it together, Sid. You need answers.

I shake my head clear. I don't have time to be lusting after this man. I need to know what's going on with getting my life back.

I take the seat opposite him and place my phone down, checking for the millionth time to see if Chloe has sent me a text. He pauses when he notices I'm not eating. Placing his fork down, he narrows his gaze on me.

"What is it?"

"Any news on my accounts? What's going on with that warrant? Is that something I need to be worried about?"

"I'll have your accounts restored by the end of the week. You don't have to worry about that warrant or any other. I've had that all taken care of. For now, you can focus on wedding planning. I'm overseeing anything trying to make its way to you from here on out and you seem to have won my father over, so he'll make it his business to look out for you as well."

I purse my lips, wanting to say more. However, I have to admit, I'm more than relieved. I'll be even more so when all my accounts are released.

I pick up my fork and start to eat. The flavors burst in my mouth. He really is a good cook.

"Tell me something, how did Delta know you could cook?"

"I've done some charities with kids, showing them how to cook. She's on a few boards and committees."

I nod as I take that answer in. He's full of surprises. It had nagged at me yesterday to know how Delta knew so much about him, but I couldn't ask while she was there.

"Where did you learn to cook?" I ask as I cover my mouth.

He picks up his napkin and wipes his mouth. I get caught in his gaze as I await an answer. This man can make anything sexy.

His presence pulls you in like a warm hug. I didn't mean to open up so much last night, but he has a way of making me want to do things I wouldn't normally do. It's like I'm safe to be a Sid I can't normally be.

"I told you last night about how we didn't get to play much. Oscar, my parents' chef, would put an apron on me and allow me to spend time in the kitchen with him. I picked some things up in travels later in life as well."

I nod. "Does Oscar still work for your parents?"

"No, he retired. His son works for them now."

"Do you need me for anything today?"

"No, I have to go into some meetings. David will be here with you."

"Is that necessary?"

"Your place was bugged. Humor me for now."

"What?" A chill runs through me as I feel totally violated.

"I had your place swept, and they found listening devices. I don't know how much further this goes, so I'd prefer David be with you when I'm not."

"And Ally and Chloe? Are they safe?"

"Chloe is with Gregor. She's more than safe. Ally, I'm working on getting her situation under control."

"Working to get it under control. What does that mean?"

"There have been some interesting developments I wasn't aware of. I had planned for her to stay at Cane's while he was away. I didn't know of their connection, and it seems like her problem is somehow connected to Cane's. I'm taking care of it."

I start to rub my temples. I'm not getting straight answers and I know so much more is going on here.

"Why is this happening to me?" I say in almost a whisper.

"Baby, I don't want you to worry about any of this. Delta sent me a text. She wants to meet with you tomorrow. You can focus on planning our wedding to get your mind off things. How about you take today to relax and maybe write?"

"I don't have my laptop."

"I had David replace the one that may have been bugged too. You can use my office to work in if you like. I might be in late tonight. Anything here is yours. Make yourself at home."

He picks up his phone and types something quickly before placing it back on the table. My phone buzzes next to my hand.

"That's my number. Call me anytime you need me."

I look at him and tilt my head. This man has known entirely too much about me. I never gave him my number.

"What don't you know about me, Clayton?"

"How your pussy feels wrapped around me as I'm deep inside you." He winks.

I bite my lip, trying not to smile at him. After the full-frontal view I had in the bathtub last night, I can't help the images that float through my head.

Damn, I need to get my life back before I'm in trouble.

CHAPTER FIFTEEN

To See her Happy

Sidney

I took Clayton up on his offer to use his office, but I can't focus enough to get any writing done. I'm starting to become so pissed with Chloe. She needs to answer my calls and texts.

I want to say this isn't like her, but there was a time when this was her. She was seeing some guy and she'd sneak off to spend the night with him while I'd watch Ally. I would have to send 911 messages if I really needed her. Otherwise, she'd ignore my pages.

Giving up on trying to write, I get up and head for the kitchen. My stomach growls as I enter the hall. "All right, all right," I mutter.

"Hey, everything okay?"

I jump and yelp as David appears. I almost forgot he was here. I place a hand over my stomach and take a calming breath. I laugh at my thoughts as I wonder if Clayton only hires handsome men. All his guards are attractive, but David is gorgeous. He has dark hair and piercing blue eyes. He's only an inch or two shorter than Clayton.

"I'm fine. I'm just a bit hungry. I was heading to see if there's anything here."

"I've ordered some Italian food. There're garlic knots, lasagna, and a salad. Clay said that's what you would like."

I smile. "How does your boss know so much about me and my preferences?"

"Clay is very thorough in his research before he pursues an arrangement. However, in your case, I do believe he was a bit more invested and thorough about understanding you."

"Understanding me? It sounds more like he's stalking me. Should I be worried?"

I start to question my decisions as of late. This isn't normal. This situation is crazy.

"Clayton is my best friend. You can trust him. He'd do anything to keep you safe and happy. I think in time, you'll learn why he's chosen this route and it will all make sense to you."

I palm my forehead. "You know what, I think I've lost my appetite."

"Please try to eat something. Mr. Hennessy will be upset if he finds out you haven't eaten all day."

I bob my head, still lost in my thoughts. "Okay, I'll try."

"Good, if you need me, you can use the intercom system. Enjoy the meal."

I stumble into the kitchen with a million thoughts. Clayton's dad didn't seem so horrible to me. Yes, at first, I was a little offended, but then I realized Clooney and Eileen were just hurt by how they found out about the engagement. I guess that kind of did suck.

I grab something to eat and then head upstairs to take a bath and relax. Sitting on the side of the bed to gather my thoughts, I pick up my phone to check for a message from Chloe. Instead of finding a reply from her, I find a text from Clayton.

Clayton: Check your accounts.

I quickly open the app and log on. I squeal and fall back on the bed as I see my funds have been released. I want to kiss Clayton and run out to do some retail therapy to make up for this sucky week.

Sound by the door grabs my attention. I look up to find Clayton in the doorway, watching me. He looks tired. I look at the time on my phone. It's after eight.

"Long day?"

He runs a hand through his hair. "You have no idea."

"Come, sit with me."

He starts to remove his suit jacket and then works on his cuffs. I marvel at how smooth he moves, as if always in control. It's like he knows each move is alluring and sexy, drawing me into his trap.

I sit up and move to the center of the bed, crossing my legs. Once down to his boxers, he sits at the foot. I sit staring at his back.

"How was dinner? Did you enjoy it? I know another place if you didn't like that one."

"It was great, but let me ask you something," I reply.

He turns and lifts a brow, reaching to place a hand on my thigh. My skin starts to hum from his touch. If it weren't for this connection and the safety I feel with him, I don't think I would still be here.

"How do you know so much about me? What made you choose me for this?"

"I know what any determined person can learn about anyone. I've spent years learning and studying you. After the first night I saw you, I needed to know more. Your beauty piqued my interest, but there was something else about you that drew me in and made me want to get to know you."

I scoff and shake my head. The first time he saw me? I don't know whether to be alarmed or flattered.

He turns and crawls up the bed, moving around me to sit behind me and pulls me into his chest. He wraps me in his arms and breathes me in.

"I know it sounds crazy, but my past has made me cautious of who I see. My intention is never to invade another's privacy. It's more so to protect me."

"So you wanted to learn if I was a nutjob by doing nutjob shit?"

He laughs, the deep rumble vibrates through my back. My nipples tighten when he kisses the side of my neck. He smells so good, even after a long day at work.

I relax in his hold, feeling more than safe. Any other guy would have reached under this thin tank top to fondle me. Not Clayton, he keeps his arms around me and buries his face in my hair.

"I guess you can see it that way, or you can see that I want to get to know you."

"Okay, Clay. You want to get to know me. Tell me something I don't know about you."

"I only live in New York part time. I have a home in Georgia, where I stay most times when I'm not in New York.

"You know I'm the middle brother of three. My father wants us to take over his empire, but we came up with a plan to build our own."

"I have so many questions about that, but go on."

"No, I'll answer. What do you want to know?"

"How is your father trying to control you? Why do we need to put on this farce?"

This is a question that's been burning my thoughts. After meeting Clooney, he doesn't seem like the monster I thought Clayton was up against. He seems more like a concerned dad.

"My dad managed to gain a controlling interest in our companies. I still don't know how. Once he knew he had us by the balls, he demanded we marry and come run the family business, or he would dismantle all we've worked for."

I gasp and turn to look up at him. "Oh wow, that's...that's—"

"Total bullshit. Yeah, I know. You don't even know how fucked up it is. We all have our reasons for not being married and Dad knows it. To force this is the cruelest thing he has ever done. And trust me, he's done some foul shit."

I can't help but feel for him. It hits me why he needs me as I look into his eyes and see the pain there. Clearly, his reason for not wanting to get married is something heavy.

I think fast to change the subject even as I tell myself I plan to help this man any way I can. I couldn't imagine having a father who's so controlling.

"And the Penthouse suites. There are three of them and all three of you live here…when you're in New York."

"Yes. You don't care for Cane, do you?"

"I don't know him."

"And yet, you don't like him."

"He has left a bad taste in my mouth. I'm particularly protective of Ally. I'm not sure what's going on with them."

"Give him time to grow on you. He means Ally no harm. I think he's become just as protective."

"Time will tell," I mumble.

"That it will."

Clayton

Sidney doesn't know it, but this is just what I needed. Coming home and finding her in my bed brought me a calm I can't explain. I still want her, but this…the intimacy of holding her in my arms is something I didn't know I'd been missing.

I hold on to the feeling and allow it to course through my body. She's the perfect fit to my life, and it's only been a few days. I'm still in awe of the fact that I'm okay with this. I want her here.

A smile comes to my lips. "You know I won't allow anything to happen to Ally?"

"I'm trying to trust you, but that girl means everything to me and Chloe. They both mean the world to me. You won't have to worry about your father if something happens to one of them, so I hope you make good on your promises."

I laugh into her neck and squeeze my arms around her. Again, I note that fierceness I love about her. I reach to brush a lock of hair behind her ear. It's hard not to touch her in some way. Not stripping her bare to take her has been a battle in itself.

It's been three days and I've shown restraint I didn't know I had, but I'll continue to as long as I can have moments like this.

She turns her head up and stares at me for a beat. I search her face, floored by her beauty.

"What are you thinking? You get this look in your eyes sometimes."

"I'm thinking about how gorgeous you are. You make me want things I never knew I wanted. You toss everything I thought I knew about life out of the window," I reply.

"Wow, you were thinking all of that?"

I chuckle. "Yes, I'm captivated by you."

She palms the side of my face. "I'm becoming very intrigued by you."

I lean in and take her lips, forcing myself not to reach into her shorts to play with her pussy. I want more than sex from Sidney. Otherwise, I would have pounded her ass into my bed days ago. Instead, I'm savoring the light she brings into my life.

She pulls away from the kiss. "You, Clay, are dangerous," she says breathlessly.

I wink at her. "I'm harmless…until I'm not."

CHAPTER SIXTEEN

Unpredicted

Sidney

I wasn't expecting all this. I've been with Clayton for two weeks and he keeps surprising me. All I mentioned was a restaurant in Vegas I'd heard about.

The next thing I knew, I was packing a bag to meet him after work. When David pulled up to the tarmac and I saw Clayton standing in front of the plane with the wind blowing through his hair, wearing a pink polo, light blue jeans and white sneakers, I was stunned.

Now here I am in Vegas, feeling like a pampered queen. Is this what being a kept woman is like? If it is, I wouldn't mind living this life. I laugh at myself and sink deeper into the warm water.

I lift my arms up over my head and stretch, trying not to fall all the way into this big-ass tub. Sitting back up, I lift my leg to allow the water and bubbles to run down it. This place has brought me so much peace. I've barely stressed about anything going on back home.

Reaching for my glass of champagne, I drain the glass and hum happily. After a day of shopping and an amazing dinner, Clayton drew me a bath to relax. Last night when we arrived, I had no idea what to expect.

The man is so unpredictable. I didn't expect him to drop everything so I could go to a restaurant I read about. Nor did I think he would dress up in the things I picked for him while shopping, but he went along with me asking him to model for me. Phew, the man can make anything look great.

"You okay in here?" I look up as his deep, rich voice pulls me from my thoughts.

He's standing in the doorway in a pair of boxers with no shirt on. His long legs look so powerful. Oh, God, wait. Is that the tip of his penis peeking through the leg of his boxers? I look up at his face quickly.

The size of this man definitely matches the size of the heat he's packing. His dick is as long and thick as he is and to think, that's not even full-mast.

"Are you coming in?"

I enjoyed our bath time last time. I wouldn't mind doing it again. However, I'm disappointed by his answer.

"I'm waiting on a few calls. I just wanted to check on you. Maybe next time."

Right as my gaze falls back to his length, it twitches against the fabric. I bite my lip and reach to pour myself some more champagne. I can't allow the romantic vibe of this place to cause me to lose focus.

None of this is real. We're not dating, and this engagement will be over before I know it. When we return home, I'll still be planning a fake wedding to help him get out of his tyrant father's grasp.

Keep it together, Sid.

All my accounts have been restored. Now I need to know who's after me and how to shut their asses down. That needs to be my main focus. Not Clayton.

CHAPTER SEVENTEEN

Couple Things

Clayton

A week later...

With each day that passes, I enjoy having Sidney in my space more and more. After our trip to Vegas, we've become more attuned to each other.

I'm beginning to believe she enjoys my company as much as I enjoy hers. I'm starting to miss her when she's not around. The sexual tension is off the charts as well.

However, I don't think Sid is ready for me. Not the way I want her to be. When I take her, I want her to crave me like her next breath.

"Call me when you have something I can use," I say and end my call.

We're in my home office. Sidney has been writing as I make
a few calls. I'm trying to keep it down, so I don't disturb her. I
love watching her get lost in her writing. She gets this look in
her eyes and I know she's off in some world only known to her.

"I'm going to break for lunch soon," she says and stretches
her arms above her head. The oversized sweatshirt she took from
my closet shows me just how comfortable we have become.

She has more than enough clothes of her own, but she takes
my things all the time. I don't mind. Something possessive
comes over me when I see her wearing my clothes.

In the last few weeks, I've come to have a hard time seeing
Sid as anything other than mine. I shake my head to focus.

"What would you like to eat? I can order in."

"I'm fine with the leftovers from last night."

"You sure? It's no trouble to make a call. Carlos will be back
from vacation in a few days. He'll be taking over the cooking."

Sidney pouts. "So no more of your delicious meals?"

"I'll cook for you anytime you want, baby."

She gives me a little smile. "Come sit with me. I have a few
more scenes to write before I break for lunch. Keep me
company."

I move over to the lounge she's sitting on. She scoots forward
and I throw my leg over the chaise lounge to take a seat behind
her. She settles back into my chest. This seems to be one of her
favorite positions.

Kissing the top of her head, I relax and take in the silence of
the room. The clicking of her fingers over the keyboard is the
only sound as we fall into a comfortable silence.

"Have you heard from your brother? How's Chloe? Why
hasn't she returned my calls?"

"They have a lot going on. I'll see if he can get her to touch base with you soon."

"I just want to know she's all right. This isn't like her."

"I understand, I'll talk to him."

"Thanks."

"How's the wedding planning going?"

"It's fine. Although, I don't know why you have me spending so much money on a wedding that's not going to happen."

"You let me worry about that. Have you found a dress?"

She turns to look at me. I peck her lips, then her nose. She's such a pretty woman.

"No. I'm going to go looking again this week. Delta won't let it go. Your mom wants me to FaceTime her next time."

I nod. Mom took off for Dubai. Apparently, whatever's going on with Gregor needed mom's attention.

"If you don't find anything soon, I'll bring in a designer. You can have something custom made."

"Clay, don't be ridiculous."

"There's nothing ridiculous about it. Humor me, Sid."

"Hmm."

"Were you this reluctant in your old relationships?"

"First, we're not in a relationship, which is why I don't want to waste your money. Second, I used to bend over backward for my boyfriends, and I was hurt every time. It took a long time for me to see I needed to know myself before I could be with anyone else."

"Is that why you haven't been dating in the past few years?"

"Clay, you're growing on me. Don't start that creepy stalking shit again."

I laugh, not even offended by her use of language. I'm learning to allow Sid to be Sid. I like her that way.

"No, seriously, a gorgeous woman like you should have men knocking down her door."

"I've gone on a date or two in the last two years. You might want to check your sources. They're leaving things out."

That earns another laugh. She places her laptop aside and turns to face me. I cup her face and take her lips. Then place my forehead to hers to absorb her.

"Clay, we're not really getting married. Can you back off on the spending?"

"My father knows I would spare no expense if this were real. Stop worrying, it's fine."

I smile and wrap my arms around her for a hug. Little does she know. I plan to get her to the altar. My goals have changed again, I want to have Sid with me until I have my fill. If going through with this wedding will get me that, I'm all for it.

Sidney

I sit at Clay's desk in his home office on the phone with Delta as I rub at my temples. I have a tension headache. Today was one of those days when all of this feels like a real relationship.

Everything feels too real. My heart is opening to Clayton without my permission. It's the attention and the warmth he gives. Yes, he's a bit domineering, but it's the care he gives that brings balance.

For example, I complained about not liking to do the business part of running my company. I'd rather focus on the writing. The next morning, Nikki, my new assistant, was waiting for me.

Clay gets shit done. It has also become clear to me that he pays attention to details. He makes sure I'm happy and taken care of, even when I don't speak up about what it is I want. That's dangerous when this is all supposed to be fake.

"Sidney?"

"Oh, sorry. What was that?"

"Did you get to look at the invitation paper I sent over? Which sample did you like?"

This is just another example of Clayton wiggling his way into my feelings. The delivery with the samples arrived and he insisted on sitting with me to make the decisions on the invitations. He was totally invested in my thoughts and gave his input as well.

"Oh, yes, we looked at them. Clayton likes the black paper with the gold writing. I'm leaning more toward the navy blue with the silver print."

"Those are both lovely options. I'll have them make a sample of each and you two can choose from there."

"Thanks, that sounds great."

"I'll need your final approval on the floral arrangements and the linens. The place settings came in and they're divine. I'll send you over some photos and bring a set by in person for our next meeting."

"That sounds awesome. Thanks so much."

"No problem, dear. Is there anything else you've thought of that I can get for you?"

"Oh, no. Everything is fine."

I rub my forehead as I think of the price of the custom place settings alone. I'm not adding a thing more to this wedding. I blow out a breath and roll my shoulders.

I moan out loud as large hands land on my neck. Clayton kisses the top of my head as he massages the tension away. Delta is forgotten before she even ends the call.

I look up and he places a kiss on my lips. "You've been in here all day. Let's go to bed."

"I was heading up for a bath before Delta caught me."

His brows wrinkle in concern. "Everything okay?"

"Yeah, she just needed me to weigh in on a few things."

"Did you tell her about the Swarovski crystal floral arrangements you liked?"

"Clay," I groan. "No, I told you those were so pricey."

"And I told you to get whatever you like. This isn't hurting me in the least. My mother and father would expect nothing but the best."

"Gah." I cover my face with my hands.

He releases me and takes his phone out. I already know he's texting Delta. Again, with that domineering personality.

If he were really my man, I know I'd feel cherished by the way he always wants to make me happy, but he's not, so this is ridiculous.

"Come on, baby. Let's get ready for bed."

I look up at him, thinking of so many things I should say. However, the words die on my lips as he holds his hand out and gives me that panty-melting smile.

I take his hand. He leads me upstairs to the room we share. As has become routine, he starts to take my clothes off. I stand staring up at him, wishing this was more than a contract agreement.

He cups my face when I'm down to my panties and bra, running his thumb across my lip. I watch him stare hungrily at my mouth. I peek my tongue out to follow his finger as he makes a second pass.

"Sidney, Sidney," he murmurs before turning to grab a nightgown for me to wear to sleep.

I release a breath of disappointment. He has to feel how much I want him. However, I'm not about to throw myself at him like a thirsty thot.

So I allow him to dress me and tuck me in before he changes into a pair of sleep pants and climbs into the bed next to me. He palms my face again and presses his forehead to mine.

He breaks the contact and backs away slightly. "Do you trust me yet, Sid?"

"I'm getting there."

He gently kisses my lips and settles back against the bed, pulling me into his chest. I snuggle into his side, wondering if I should have answered differently.

Damn it, Sid. Take your ass to bed. None of this is real.

CHAPTER EIGHTEEN

Romantic Dinner

Sidney

"Thanks, David. You can leave those there," I say as we enter the apartment.

I've been out dress shopping with Delta all day. I just can't bring myself to purchase a dress I know I'm not going to wear. I've tried on dress after dress and found something wrong with all of them.

Once Delta said she had to leave to meet with another client, I took advantage and went to do some real shopping on my own. Well, as on my own as Clayton will allow these days. Poor David. I know he has to be tired of me.

"Mr. Hennessy is expecting you. I'll see you later."

"Thanks."

I turn, walking deeper into the apartment. The aroma of something delicious hits me. My mouth starts to water. The deeper into the apartment I go, the more I salivate.

Clayton appears, wiping his hands on a towel. He looks as delicious as the room smells. He has on a pair of black slacks and a black dress shirt with the sleeves rolled up over his elbows.

He has a bit of a beard going on. I love the red contrast to his skin. His beard shows more red than the hair on the top of his head.

He purses his lips. "Still no dress?"

I shake my head. "No."

He opens his arms. "Come here."

I walk over to him and into his embrace. He kisses the top of my head. I look up at him and he captures my lips. I'm expecting just a peck, but he devours me instead.

I moan into his mouth the same time as he groans into mine. My pussy starts to throb as he palms my ass and holds me to him.

Maybe tonight will be the night we finally have sex. I appreciate that he's been taking things slow. However, the contract did say we would be intimate, and it's kisses like this that have me looking forward to when that time comes.

He breaks the kiss. "I'll call Delta in the morning and let her know to bring someone in. They can design whatever you want."

"Clayton, no."

"Yes." He kisses my nose.

Well, that just backfired. I didn't want to waste his money on the gowns I've been looking at. Now he's going to spend a fortune bringing someone in.

In the short time I've gotten to know him. I've learned that when he gets something in his head, it's final. I'll be getting a dress designed for this nonexistent wedding if I don't find a way to put a stop to this.

"Listen, Delta has a few more shops she wants me to go to. If I don't find a dress in one of those, then we can do it your way."

He eyes me suspiciously. "Fine." He pecks my lips. "Come, let's eat."

Clayton

"This is so romantic. It must have taken so much time for you to do all this," Sid says as she looks around at the roses, candles, and the table set for two.

I shrug my shoulders. "Not really, Levi was here to help."

The look on her face is beyond what I was expecting. I'd do it all again to put that look there. The candlelight highlights her beauty. I've never wanted to do so much for any other woman.

"Speaking of assistants. How is Nikki working out? Are you happy with her?" I ask.

"She's great. I'm getting so much more writing done. Thanks again."

"No problem," I reply.

"You know, having her has led me to think about writing an actual full-length novel."

"So why don't you?"

She shrugs. "Fear, I guess. A short story is miles away from a book. I'll need to find editors and I'm thinking about self-publishing, so I need to do my research on how that all works."

"I'm sure you can pull it off. I'll help with finding the editors. I'll have Levi get on that first thing in the morning. Go for it. If anyone can do it, it's you."

She gives me a cute smile and tilts her head to the side. "You have such confidence in me. It means a lot. Thank you."

"Anytime. Let me know how I can help. I'm here for whatever you need."

"And why is that?"

I place my fork and knife down. I take her in and allow a small smile to take over my lips. Why am I here for her every need? I've asked myself the same thing since she signed that contract. I've never been this invested in my past arrangements.

Yes, I take care of my women and their needs. However, none of those women have answered the deep needs I have the way she has. I'm willing to give her anything she needs because she gives me all that I need without knowing it.

"You're mine."

The awed look on her face is the most satisfying look I've seen all night. However, no lie has been told. She is mine.

"All right then," she breathes.

CHAPTER NINETEEN

On Fire

Sidney

A week later…

"Sid, Baby, what's wrong?" Clayton grumbles tiredly while spooning behind me in bed. My skin is buzzing from his nearness. My nipples are so hard they could cut a diamond.

"Nothing," I reply quietly.

It's been a month since that night I opened up to Clayton in the bathtub. I hadn't expected to bare my soul to him the way I had. That was only the start to me losing a piece of myself to him. There's just something about him that always has me doing the opposite of what I think I would.

For example, I'm not quick to bed any man, but after his romantic gestures over the last four weeks, I've been ready to lie down with Clayton. Only, he never takes things there.

That night all those weeks ago, instead of having sex, he dried me off, carried me into the bedroom and dressed me in a nightgown like I was the most precious thing in the world to him.

That has become a routine. He will undress me to dress me for bed, but it never goes further than that.

I've been both blown away and disappointed by the restraint he's shown in the last four weeks. I see the lust in his eyes, but he's content with holding me close and falling asleep with me in his arms.

At first, I was grateful to him for this since my mind seemed to be malfunctioning. I needed to get all my lust-filled thoughts and feelings under control. Thinking clearly is necessary.

Yet now, it's all pissing me off. I go to bed every night with one of the sexiest men I've ever met in my life, and he hasn't made a single move to take our relationship to the next level of intimacy.

If only he could be as determined about getting into my drawers as he is about planning this fake wedding. Clayton has ensured that I cover every single detail for the wedding. You would think we were really going to get married.

I mean, he seems to be attracted to me. His heated kisses say he is. Yet, I'm the most sexually frustrated I've ever been in my life.

I've even started to work out. After all, I could stand a little toning here and there. Lord knows I need to work off this frustration.

I've tried flirting. Which, by the way, I think I totally suck at. I've even wiggled my ass on that morning wood a few times in hopes he'd share.

It hasn't happened yet. I'm starting to think that maybe he has a supplier on the side. Some chick who's giving him a release, while he keeps me tortured with need in his bed.

"I would have believed that lie an hour ago, before you spent an hour sighing and wiggling in my hold." He sighs, the exhaustion in his voice clear.

I'm exhausted too from running around looking for a wedding gown. Eileen has had me FaceTime her each time since she hasn't returned from her trip. She truly is a sweet woman.

I hate that she believes I just haven't found the right dress, when in truth, I haven't chosen one because I'll never wear it. I'm still trying not to waste Clayton's money, no matter what he says.

Since I still haven't found a dress, he's already commissioned a designer to come in and design whatever it is I want. I honestly don't understand this man at all.

He kisses the top of my head, drawing me in closer to his heat. The erection I feel poking me in the ass has me throbbing. I don't understand how it can be so clear that he wants me, yet he denies us both—leaving me utterly confused.

"I have a lot on my mind. Things have been…" I pause, thinking of the right words. "Too silent, I guess."

Clayton groans. "Never, ever say those words," he releases me, rolling onto his back. "Those words almost always fuck shit up."

I turn to look at his face. He has a sour pout that's adorable. Honestly, those words were the first thing to come to mind as a cover. They weren't my actual thoughts. There's no way I'm telling this man that I want to fuck him more than I want my next meal.

However, I do have questions now that I have his attention. It's been a month and though I haven't been threatened with jail time and my accounts have been released, I have a feeling all of this isn't over. Clayton hasn't mentioned much about what's going on since briefing me the morning after I met his parents. He told me to let him handle it.

I reluctantly gave in at the time and he's been keeping me so busy with wedding planning I haven't had time to focus on anything other than the wedding and my book. My website has seemed to double in membership, which probably has something to do with the fact that I've been writing my fantasies of the giant lying beside me.

"Are you ever going to tell me who's after me?" I blurt out.

"Sid," he groans.

I almost smile. He's been calling me Sid more and more in the last few weeks. I think we've reached a new level of comfort with each other. I'm seeing more and more of his humorous side.

"What?" I huff.

"I'm so fucking tired. Can't you just lie your ass down on me and help me fall asleep? Stop fidgeting, quiet down your thoughts, and go to sleep. In the morning, I will answer anything you want me to," he rumbles while rubbing his eyes.

I sit and think for a moment. I have a million things I'd like to say. All of them nasty. I wonder if I let one of them slip, will he still be too tired?

I'll lie my ass down if you lie on top of me. Why don't you quiet my thoughts down by making me scream your name? I can go to sleep after you finally put it on me.

Yup, I have a bunch of things I want to say, but I just bite my lip and stare into his tired gray eyes as he looks back at me. His eyes drop to my rock-hard nipples. For a brief moment, I think I detect lust in his eyes.

He licks his lips before they part to speak, but his phone rings, cutting off his words. He growls, rolling to reach for the phone on the nightstand. His brows crease when he looks at the screen.

Sitting up, he leans in to kiss my forehead before standing and leaving the room. I fold my arms over my chest and stare after him. Clayton never leaves the room to take a call.

I don't think of myself as insecure, but this right here has me second-guessing myself in all types of ways. I don't like it and I damn sure won't allow it. Enough is enough.

You know something, I'm glad we haven't slept together. That's going to help me make this exit swift.

I don't need to be anymore tied to this man than I already am. All of this is for the birds. If he's seeing someone, he's welcome to it. I'm officially over it.

CHAPTER TWENTY

Ten Steps Back

Sidney

I'm sitting on the chaise lounge in Clayton's office, working on a few blog posts for today. Which is driving my horny ass crazy.

I'm typing about this guy pounding this chick out and all I want is for Clayton to come over here and fuck me against this chaise. In my defense. It's been so long since I've been with a man. Clayton is all man and looking at that body and smelling his manly cologne and aftershave is doing nothing to help me.

"You were gone when I woke," Clayton rumbles as he appears.

He grasps the back of my neck and tips my head back for a kiss. I turn my face and his lips land on my cheek. I ignore him and keep typing.

"I wanted to get in a workout and get these thoughts down," I reply.

"I was surprised, is all," he says, sounding a bit frustrated.

I stop typing to look up at him and frown. His hair is damp from his shower and his dress shirt is sitting open as it's tucked into his slacks. Gah, why me?

He goes to throw his leg over the chaise to sit behind me, but I get up, take my laptop, and move across the room to sit on the floor.

I go back to work as if nothing happened. His eyes are on me, but I refuse to look up at him. I'm too charged up to allow him to be so close to me.

His phone rings, causing him to stand and leave the room as he starts to bark orders into it. I watch his ass as he goes.

"Thank God," I murmur.

Clayton

"Sidney." I blow out a long, exasperated breath. "I'm not a mind reader, but it's clear we're having a problem. Would you like to tell me what's going on?"

"Nothing," she replies, not looking up from her plate.

I've been in a shit mood since last night. It's been a long week full of shit to keep me on my toes. I was already tired when that call came in.

It should have been a simple task, pick up the jewels from Georgia and bring them here to New York. That's all the guys had to do. I wanted to have them cleaned and maintained before handing them over to the woman that has made her way into my heart without so much as knowing it.

How a simple task turned into two of my men being arrested and detained for questioning, I have no idea. Another well-aligned tip that has only served to piss me off. Sidney thinks things have been quiet.

They haven't, I've just been ahead of her finding out about any of the bullshit that's happening. One of my companies is in the process of being audited and a few of my permits have been paused for a couple of new projects. It's nothing to really hurt my business, but it's enough to be a nuisance.

Someone's trying to get under my skin. I could easily make this all go away if I go to my father for his help, but I'll be a dead man before that happens. I've done everything I can to keep a lid on this since my father decided to stick his nose into Sid's situation.

If all of that wasn't enough to piss me off, now I have my woman trying to freeze me out. I've been taking my time to build a relationship with Sidney. She hasn't even realized how much she's opened up to me in the last four weeks. It's been so natural.

We've fallen into a routine. Sid has fit into my life so effortlessly. I enjoy our weekends the most. The hours when she sits between my legs as she clicks away on her laptop, while I make calls and hammer away at my own business.

That was the first clue that something was wrong this afternoon. When I went to climb behind her on the chaise lounge and she got up and sat across the room on the floor. At first, I let it slide, thinking maybe she was in the middle of a scene and didn't want the distraction.

I try to respect her creativity. Already frustrated with the delivery that should have arrived today, I let it go. I spent most of the afternoon barking orders anyway.

It was when Ashley arrived to get Sid ready for dinner that I was no longer able to ignore her change in temperament. I'd forgotten to tell her we were going out for a dinner date. I've been so busy this week, I wanted to spend a little time with her.

One of my restaurants just received an amazing review. I thought I'd bring her here to celebrate. I also wanted to inform her that we'll be traveling to Georgia for a bit in the coming months.

I've been here in New York longer than I planned. It's time for me to start making my rounds. Gregor still isn't back, he has his own shit to deal with, which has left me with more on my plate than I expected.

What I also wasn't expecting was to have Sidney decline dinner, repeatedly. We damn near had a fight just for her to get ready. The woman is lucky she's the only person in the world I have patience for at the moment. Although, I feel like we've somehow taken ten steps back.

"You haven't said two words to me since we got in the car," I retort.

"I'm not in a talkative mood." She shrugs.

"Would you like to tell me why?"

With a sigh, she places her fork beside her plate. Her pretty eyes lift to mine, and they're guarded. I don't like it, so much so, my jaw tightens, and I sit back in my seat.

"Clayton, this is an arrangement. We don't have to pretend it's more than that. All the talking and getting to know each other can stop. When this is over, we're going to go our separate ways and you will be free to talk to whoever you like, whenever you like," she says coolly.

I snap my head back. I didn't see that coming. We were getting along fine. I narrow my eyes on her. I don't know what's been going on in her head, but I'm about to fix it for her right now.

I tilt my head, still studying her as her words roll through my mind. I lock in on the words that stick out to me most. Clearly, Sidney is missing some of the larger pieces here, but I'll be glad to point them out.

"I'm not sure who's pretending. I'm a grown-ass man, Sweetheart. I don't have time for games, nor do I play them. What need do I have to talk to anyone else when I have the most beautiful woman in the world already?" I lift a brow.

"Furthermore, this"—I wave between us—"won't be over for a very, very, very long time. Maybe you should spend more time getting to know me. That way, you can save us these little talks."

She rolls her eyes and works her jaw. Her eyes ignite with anger. I'm ready to match her energy. Enough is enough.

"Someone has your attention, because I sure as hell can't get it and since when can't you talk on the phone in front of me?

"Obviously, you have someone that's keeping your interest. I'm a grown-ass woman. I don't beg anyone to want me," she snaps in a hushed tone, clamping her mouth shut at the end as if she's said too much.

Ah, we've gotten to the root of all of this. The corners of my lips lift into a smile. My little kitten wants to be stroked. As exhausted as I was last night, I was more than tempted before that call came in. I only left the room because it concerned a surprise for her.

Catching her eyes, I lean forward so that she hears every word that's about to come out of my mouth. I want there to be no misunderstandings from this point on. I let all the feelings I've been concealing show in my eyes.

"You always have my attention. How can anyone else keep my interest when all I think about is you? I wake up wanting to taste you, wanting to push your thick thighs apart to bury my head between them. I go to bed hard as fuck, wanting nothing more than to push inside you to feel your tight walls clamp around me.

"I bet that pussy is nice and tight. The type of pussy that makes you want to throw your head back and lose your mind. While I watch you sleep, I think about sucking those gorgeous tits. I've been tempted to knead those beautiful mounds until you open those pretty eyes and look at me.

"I want to get behind that lush ass and watch it bounce on my cock. And when I feel you on the verge of coming, I want to stop to eat that sweet pussy until you come, just so I can fuck you again. My cock doesn't get hard for anyone but you, precious.

"Last night's call wasn't for your ears, but it wasn't because I had someone else to entertain my interests. You never have to worry about me and any other woman. This cock has your name on it." I pause, licking my lips as my gaze roams over her. "Now, Sid, if I've been keeping my baby waiting too long. You say the word.

"I've been dying to fuck you to the brink of insanity. You want to drip that sweet cum on me, I'll be happy to oblige you. One word, Sid. Just one word. Yes, is all you need to say," I purr.

Her eyes are completely dilated. Her lush lips are parted, that sexy tongue peeks out to wet her lips. Her breasts heave in that sexy black dress.

I've been staring at her tastefully exposed patch of skin all night. Her chocolate breasts are one of my favorite parts of her delectable body. I want her to say the word more than she knows. Just give me a reason to have her breasts in my mouth tonight.

The table remains silent as I wait for her response. It's always been Sid's choice. I've noticed her flirting, but she wasn't ready. Now, I see it. I see how ready she is.

"Yes," the word is finally breathed through her full lips.

I stand from my seat, gesturing for the manager to come over. Buttoning my suit jacket, I wait for him to rush to our table. Phillip has been with me for years.

"Is everything to your satisfaction, sir?" Phillip asks as he approaches me.

"Shut the kitchen down. Send the staff home. You're all done for the night," I reply, not taking my eyes off Sidney.

"Excuse me, sir. Was something wrong with the meal?"

I ignore his question, reaching for my glass and knife. I tap the glass to get the attention of the patrons that are still dining. The entire restaurant comes to a standstill around me.

Sidney and I have been sitting at the table in the center of the restaurant. I wanted diners to know I was in the building, enjoying a meal just as they were.

"Good evening, everyone. I hope your dining experience has been stellar this evening. I want to apologize for this, but the restaurant will be closing immediately. As a thank you and an apology, I will be covering everyone's tab, and you will all receive a voucher for your next visit. Please see Phillip on your way out, he will take care of you," I announce.

I finally turn my gaze to a stunned Phillip. He instantly shakes the shock off, nodding. He rushes the staff into action as I return to my seat, giving Sid all my attention.

Her brows are furrowed as she looks at me. Confusion and curiosity are written all over her face. I remain silent as the restaurant buzzes with murmurs and grumbles. I reach for my wine, finishing the glass and pouring another.

I wave over our waiter and have him clear our table. Sid hasn't touched her meal since our conversation started. I think it's clear that dinner is over. I have other plans for dessert at the moment.

I can feel the anticipation building within Sidney. It's rolling off her in waves. It's exactly the reaction I was going for. By the time this place clears out, we'll both be coming apart from desire and uncontained need.

I lounge back in my seat, tossing an arm over the back of my chair. The picture of a relaxed and restrained man on the outside. From looking at me, one would never know I'm coming out of my skin on the inside, dying to get my hands on her.

Sidney, on the other hand, can't stop fidgeting under my gaze. It's like watching my prey. She knows what's coming. The trap has been set and she has been cornered. There's no place for her to go.

"Will that be all, sir? Can I get you anything else before the staff and I leave?" Phillip comes over to ask after the last patron has left the restaurant.

"That will be all. You can cut the lights in the front and dim the ones in the main dining room. Lock the front door, we'll be leaving through the back," I reply.

"Will do," Phillip says, still looking perplexed. "Have a good evening, Sir."

The lights dim and the restaurant falls completely silent after the workers leave through the front. I stand from my seat, removing my suit jacket. Sidney's eyes follow mine, craning her neck to do so.

"You do understand I'm about to ruin you," I say, releasing my cuff links.

"Wow, you're awfully cocky," she says huskily.

"You have no idea." I lick my lips, removing my now unbuttoned shirt.

I round the table, lifting her from her seat and turn her back to me, pulling her into my front. Her round ass moves into me, fitting her body to me perfectly. I splay hands over her belly as I lean into her ear.

"This is it, Sid. Once I take you, you belong to me," I whisper in her ear.

"You're all talk, so far," she breathes out.

I laugh, bending my head to kiss her neck. Slowly, I move my hands to release the zipper on the back of her dress. The fabric of the tight satin dress parts to reveal the soft skin I've longed to caress. I slip my hand into the parted fabric, gliding my hand from her side around to her front.

I cup her heavy mound, kneading it while nibbling on her neck. Sid gasps when I suck her flesh into my mouth. It's a sound I will be committing to memory.

I edge my free hand into her dress to push it from her body. Pure satin greets my fingertips. I've never felt skin as smooth and soft. She shivers as goose bumps rise on her flesh.

I push the dress down far enough for it to fall at her feet on its own. Slowly, I retrace the path my hand just followed, I reach the clasp of her bra and release it, letting the garment fall to the floor with her dress.

"Bend and grab your ankles," I command.

I grin when she follows the command without hesitation, both hands wrapping her ankles. I step back to take in the view. The lace thong she's wearing is soaked through. The purple lace fabric has darkened from her juices.

I run my hand down my face, as long as I've waited for this, I don't want to rush a moment. I just stare and take my time. Not only are her black suede heels complementing the sight, but they're also bringing her to a nice height. Her plump globes, thick thighs, and sexy calves have my mind bellowing for me to hurry up and fuck her.

I ignore my eager thoughts, removing my shoes and slacks instead. I move closer, smoothing my hands over her ass, over her back, then repeat. On the third pass, I spread her cheeks, hissing at the gorgeous sight her fat pussy makes. Reaching for her thong, I peel it down her legs, dropping to my knees as I pull the fabric down. Her pussy lips glistening back at me.

I lean in and inhale, loving the scent of her essence. I kiss first her right cheek, then her left. I watch as I run my thumb through her wet folds. My finger comes away completely soaked.

I stick the digit into my mouth and suck, enjoying her flavor and the sound of her panting with want. No longer able to continue torturing us both, I dip my head, going in for my first lick. I groan when a full sample of her sweetness blesses my tongue.

She tastes better than I could ever have imagined. I've tasted some of the most expensive and fine wines, liquors, and divine chocolates. None of those can compare to the succulent flavor of her core.

It's so juicy and sweet, I feel like I might drool on myself. I devour her, adding more vigor when her cries ring out across the empty restaurant. I eat her up like she's a five-star, four-course meal. I pry her open with my thumbs for my full feast. My face is drenched in her honey.

"Clayton, I'm…oh, God," she purrs out.

I growl into her when I feel her release bloom and explode. I want another, but I know I can't wait any longer. Standing, I pluck her up into my arms. Her heels fall from her feet as I turn her and swiftly place her on the table.

"Grab your knees and spread your legs."

I watch with a thrill at her quick obedience. The vision of her spread before me tugs at something deep within. I reach for her hips and pull her body down closer to the edge of the table.

My hard length throbs painfully, demanding I put an end to his waiting. Wrapping my hand around my impatient member, I run the tip through her soaked lips. I come away glistening from her juices.

It's the end of the last thread of my restraint. I line up with her entrance, covering her hands on her knees with mine and making sure to lock eyes with her just before easing into her tight center.

It feels better than I thought it would as she swallows me into her warm haven. The snug fit squeezes and ripples around me, sucking me in deep. I drive into her to the hilt. She is so slick, I slide right home.

Sid's pussy is so warm and wet, I'm holding on with everything I am, not to take her hard and fast. Reaching for her ankles, I lift her legs in the air and pump into her, rolling my hips slowly, then picking up the pace.

"Ah, oh shit," Sidney groans and gasps. "Oh, my, God."

I grin, as I slow down again, only to quicken my pace, while pushing her legs farther back into her chest. It feels so amazing. I throw my head back, gritting my teeth. Sidney's screams fill the room, pulling my eyes back to her.

Her gorgeous breasts bounce, and the sexy ass look on her face—as her perfectly imperfect teeth bite down on her lip—pulls a deep grunt from my chest. I feel the tingling at the base of my spine, but I'm not ready for this to end. I pull out to the tip, my eyes dropping to where we're joined.

"Play with that pussy for me, baby," I command in a throaty rasp.

Sidney's eyes widen in surprise, but she obliges my command. She reaches for her clit, strumming the bud before my eyes. I slam back into her, pulling a loud whimper from her lips. Her hand falters in its motion, but that just won't do.

"Don't stop, give me all of that wet pussy. Play with it for me, show me what you like," I rumble.

"Clayton, yes," she cries out.

I pound into her, reaching for that orgasm I feel rippling through her. She's so close, so close I roll my hips and hit the right angle to pull it to the surface. Sid bows off the table, her toes curl, while I hold her ankles in my palms. I turn my head to suck her toes into my mouth, not pausing in my thrusts.

I feel like I just stuck my cock into a waterfall. Her juices gush all over me. Yet, I plow through. Releasing her legs, I lean forward, wrapping my lips around her nipple.

Sidney keens loudly while wrapping her shaking legs around my waist. I grasp her hips, pinning them to the table to keep her from rocking against me. Instead, I nail her ass to the table with my cock.

"Clayton, shit," she moans, trying to wiggle free from my lips on her tightened peak.

She reaches to lace her fingers in my hair, holding me to her breasts while pulling me at the same time. I grin around the chocolate morsel in my mouth. Lifting my head, I move to capture her lips.

"You feel how hard you make me? I've never wanted anyone the way I want you," I breathe into her mouth.

Sid explodes around me again, much to my pleasure. Lifting up, I slide from her body. Flipping her onto her stomach, with her ass in the air over the side of the table, I nudge her legs apart with my foot. Her legs are like jelly when they hit the floor, she can hardly stand. I reach between her legs, cupping her sex, using my hold to keep her up.

With my other hand, I guide myself back into her waiting heat. Sidney reaches back to lock her small hand in my hair again. I grasp her face in my palm, lifting it to devour her lips. I kiss her with a hunger like none other.

Reality sets in. The chase has been longer than Sidney will ever know. I've waited patiently for this day, the day I get to claim her as mine. It also slams into me that I didn't think twice about sliding into her bare.

Sidney has caused me to lose my mind over her. She sleeps in my bed and here I am, riding her hard without a barrier between us. Just the thought has me wanting to spill inside of her.

It's not a possessive desire, it's one born out of thanks. Sidney will never know the gratitude I have for the comfort and peace she's brought me. A man doesn't want to live his life on an island alone forever. I've been on an emotional island since I was seventeen. I desire this lifeline she's unknowingly offered me with every fiber of my being.

I remove my hand from her sex, lacing my fingers with hers. I pin her hand to the tabletop as I deepen the kiss. It feels like something is unlocking within me. The feel of Sidney melting into me, bonelessly, yielding her will over to me—it's all more of a turn-on than I could express in words.

Which is why I don't use words, I use my body. Reaching for her inner thighs, I lift her body and straighten mine. I use my arms to bounce her on my length. We're both going over this time, I'm demanding it.

I press my lips to her ear, breathing hotly. My words don't come right away. I let my presence fill her, drawing on her anticipation.

"When I come, you come," I command roughly. "You understand me, baby?"

"Lord, yes," she purrs.

"Now," I roar. "Give it all to me, now."

I come so hard, spots form before my eyes. I stumble toward the table to support us both. Sid is still impaled by my semihard dick. Her sweaty back plastered to my front, her legs clinging to my sides loosely.

You have a problem, Clayton. That was not ordinary pussy.

CHAPTER TWENTY-ONE

We're leaving

Sidney

I wake and lift my arms above my head, stretching my sore body. A grin comes to my lips. I don't think I've ever had sex so good. Clayton is a beast in the sheets. It was well worth the wait.

All thoughts of him not wanting me went out the window last night. Once we got home, he showed me what he did to me at the restaurant was nothing compared to the coming attractions.

I clear my throat, feeling my voice may be gone. "Oh my God," I say to test it.

Yup, gone and so worth it. I cover my face with my hands and shake my head. I need to pull it together. I can't catch feelings. When this is over, I need to make a clean break.

I reach for my phone to check for a message from Chloe. Still nothing. I roll my eyes. I'm going to need some answers soon. She has to know this isn't cool. I'm starting to get concerned.

Putting the phone back down, I get up and head for the bathroom. A bath is in order. While thoroughly satisfied, my body is protesting all the stretching it had to do to accommodate Clay's intrusion.

After a nice soak in the tub, I decide to climb out and shower. I want to shave since I plan to have more visitations. Even with all that's going on around me, this is the most relaxed I've been in a long time.

I place my forehead against the cool shower tiles and allow myself to absorb the silence. Telling myself I would feel it if something were truly wrong with Chloe. Besides, I do think she spoke to Ally. So someone has heard her voice.

A smile comes to my lips as an inferno of heat covers my back. When he covers my breasts with his warm, large hands, I sigh as if my world has come to order.

"You can expect a call from Chloe today," he says in my ear.

"Really?"

"Yes. I told you I'd talk to my brother." He kneads my breasts as he talks against my neck. "We're leaving out this evening."

I freeze and turn to face him. He straightens to his full height and looks down at me. I cross my arms over my chest.

"Leaving to go where?"

"Georgia, I need to head back. I've been away too long. I need to check on some things."

"Wow, you didn't think I needed to know this sooner? That's a no for me, Clayton."

"No one will be looking for you in Georgia. You can take some time to relax and regroup. You've done most of the wedding planning, now you can kick back and get to know me."

"But why? In five months, I won't even exist to you."

He crowds my space and my back hits the shower wall. "I guarantee you, in a year, you will still feel me inside you. Your pussy will throb in memory of me. I'm pretty sure I will have the same lasting impression of you."

He dips his head to take my lips. I moan in his mouth as he lifts me onto his waist. He breaks the kiss and looks me in the eyes. "I've felt the ghost of your tight pussy around my cock all morning. I will know you exist, Sid. Trust me."

I pant against his lips, hoping he'll slide into me. I can feel his erection pulsing against me. I can't help pouting when he places me back on my feet.

"Let me wash your back."

Still disappointed, I turn to face the shower wall. Clayton reaches for the shower gel and pours some in his palm before he rubs it on my back. He massages it into my skin, pulling a moan from my lips as my muscles loosen.

This is just what I need. I used muscles I didn't know I had last night. I savor the rubdown Clayton gives me. He works the muscles of my inner thighs. Lord knows I used those last night to ride him until the muscles in his neck strained and he bellowed my name.

I melt against the shower wall as he massages my calves. *This is heaven.*

No sooner than I have the thought, he takes a bite of my ass and moves to eat my pussy. I stand corrected as he takes me to Mount Olympus and drops me back to earth.

Clayton

I have a grin on my face as I carry Sid's limp body into the bedroom. I didn't think it possible to be satisfied from eating pussy with no release of my own. However, Sid's pleasure is my pleasure.

I'd do it again to have her this sated. Last night was amazing. The connection was beyond what I was expecting. I find myself changing my plans once again.

Five months isn't enough. I want too much more of Sidney. I place her in bed and pull the covers over her.

"I hope I don't scare you away," I murmur as she sleeps. "I'd give a million more to keep you."

CHAPTER TWENTY-TWO

Trust Me

Clayton

Three weeks later…

Sid walks out to the pool in a black bikini, and I lift my shades, taking her in. A frown comes to my face as I think of my security. I lift a hand to beckon David over to the lounge chair I'm sitting on.

"I've sent them all to the front of the house," he says before I can give the order.

"You can go too. Stay close, but out of sight."

He nods and turns to leave. I turn my attention back to Sidney. That body is going to make me commit murder. However, for now, my plan is to kill that pussy.

Taking off my shades, I set them aside and get up. Sauntering over to the pool, I dive in. Cutting through the water, I swim over to where Sid sits with her feet in the water.

She has her cute toes skimming the top of the surface. I've yet to see her go for a swim. I've assumed it's because of her hair. I've been meaning to find her a stylist here. If not, I'll see if Ashley wants to come in for the rest of the trip.

I pop out of the water and peck Sid's lips. "Hey," I breathe.

She looks at me in surprise at first, then she allows her gaze to roam over me. Lust fills her eyes. I move between her thighs and wrap her legs around me, then take her lips for a deeper kiss.

She wraps her arms around my neck and melts into the kiss. I start to back away from the edge of the pool. She breaks the kiss and looks at me with wide eyes.

"Clay, I can't swim," she says frantically.

"I've got you. Trust me."

"But I can't swim. Please, put me back."

I kiss her chin. "Trust me. I'm not going to let you go. Relax, baby. I've got you."

She eyes me warily. I nip at her lips, willing her to calm down and relax in my hold. She only gives in as I start to knead her ass in my palms and kiss her passionately.

The water is forgotten as I devour her mouth. I move back to the pool wall and pin her to it. I groan into her mouth as I grow hard.

"Clay," she cries out as I move my lips to the tops of her breasts.

I love the way she cries my name. I can't get enough of the sound. I reach to push my swim trunks down as I suck at the flesh of her breast. Then I reach for her bikini bottom to push it aside.

"Oh shit, Clay," she whimpers as I slide into her tight sex.

I capture her lips again as I start to pound into her. Water splashes around us. Her legs are locked tightly around my waist. I break the kiss and hiss out a breath as she starts to rock her hips into me, riding me as I stroke into her hard.

I clench my teeth and stare into her sexy eyes. In the three weeks we've been here in Georgia, our relationship has changed. Sidney has let her guard down and I'm falling for her more and more.

I bring her to climax over and over as it hits me how much I've fallen for her. I'm only making this harder for myself.

Sidney

I'm trying so hard not to fall for this man, but he's making it damn near impossible. It's not just the sex. It's moments like this.

After our time out in the pool, Clayton wanted to cook for me. He insisted I take a nap. When I woke and showered, I came downstairs to find this romantic setting waiting.

He has candles lit all over the dining and living room. We eat by candlelight and then move into the living area in front of the fire. I'm full and ready for another nap.

However, I wouldn't want to move for anything in the world. I sit straddling Clay's lap with my legs around him. He has his hands palming my ass as he nuzzles my nose with his.

This is more intimate than the sex we had in the pool. As much as I want to deny my feelings for him, that's becoming harder by the day.

"What are you thinking about?" he murmurs.

"I picked an editor for my book. I'm excited for the next steps," I reply to keep from saying something stupid.

"I'm so proud of you. This is a big step up from the blog."

"Yeah, it is. It's scary, but I'm glad I'm doing it. I just feel super vulnerable. You know what I mean?"

"That makes sense, you're putting a part of yourself out there. That can't be easy. I admire you even thinking about it."

I cup his face and smile. Kissing his lips, I then pull back and stare into his eyes. A pang of jealousy comes with my next thought.

"Your wife will be a lucky woman."

"Yes, she will."

"Ugh, you don't have to be so cocky about it."

He runs his hands up my back as he stares into my eyes and breathes me in. I look away from the intensity in his gaze. It's pulling at all my emotions.

"I know for a fact I plan to spoil my wife. She will be the best-cared-for woman on this earth. I plan to make all her dreams come true. For as long as I have breath in my body, she will know she's loved." He shrugs. "My wife is very lucky."

I narrow my eyes at him. There's something in his words that tugs at my brain. It's more than the jealous fit I want to throw.

He pecks my lips. "Stop overthinking, Sid."

"I'm not overthinking. I'm just wondering what your future wife will think about all of this. Our fake engagement, the wedding we've planned."

His face shuts down. I can't read him like I normally can. "You can't tell me you haven't thought about it," I say softly.

"No, I haven't."

I tilt my head to the side and study him. Something tells me not to push with this subject. If this were real, I would pry, but Clayton owes me nothing. He can keep his secrets. I'll leave something for his future wife.

CHAPTER TWENTY-THREE

Opening Up

Sidney

It's a lovely day, so we decided to take a walk on the back of Clay's property by the lake. He has my hand in his as he brushes the back with his thumb.

The motion is calming and draws me in. I haven't had this in a relationship in a long time. Not that this is a relationship. I constantly have to remind myself of this.

"When was the last time you spoke with your mother?"

I frown and tug my hand away from his hold to wrap my middle with my arms. He places his hand on my back and starts to rub up and down. It's that comfort he offers that makes me open up.

"Not long after I graduated college. I thought she'd be proud of me. I wanted to share the moment with her. It took me weeks to get up the nerve to go," I reply.

He tugs me into his side and tightens his hold. I lean my head against his side.

"She was so fucked up. I don't think she knew who I was or even cared."

"I'm sorry."

"For?"

"I know that had to hurt. Sometimes all you want is for your parents to tell you they're proud of you. That had to sting."

I shrug. "I got over it."

We continue to walk in silence for a bit. He takes my hand back into his as I release my arms from around my middle.

"So you moved in with Chloe after her mother died? To help with Ally, right?"

"Yeah, we lived in East New York, but Ally started running with gang members, so we moved to Clinton Hills trying to get her away from all that.

"It wasn't that far, but it was the best we could do. When the boy she was crushing on was murdered, we thought that would be the end of it, but Ally is Ally. I think she fell in deeper because we told her not to. It took a few years before we could move into a place in Manhattan. A lot changed then."

"You guys were so young yourselves. I admire Chloe and you for sticking in there with her."

"That's my ride or die. You know, I wouldn't have come to your club if not for her."

He winks at me. "I know."

"Which is why you sent the invitations to her. You think you're so slick," I bump his hip with mine.

He ignores my comment. Flexing his hand around mine. "You're a great friend."

I look up at him and smile. "You sound as if you want to be my friend, Clay," I tease.

He wraps an arm around my head and kisses it. "I want to be your everything."

My heart starts to pound, and a face-splitting smile comes over my lips.

Calm down, Sid. It's all an act.

Clayton

I don't want to go back to New York. It feels like when we do, everything is going to change. However, Sidney's problem is in New York and that's where I need to be to get a handle on this.

I need to get my eyes on one of my targets and the opportunity to do so is coming up. Her laugh brings me out of my thoughts. I look up from the popcorn I just popped.

She has her head thrown back and her shoulders shake with her laughter. We're bingeing comedy shows on Netflix. Something I would never do by myself. I don't make time for this type of thing.

However, to spend time with her, I'm willing to. I grab the bowl and walk over to the rug where she's sitting. Moving behind her, I sit with my legs caging her in. I place the popcorn in her lap and take a handful.

"You missed the best part. Let me rewind it," she says as she snuggles back into my chest.

"You don't have to."

"I told you I should've paused. You have to hear this bit. The setup is perfect."

She rewinds it and grabs some popcorn for herself. My eyes are on her as I listen for the joke. She looks up into my eyes and we both laugh at the punch line.

I can't help kissing her smiling lips. It's a funny joke but seeing the sparkle in her eyes is what does it for me. I nuzzle her nose with mine, not able to lose our connection.

"This hasn't been so bad. I'm still a New York City girl all day, but I like the peace this place has."

"You can come here to write anytime you want."

"Even after our time is up?"

"Anytime."

I hold her gaze with the promise. I think back to her words earlier. *You sound as if you want to be my friend, Clay.*

I'll be honest, the thought of growing a friendship with her has taken root. It's the smiles and laughter she brings that make me want to be more. Her friend, her man, her protector.

I want to be all those things to Sid and more. It's not just the sex I can't get enough of, it's her.

I wake with her on my mind, and I go to bed the same way. At night, I find myself waking just to watch her sleep. Sidney became my obsession a long time ago, now I'm consumed by her and I'm good with that.

CHAPTER TWENTY-FOUR

Loving Father

Sidney

"Welcome back to New York, Sidney. Thank you for coming by," Clooney says as we sit in the drawing room. I was surprised when he called and asked me to come by.

"Thank you for having me."

"I'm assuming the wedding planning is going well. Is there anything Eileen and I can help with?"

"No. We have it all covered. Eileen was on FaceTime with me as I talked to the new dress designer."

"Good, good. I'm glad you're allowing her to be a part of things. She's already so fond of you."

"I'm fond of her as well."

"Sidney, I wanted to talk to you because you still don't know me well. You don't see me as the villain my sons do. At least I hope Clay hasn't tainted your view of me."

"I have to say, I've heard some things, but I always like to form my own opinion."

"What my sons don't see is that I want the best for them. I'm trying to get something to them, not take anything away. Marriage enriches a man. Children create a family bond. I believe grandchildren will close the gap and fill the void of my own failures as a father. I'll get to make up for my wrongs."

"I don't know about Cane or Gregor, but Clay can be as stubborn as the day is long. Good luck with that one."

Clooney chuckles. "You're right. However, he's changing, and I think it's because of you. Love will do that to you."

I want to tell him his son isn't in love with me, but I keep my lips sealed. I was already wary of coming here to begin with. I don't want to say or do anything that will derail Clayton's plans. However, I also didn't want to leave him suspicious of us.

"Your son has changed my life as well," I say instead. "I think he will make a great husband and father someday."

"I can't wait to be a grandfather. At least an active grandfather," he says.

I furrow my brows as he says the last part. Yet I remain silent. I get the impression this man isn't as bad as Clayton paints him to be.

"I hope you get the opportunity soon," I say, not knowing what else to say.

"Give Clay a chance to figure out what he needs, Sid. When he does, he'll surprise you. He's guarded because of his past. I regret how I handled some things, but I'll always do what's necessary to keep my boys safe and protected."

I'm not sure what to say. I might be falling for Clay, but I'm not expecting him to return the feelings. However, I don't want to crush the hope I see in this man's eyes. It's bad enough the wedding isn't going to happen once Clay figures out how to outsmart his father.

I look into the old man's eyes, and I wonder who will outsmart who in the end. I might be rooting for Clayton, but I don't think he should underestimate his father. He's still holding cards.

"Sidney, I think you're just what I was looking for," he says and winks at me.

Yup, Clayton better watch this one. He's definitely up to something.

CHAPTER TWENTY-FIVE

Jealous Past

Sidney

Ahem, remind me never to question Clayton again in my life. The man has put it on me every single day and night since that evening in the restaurant when he cleared it out. I still tingle and shiver whenever I think of that night.

The man has talent. Sex appeal isn't just something that oozes off him, he delivers on that pulsing promise every single time. I can't look at him without having a ton of dirty thoughts.

I'm not a small girl, but Clayton will flip me and toss my ass around in a heartbeat. He has left me breathless on several occasions. I swear, at this point, some days I have to check my ID just to remember my own name.

I've been so distracted by Clayton's sexual prowess I've hardly noticed the time fly by. It's been three months since I moved in with him and two months since we've taken a simple arrangement into not so simple territory.

As much as I try to ignore it, something has changed for me. It's more than a sexual attraction, which scares the shit out of me. Clayton is complicated. He's revealed so much of himself, but so much more is hidden behind those gray eyes.

I'm not sure I'm ready to deal with that type of complicated. I still need to get back to my own life. When this is over and Clayton has solved all our problems, then where does that leave me?

I knew coming into this not to be stupid enough to fall for him, but my heart had plans of her own. Sometimes, I tell myself I should have said no that night in the restaurant. Yet, I know what's happening to me started well before we slept together.

"Sid," he calls.

I hear him moving in the hallway. I've been in his home office editing this morning. I needed to focus and get some work done. I just got back the revisions from my editor. I feel like I'm under so much pressure.

I roll my eyes at the interruption. I'm finally making some headway through the tons of notes and red marks. My eyes feel about ready to cross. I can't believe I'm so close to having this done.

"Sid," Clayton calls again, stepping into the office this time. "Baby, do you see what time it is? Ashley is waiting for you."

I look at the clock on the laptop and groan. It's after five in the evening. I hadn't noticed I'd been sitting here all day. I thought it was only lunchtime. No wonder I'm suddenly starving.

Clayton comes over, cupping my chin to lift my face to his. He seizes my lips in a devastating kiss that dazes me for a moment. When I blink the haze away, his eyes are twinkling down at me.

"I lost track of time." I manage to respond after a few beats.

He plucks me from the desk chair, pulling me between his long legs while he leans back against the desk. His big arms go around me and I notice—not for the first time—how safe and at home I feel in his embrace. I place my arms around his neck automatically. It's so natural, I don't even think about it before I do it.

"I've wanted to give you something for a long time," he dips his head to say against my lips.

"I don't think we have time for that. What time do we have to leave for the gala?"

He gives a hearty laugh. "There is always time for that. However, *that* isn't what I'm talking about." He pecks my lips while reaching into his pocket.

When he holds the box up between us, I look at him, perplexed. I know he can't possibly be replacing my engagement ring. I've asked him repeatedly to stop buying me expensive gifts.

They all make me feel so guilty. It's like I'm taking these gifts, knowing I'll be leaving at some point. The cost of the wedding has gotten so out of control, I just can't take the amount of money being wasted.

"What's this?"

"Don't just look at it, open it," he says through a sexy grin.

"*Clay*," I warn.

"Open it, precious. I went through hell getting this ready for you," he says like an excited child.

His behavior piques my interest. I pluck the box from his hand and open it. Inside the velvet box rests the most beautiful diamond and blue sapphire earrings I've ever seen. Simply breathtaking.

"These are gorgeous," I gasp.

"Not as gorgeous as you are. I wanted you to have them. They—" His words are cut off by his phone chiming.

He takes his phone out, a scowl taking over his handsome face. I watch a storm enter his eyes. I've seen him pissed off before, but never like this. The rage that consumes his face has me wanting to take a step back.

Instead, I move closer to him, placing a hand on his cheek. His eyes lift to mine, clearing just a bit. He clasps my hand in his, holding it as he turns his face to kiss my palm. My heart skips a beat, and butterflies take flight in my belly.

"Wear the earrings tonight. Go, Ashley is waiting, we leave in an hour," he says, using that tone that I've grown to know means no questions are to be asked.

I sigh, not knowing when I became so compliant. I turn to save my work and shut down my laptop. Clayton crooks his finger for me to come to him before I leave out of the room.

I stand before him again, looking up into those intense eyes. He wraps my waist with one arm, making sure to kiss me thoroughly. One hand cupping my backside as he deepens the kiss.

There's something possessive and urgent in his kiss. My brows knit as the desire to understand him takes over. Something has shifted and I think that text has something to do with it.

When he breaks the kiss and nods for me to leave, I hesitate for the briefest moment, ready to pry. Only, I hold my tongue. This isn't a real relationship. I've been trying more and more to remind myself of that.

I leave the room, clutching the jewelry box in my hand. My mind races. What would make him give me such an expensive and gorgeous gift? What was he about to say before that text?

Again, I ask myself, when did I become so obedient? I've fallen into this routine with Clayton. I never have to worry about a thing. With most of the wedding planning out of the way, all I've had to focus on has been my blog and book.

Clayton allows me to get lost in my head for hours. His hiring of Nikki has been just what I needed. I get so much done and don't have to worry about losing a thought to send emails or fix website issues.

I hate having to stop in the middle of developing a scene to focus on non-writing things. Sometimes, I have no idea how I made it so far in the financial district. My ability to multitask has fallen off.

I'm spoiled in this safe nest Clayton has created for me. Even the time we spent in Georgia in the last month was like being on a writing vacation. While there, I was able to finish my book and send it off to the editor.

With Clayton making all of that happen, I haven't thought much about the reason I agreed to be in this relationship or the fact that he hasn't updated me on what's going on. I believe that's where my problems lie. I've fallen into a relationship.

As much as I try to tell myself this isn't one, it looks, smells, and breathes like one. Actually, I've fallen into more than just a relationship. My mind keeps tripping over my thoughts as I get ready for the evening.

"I have some new looks for you," Ashley says, bringing me out of my thoughts. She hands me a binder as I sit at the vanity in my robe. I take it from her and start to flip through. "Here, I made a book for you to look through. You can pick which you want to try first. It's mostly hair and makeup for now. I was thinking I can come in during the week to get pictures of your wardrobe, that way you can mix and match to your liking, and I'll know what you want to do when I arrive."

"This is a great idea," I reply. "I like this one for tonight."

I hand the book back as she continues to go on and on about different looks she wants to try with me, but I'm stuck in my head. I get ready on autopilot and remain that way well into the evening.

****

"Where are you?" Clayton croons against my temple, his thumb caressing the side of my neck.

I shiver at the sound of his voice, along with his touch. The fact that Clayton is flawlessly wearing the hell out of his navy tux tonight isn't lost on me. The color in contrast to his eyes is stunning.

When I look up into his gaze, he searches my face with concern in his probing eyes. I blink away my thoughts. We've shared a lot with each other, but he doesn't need to know that I'm trying to figure out how and when I happened to fall in love with him. I'd also like to know how he managed to wrap me around his finger.

"Just thinking. It's been a while since I've heard from Chloe. I should text her tomorrow," I reply, avoiding my thoughts totally.

Clayton pulls a face, his eyes clouding over a bit. "They'll be returning soon," he says in that dismissive tone of his.

"I hate when you do that," I blurt out.

"When I do what?" He lifts a brow.

"Say things with such finality. Like I'm supposed to just take your word for whatever and move on." I narrow my eyes at him.

He presses his hand on the small of my back, drawing me into him. I suck in a breath when I feel his erection poke me in the belly. The cocky smile on his lips causes me to frown at him, which in turn increases his smile.

"Have I ever told you how much it turns me on when you challenge me?" he croons low enough for my ears only.

"No, but I think I get the picture." I purse my lips at him.

He laughs before pecking my lips. I get ready to fuss some more, but a throat clears, drawing both our attention. Two tall brunettes stand to our right, watching us, one with narrowed hawk eyes, the other with a look of longing on her face.

Clayton stiffens beside me. I turn to look up at him. He looks like he smells shit. The level of disgust on his face is palpable. Whoever these women are, he doesn't care for them very much.

I look back at them. They both look to be in their thirties. Neither one can be called gorgeous, but not ugly either.

The shorter of the two is more attractive, her hair cups her face, her light blue eyes are large but fit her features. However, there's something mousy and timid about her. The taller of the two gives off a different vibe, as if she's full of herself.

Her hair falls to her shoulders, her light-blue eyes holding something different than the woman next to her. Her gaze seems colder, almost calculating and rather dismissive. They're both a bit long nosed in the face, with thin upper lips. I'd say the taller one just made it on the right side of pretty.

"It's so good to see you, Clayton," the taller one purrs, keeping her attention on him.

"Um," Clayton grumbles.

I lift my brow at his reply, but he's too busy frowning at our new guests to see. I can't help wondering who the heck they are. From the tight hold he has on my waist, I don't know if he's restraining himself or me.

"It's good to see you, Clay," the other one says.

"Leeann." Clayton nods.

"You know, I couldn't believe my ears when I heard you were engaged." The first one continues with a phony laugh.

Oh, yeah, I don't like this bitch. I'm already coiled to lunge at her. She still hasn't acknowledged that I'm standing here.

"Not sure why that's any of your business," Clayton grits out.

"Congratulations, I'm happy that you're happy," Leeann says.

She turns to me and gives a shy smile. She seems to want to say more, but that timid look takes over. I can see her curling into herself as if she would rather hide.

"Oh, come on, we know him well enough. He can't be serious about this. Isn't that right, Clay? You're just having fun with another plaything," the tall one pouts.

"I don't share my bed with playthings," Clayton snorts. "Be careful what you say, Fran."

Her head whips in my direction, her lips parting for just a moment before she regains her composure. Leeann's face seems to crumble in the same instant. My curiosity rings loud, but Fran's reaction arrests my attention.

She looks me over from head to toe. A look of disgust curls her thin lip. She has a lot of nerve.

"Surely, you don't mean *she* sleeps in *your* bed," she mutters.

"Every single night," I reply, returning her look of disdain.

Her eyes roll over me again. Out of the corner of my eye, I see Leeann assessing me as well. My attention turns to her when her shoulders sag, her eyes lingering on my ears. Then her head bounces between me and Clayton a few times.

"Are those—"

"My grandmother's earrings," Clayton cuts her off. "Yes, they are."

"But...but you would never allow anyone to wear those," she stammers out.

"Never," Fran breathes, shock crossing her face.

My chest swells at the sweet sound of her feelings crushing. Although, I wonder who these women are that they have so much information I don't. I had no idea these were his grandmother's earrings. The significance of that tugs at the back of my mind.

"Correction, I would only allow someone I care about to *have* them," Clayton grinds out. "You may leave now. My fiancée and I are none of your concern."

"Your fiancée," Fran seethes. "Does she know my sister was once on her way to being your fiancée?"

This time I stiffen at Clayton's side. I look up at him and his face tells a million stories. I don't know what happened between them, but it wasn't pretty. At least, it must not have ended well.

"Leeann was never close to any such thing. Once upon a very long time ago, I thought she was a friend. Never once did I have intentions of marrying her.

"Our *friendship* and wanting to keep my father from up my ass are the only reasons we carried on for as long as we did," Clayton bites out.

"Two years is a long time to date someone you don't care about," Fran tosses back, giving me a sly smile.

"Fran," Leeann admonishes, looking to be on the verge of tears.

"I see the game you're playing." Clayton gives a dry laugh. "Sidney isn't an insecure woman like yourself, Fran. She knows she doesn't have to worry about my past.

"If you want to toss out and manipulate facts, share the fact that your sister turned her back on me not once, but twice. She turned into someone I didn't even recognize. She became you.

"Share with Sid that the reason I loathe your sister is that not only did my father have her spying on me—her so-called best friend and boyfriend. She also fucked my security guard and twisted his mind until she got him to try to help her blackmail me," he hisses.

Both sisters turn beet red in the face. Clayton just earned a new level of respect from me. Now, that right there is a new level of petty.

Fran wasn't expecting that. Homegirl's face looks like it just cracked in two and I didn't even get a chance to throw a jab.

"You still can't prove that," Leeann says brokenly.

"You're still always pleading with him," Fran fumes in disgust.

Clayton throws his head back and laughs. Yet, there's no humor in his eyes when he looks back at them. I feel a chill run through me.

"It's not worth my time. Now, if you will excuse us. There are actually important people here to talk to," he delivers the final blow.

We turn to leave, but Mrs. Thing isn't finished. I've had enough of her and her big mouth. However, her words serve as intended. My interest is piqued immediately.

"She mustn't know *our* history then," Fran hisses, causing Clayton to pause in his tracks.

He spins around sharply, but I'm not about to let my man go down for losing it and hitting this chick. Not that I think Clayton would actually hit a lady, but this heifer isn't a lady and I want to give her a good punch at this point.

I step forward, getting all up in her face. Well, as in her face as my small stature will allow. It doesn't matter that she's taller than me, I still look at her as if she's beneath me and I'm the one who has to look down.

"You don't know what I know," I hiss at her. "But what you need to be crystal clear on. I don't give a shit about the garbage you have ready to spill out your mouth. You've reached your quota for words to say to Sid and Clay. Button up those lips, before I rip them off your face and feed them to you. Understand?"

I don't wait for her reply. I turn, lacing my fingers with Clayton's and allow him to lead the way. Although, my mind is burning, wondering what secrets she has that I don't.

CHAPTER TWENTY-SIX

Troubled Family

Clayton

I can't release the smile from my lips as I watch Sid across the room. I didn't want her anywhere near that pariah, Fran, but watching her defend me as her man almost made me call it an early night. I wanted nothing more than to bend her over and fuck her senseless.

Sid doesn't even begin to understand the things she does to me. I've taken her every chance I can and it's still not enough. I think I'll forever want more of her.

Just the sight of her glowing face makes me ache to be near her. She looks stunning tonight in her navy-blue gown. It forms to her body like a second skin. I will have to talk to Ashley about the amount of skin this one shows. Especially the split showing off one of those brown thighs I love so much.

I don't think Sid sees how quickly she's melded into my world. People seem to gravitate to her. That smile alone is infectious.

"You watch her as if she's going to fly away," my father's voice rumbles in my ears.

I turn to the old man to see him looking in Sid's direction. He lifts his glass to his lips and takes a sip. I turn back to Sid just as she throws her head back in laughter. It's a sight I want to see as she's beneath me. That twinkle in her eyes, the curve of her luscious lips.

"Just taking in the night. It's been good for business," I reply, removing all emotion from my words.

"I see you still haven't gotten over your little tiff with Leeann." He changes the subject.

I snort. "Tiff? You used the only friend I had against me. You turned her into one of your minions," I growl, allowing my composure to slip just a little.

"You tend to see things from a narrow gaze. You always have. I had no involvement in the things Leeann has been accused of. I warned you to beware of those two many times. I figured burned by one, you'd be cautious of the other, but I left you to learn that lesson on your own.

"Everything I do, I do it to protect my boys. The three of you think I'm your enemy. All your lives, I've allowed you to learn to be men. Someday, I hope you'll see that." I feel his eyes on me, but I refuse to turn to face him.

I feel the rage building inside of me. I fight back the memories and the hurt. I've come too far.

I will not allow that time in my life to ruin my good mood tonight. Surprisingly, Fran didn't ruffle my feathers as much as she would have in the past. There was a time I refused to be in the same room with her.

I snort deeply at his words and the memories. "Guess that's why you allowed me to go to jail," I fume.

"Another moment that defined you and made you a better man," he replies.

"You keep telling yourself that," I grumble, taking a sip of my drink.

My father sighs. "I'm not going to be around forever." His voice wavers, grabbing my attention and causing me to turn my head this time. "I've done everything in my power for you boys. I know I pushed too much at times. I have my regrets, but in the end, I think we will all land on the same page."

I stare at my father, eyeing him intently. I hear his words, but I also hear something else behind them. Something crosses his eyes, but he turns his attention back across the room before I can pinpoint what I'm seeing.

I follow his gaze, only to stiffen. My eyes land on Sidney just as my cousin, Wade, walks up to her. I watch as the smile fades from her lips. I don't blame her for the reaction.

Wade's a pompous asshole. For years, he has wanted everything my brothers and I have. When Gregor walked away from the path that would've landed him in the governor's seat, Wade was there to lick my father's ass and step into the shoes that were still too big for his entitled feet.

Wade is my father's sister's son. Aunt Evelyn spoiled his ass rotten from day one. My father isn't any better.

He never used the heavy hand he used with me and my brothers on Wade. Now, my cousin runs around like he's owed the world, while living in the shadow of my older brother. If my father says jump, Wade asks how high midjump.

I've been wanting to see Sid and Wade in the same room. Watching her body language shift is more than revealing. Wade has his back to me, but I can read Sidney's lips clearly. It's a gift.

I watch as her pinched lips form the words. *It isn't good to see you again.*

I start moving across the room, my father forgotten. His voice calling my name is just a buzz in my ears. I ignore it like an annoying bug.

"Wade," I grumble, sliding an arm around Sidney's waist.

I savor how her soft body melts right into me. She leans her lush curves against me as naturally as if it were something she's done for years. I dip my head to kiss the top of her head.

"Clayton, you lucky bastard. I don't know how you did it. Sidney here is one hard nut to crack." Wade's smug ass grins at me.

"Wade, I'm warning you. You're treading on thin ice. Swallow the rest of your dumbass comments before you're swallowing teeth," I say through tight lips.

He pulls a mock surprised face. Only an idiot would try me when it comes to Sid, but Wade's an idiot for sure, always has been. He picked the wrong night to piss me off.

"That temper has always been a problem, hasn't it?" Wade snorts.

"Being an asshole has always been a problem for you, hasn't it?" Sid snaps before I can hiss out my reply.

"Ouch, still a little fireball, aren't we?" he purrs while letting his eyes roam over Sidney.

I snap. Before I think better of it, I have my cousin by the collar. His face is bright red despite the fact that he continues to grin. Sid's hand is on my forearm, but I don't release my hold on him.

"My cousin here never knows how or when to shut his fucking mouth," I hiss low.

"Your cousin?" Sidney gasps. "Clay, baby, you're choking him."

"That's the point," I snarl, shoving him back when I release him.

"Be careful, dear. Your taste in men will lead you down a dark road." Wade coughs.

"If you don't shut your mouth, I will permanently shut it for you," I snarl.

"My taste in men is just fine. I avoided you, didn't I?"

I spin to face Sid, my head feeling like it's about to burst. I was aware of Sidney having dealings with Wade, but this is hinting at more than what came up on my radar. I narrow my eyes at her, trying to grab hold of my restraint. I know I must be hearing things.

Her comment about dating and my sources failing me comes back to mind. *I've gone on a date or two in the last two years. You might want to check your sources. They're leaving things out.*

"What exactly does that mean?" I ask, with a calm I'm certainly not feeling.

"He was a potential client. When I wasn't assigned his account, he asked me out on a date. I agreed, not knowing he was a total jerk," Sid replies, her eyes bouncing over my face.

"Don't worry, little cousin. I didn't dip into your sweet little thing. She still doesn't know what it's like to be with a real man." Wade chuckles.

I slowly turn to face him again. He has the good sense to stiffen this time. I take slow, deliberate steps toward him. When I reach him, I dip my head to get in his ear.

"Walk away, Wade. Walk away quickly. The next time I see you, be prepared for me to hand you your ass. Oh, and if I prove what I believe I already know, you and I will see each other very soon," I hiss.

His head snaps back, a frown marring his face. His eyes are hard as he glares back at me, his jaw working.

"It's always about you. Even when you're winning, you don't see it. The three of you should be thanking me," he says tightly and snorts. "Enjoy your night, *cousin*."

I nearly lunge at him, I see nothing but red. Wade and I have a deeper history, one I won't dig into at the moment, but it's one that makes my mind boil. Sid's hand on my back both calms me and reminds me why my judgment has been so clouded. I need to watch the snakes around me a little more closely.

"We're leaving." I grab her arm and start for the exit.

I can feel the beast inside me clawing his way out. Just the thought of Wade even trying to get his hands on her has me ready to destroy something. She's mine.

No one has a right to what's mine. I don't care how long ago their interaction was. Irrational, absolutely and I know it.

I've said it before, and I'll say it again. I'm a man that needs control. Tonight, Sid will learn what that means.

I haven't allowed that door to open before tonight, but it's been forced open. Tonight, I've been pushed to the edge. I thought I hadn't let Fran get to me. Now, I know her taunting words meant for Sidney cut into my old wounds.

I won't even touch my raging thoughts and suspicions concerning Wade. I'll give him a bit more rope to hang himself before I cut the rest of his air off for him. He better pray I'm wrong.

"Clayton, will you let go," Sid snaps when we reach the car outside.

I only release my hold to allow her to get inside the car. "Never," I mumble to myself after she's securely inside.

CHAPTER TWENTY-SEVEN

Unleashed

Sidney

Wade Claremont is a jerk, but Clayton's anger seems a bit over the top. Sure, every time I run into Wade, he rubs me the wrong way. I still will never understand why I agreed to go out on that one date with him.

Wade is handsome in that tall, brooding type of way. However, when you get to know him, you realize that he's too aware of his good looks. I wasn't interested in entertaining that mess.

It doesn't help that he's into politics and has become used to people catering to him. I learned the hard way that he doesn't like to be told no. He just picked the wrong one to think he could push over.

Since that date, we have had choice words for each other every time we meet. I had no idea he was related to the Hennessy family, let alone Clayton. I feel for Clayton.

I'd be pissed, too, if I had that type of filth related to me. Yet, the steam coming off him at the moment tells me this is deeper than what happened before my eyes this evening. At least what I saw with the naked eye.

He's silent the entire ride back to the apartment as well as the ride up in the elevator. I'm ready to give up on getting through to him tonight. I start for the bedroom after he lets me into the front door.

Only, as I make my way in that direction, his arm bands around my waist, plucking me off my feet. A yelp leaves my lips as I cling to his forearm. We're moving toward the stairs that lead down to the floor beneath us.

I rarely go down to the other levels. There's so much apartment for me to occupy on the top floor. However, my curiosity rises as he descends the stairs.

"Clay, what are you doing?" I ask while bouncing against his side.

He just grunts at me. I can still feel the anger rolling off him, but there's something else. I think about kicking and protesting, but I'm not looking to break any bones—his or mine.

My brows knit when he turns up a hallway and walks to the very last door. I hear more than see keys jingle. The next thing I know, he's pushing the door open, revealing the last thing I expect.

The room is painted a lush gold color, the walls shimmer as the lights automatically come on. Anchoring the back wall of the large room is a huge bed covered in a red spread. Shear gold fabric hangs from the four posts, but what gets my attention is the golden chair swing in the center of the room. I tilt my head looking at it, blinking to focus on what I think I'm seeing.

"Are those…cuffs?" I ask, looking at the set of gold restraints dangling from the swing's sides and the set resting in its red seat.

He doesn't respond, instead, placing me on my feet. I've lost a shoe in the process. I swing my gaze around the room and bite my lip as I take in the gold cabinet doors. My imagination runs wild.

I start to think of a way to get this room into one of my next blogs or books. I'm so absorbed with taking it all in I forget Clayton until he snakes his hand around my throat. He doesn't squeeze hard, but it's enough to get my attention.

"You should've read the contract, Sid," he hisses in my ear.

"What?" I gasp.

"Do you know you signed your body over to me?" he asks in an eerily dark voice.

"Clay, what the—"

His fingers flex, cutting off my words. I purse my lips and roll my eyes, even though he can't see my face. I curse my body when it melts into him as he pulls me closer to his heat. I hobble on my one heel, my back pressed to his front.

"You will watch that pretty mouth, Sid. When I'm fucking you mindless is the only time you're allowed to let that dirty mouth slip," he demands.

I nearly tell him to fuck himself just to see what he'll do. The words never make it out of my mouth. He tips my head back roughly, capturing my lips.

The kiss is the most possessive I've ever had in my life. I can't do anything but anchor my fingers in his hair and hold on. My knees go weak, I feel him in every part of me. My bare toes curl into the plush surface beneath them as my others curl in my shoe.

I feel like I'm drowning in him. Those feelings I've been trying to deny are swirling their way forward. I want to pull away and curl away from the fire that's Clayton, but it's calling me to go up in smoke. It whispers for me to come forward like a snake charmer. I'm powerless against it.

Wordlessly, he breaks the kiss and turns my back fully to him. A ripping sound fills the room. In a single tug, my beautiful dress is in ruins at my feet. I stare down in shock. I'm left in just a blue corset, panties, and a single shoe.

"Clay, the hell," I gasp.

With an action swifter than I knew the man could move, he's seated in the swing in the center of the room and I'm across his lap. I don't have time to catch my breath before his hand comes down on my ass. I suck in a sharp breath before releasing a moan as he caresses, then kneads the spot he just slapped.

"When I say watch your mouth, I mean it," he says sternly.

"*Clayton,*" I say in warning.

His hand disappears from my flesh, only to come down twice more. I squirm in his lap, my back arching. His groan fills the air and my nipples tighten. I knit my brows—I've lost it.

Clayton proves my assumption when he moves his hand between my legs, pushing my panties aside. His fingers glide through my wetness. I try to squirm away defiantly, but his probing fingers still me.

He slips two digits into me, like a key turning to access control of my body. I bite my lip, breathing through my nose. When he starts to pump his fingers through my juices, I can't keep my hips from moving in sync. He reaches his thumb to massage my other opening, sending shock waves through my body and surprise to my brain.

"Do you want to learn what your body's capable of?" His rough voice pierces the air.

I refuse to answer. I'm pissed at him for putting me over his knee, no matter how traitorous my body is. I will my breathing to even out.

Here we are, back in the middle of one of our power struggles. It's been so long since I've pushed back. This time, I'm not willing to bow.

Enough is enough, he's pushing me too far this time. I feel like if I cave now, I'm giving too much. It's a point of no return. I just feel it.

He stops his ministrations. Again, his hand comes down multiple times, rapidly, never in the same spot. It stings in such a sensuous way. My cheeks warm, both on my face and ass. I can't believe I'm gushing for this.

"Your body is answering for you, baby, but I want to hear it from your lips. Say it, Sid. You want me to show you what your body is capable of," he demands.

"No," I bite out.

"Say it," he demands again, his voice growing harsher.

"I'm not giving you that kind of control," I hiss back.

He slowly caresses my ass, but he doesn't say a word. One fingertip starts to trace a pattern against my skin. My forehead wrinkles when he seems to repeat the pattern a third and fourth time. It's his name, he's spelling his name out on my ass.

"I thought I wanted control with you." His voice comes out tightly. "I can take it. I know how to get you to give it to me willingly, but I still wouldn't have it. I'll never have control when it comes to you."

He falls silent again. I don't realize I'm holding my breath until he lifts me, positioning me to straddle him. The swing gently sways beneath our weight. He wraps both his hands around my throat and looks into my eyes.

There's so much emotion there. Like he's unlocked a vault to allow me full access. He caresses my jaw with his thumbs. He's watching me as closely as I'm watching him. He tilts his head, his thoughts running across his face too quickly for me to catch them.

"Say it," he says quietly. "Say the words. Let me give you what you want. Let me open your desires. Say it."

My lips tremble. I lower my lashes. I know I'm already in love with him. I've lost so much control. However, I don't know how not to be in control on some level. I've always had to take care of myself.

I've already allowed him so much, not even knowing when. In the past, putting my trust in others has always burned me in some way. Chloe is the only person in the world who I trust fully.

I love Ally like my own little sister, but I'd never burden her with my adult issues. She'll always be the baby sister I need to help care for.

No, I need control because I have no one I can fall back on. Chloe has always had enough on her plate. I know she would be there for me, but I can't ask that of her.

"Trust me, Sid. I would never weaken you. I'm offering you power," he whispers next to my ear, pulling me from my thoughts. "Have I failed you yet?"

"No." I lift my eyes to his.

"Then, say it."

It's more like a plea. His eyes tell me he needs this almost as much as I know I do. Yes, I know I need this. I need to let go, but am I ready for that?

My white-knuckle grip on the control I've always held on to tells me I'm not. My pounding heart echoes the same. If it's this invested already, he'll destroy it when this is all over. I don't think I can take the devastation I felt the day I realized my mother wasn't coming back.

My last year of high school, she abandoned me. I'll never forget the uncertainty and fear I felt. I had no control over the things going on around me. At least, it felt that way for weeks until it hit me that she wasn't coming back, and I was all I had. Ms. Sinclair had her own two girls to think about.

Chloe's mom did all she could for me, but I had to take care of me. I've been taking care of me ever since. I don't know how to let that go. Yet, for three months, Clayton has allowed me to do just that.

I lift my hands to cup his face. Such a handsome face. I commit it to memory to keep me warm and safe when he breaks my heart and abandons me. I lower my lashes and shudder. He runs his strong hands up my back, settling midway to give a gentle squeeze.

I open my eyes and let a breath push out past my lips. I nod my head before I have the strength to speak the words I know he wants to hear. I need a few more seconds.

"Say it," he whispers the demand.

"Show me."

"Show you what?"

"Show me what my body is capable of," I amend.

He places his forehead against the side of my face. "You don't know what you've just taken from me," he says in a pained voice. He swallows hard. In a harder voice, he barks a rough command. "Stand and strip."

I blink at the harsh and rapid change. I stand, hobbling on my one heel again. I go to kick the shoe from my foot, but he shakes his head no. A dark smile graces his lips, sending a shiver through me.

I reach behind me for the zipper of my corset, releasing it slowly. It falls to the floor, and I reach for my panties. I shift my hips from side to side as I wiggle free of the fabric. The scrap of damp fabric floats to the floor.

I stare back at Clayton, fully dressed in his tux. Not a stitch of clothing out of place. His relaxed position makes me squirm on my feet. He can't possibly understand how sexy he looks without so much as trying.

It doesn't register with me that I'm waiting until he lifts his hand, beckoning me forward. Still in one shoe, I move to him, feeling awkward. He moves his hands to my hips, stopping me before him.

He stands, towering over me. I tip my head back to look up at him. He moves us so my back is to the swing. My bottom hits the seat gently and Clayton is on a knee before me.

He glides his hands up the backs of my calves and back down again. It dawns on me I'm not sitting on the cuffs I'd seen in the seat earlier when I hear the clinging sound and feel the cool metal around the ankle of my shoeless foot.

His eyes drop to my hands in a wordless command for me to put them at my sides to be cuffed as well. I oblige him. Swiftly my hands are restrained with the cuffs attached to the chair swing.

Clayton grasps my hips, tugging me forward in the seat. My butt meets the very edge. Next thing I know, my free leg is over Clayton's suited shoulder.

He dives in like a man possessed. His warm mouth consumes me. I'm hyperaware of his touch. It's all over, but not. Never have I had my pussy eaten to the point that my entire body feels like it's being stroked at once.

I flex my foot over his shoulder, the toes of my cuffed leg digging into the rug. The movement sends the swing rocking and swaying. It's the most amazing feeling of my life. He's gone down on me hundreds of times, but never like this. I feel like he's trying to suck my secrets out through my core.

"Clay," I moan.

His answer is a long lick from my crack up through my folds. I go to reach for his hair, only to be reminded of the cuffs attached to my wrists. The slight bite into my flesh and his simultaneous sucking at my clit, sends my body into convulsions.

He doesn't stop, that was just to prime me up. He continues to eat me up, but just when my orgasm surges and gets ready to hit, he backs off, looking up at me as he slowly licks his lips. Panting, I watch him.

He reaches to run his fingers through my soaked petals. Lifting his digits to my lips, he nods for me to open my mouth and take them in. I open, allowing him to stick his long fingers between my lips.

"Do you see how good you taste?" his voice is so husky. A total turn-on.

I nod while sucking his fingers clean. He pulls them from my mouth with a pop. Then reaches for his bow tie, tugging it free, tossing it behind him when it's loosened from around his neck. Turning his head toward my leg over his shoulder, he begins a trail of kisses. Moving randomly around my skin, he's prolonging the anticipation.

My chest heaves, knowing when he reaches his destination, pleasure is sure to greet me. However, his trip takes a turn, and my leg drops from his shoulder.

Clayton moves to cup my breasts. His eyes remain on me as he sucks a nipple into his mouth while toying with the other one. My back bows, my fists ball. His warm mouth pulling and heating my skin has me grinding at the air. I want to have him where I need him most.

He begins alternating between breasts, driving me insane. He allows his body to press against mine, finally giving me the friction I need. I know I'm soaking the front of his tux.

The swing aids in me rocking against him. His pulsing member is trapped in his pants, throbbing against me with each wiggle and pass.

My head falls back, I'm right on the brink of coming and can't believe I'm going to come so hard. I bite my lip, my eyes cross, and my ears feel like they're ringing. Just when the explosive release is about to let go, Clayton backs off.

"Wha—" I pant.

He gives me a sexy grin. This time, shrugging off his tuxedo jacket, he tosses it aside. I close my eyes, trying to regain my sanity.

Wrong move, I gasp when his warm body presses to mine and he latches his mouth onto my neck. He's not playing fair.

I cry out. This man knows my weakness. His mouth plays against my throat, causing me to begin to build again. I grind on him until he shoots his hands to my hips, pinning them in place.

My clit is pulsing so hard. I need relief. When his hand slips between my legs to pinch my needy nub, I see stars, my body trembles, but he lets go just before I peak. I whimper in frustration. The orgasm he let me have seems like it was so long ago. I'm starting to feel fatigued from the suppression.

I peer at him through heavy lids. I'm too drained to pout at him. I watch his muscles ripple as he removes his dress shirt. His broad chest makes my heart flutter. He is simply art—designed to give pleasure—visually and physically.

He moves to hover over me, my body yearning to know where he'll torture me next. I wait, but the touch never comes. Instead, he leans into my ear, his warm breath fanning my sensitive skin.

"When I step into a room, I want you to remember how I made you come without being inside you. I want your thighs soaked, knowing just my words sent your pulse racing," he rambles in my ear.

He flicks his tongue out and licks the shell of my ear. I shake hard, my eyes rolling in my head. My mouth falls open, his voice alone strokes me like a deep stroke from the back.

You have to be fucking kidding me.

"Look at me, baby," he orders, pulling away from my ear.

I train my eyes on him, not daring to blink as he slowly unzips his pants and peels them from his hips. I watch as his length springs free, looking angry and needy, just like I feel. I've never wanted to taste something so bad in my life.

"You're eyeing my cock like sucking it would bring you pleasure." He chuckles darkly.

I swallow, unable to find my voice. I nod when I still can't find the words. His eyes darken, but he doesn't place the offering before me. He's back between my legs, with his face buried in my cove.

I'm crying out his name, begging in no time. I pray that he doesn't stop as I feel my orgasm steamrollering its way toward me. I no longer know if the rocking motion is from the swing or from me trying to hump the shit out of his face.

"Please, I'm there, please don't stop," I whimper.

It's to no avail. He pulls back right as I begin to crest. However, to my relieved surprise, he thrusts into me before I can come down too far.

"You belong to me, Sidney," he growls as I pulse and gush around him.

I come so hard my head hurts. I mean, I feel it throbbing and it feels like my skull is tingling. This man has taken me to a new high. He wraps my legs around him, my one heel digging into his ass.

It seems to spur him on. He keeps pumping through my multiple orgasms. Rough and possessive is the best way to explain how he's fucking me. My fingers hurt from digging into my palms.

At some point, I feel like I'm out of my body, watching him fuck the shit out of my pussy. My voice is raw from screaming. My ass is soaked from dripping into it and the seat beneath me.

"Stop fighting it," he demands, pumping harder.

"Clay," I cry, coming all over him again.

I dig my heel in deep, pulling a groan from his lips. "Fuck yeah, baby. Give it to me, Sid."

"I'm coming," I cry out the obvious.

"That's my girl. Now you're ready to see where I can really take you," he coos.

"What?" I gasp hoarsely.

He chuckles, spilling into me. I open my mouth on a silent scream when his release triggers another from me. I'm wrung out, there's no way he can be serious.

He has to be kidding.

CHAPTER TWENTY-EIGHT

Don't Run

Clayton

I grit my teeth in self-loathing. I went too far last night. It shifted something in me when Sidney defied me while I spanked her ass. I realized I didn't want to spank and fuck the defiance out of her. I didn't even want to rein in her defiance to my control. It's one of the things I love about her.

Which leads me to my other problem. Sidney owns me. I'm in love with her. The moment she gave herself to me, when she trusted me to bring her unlimited pleasure, I knew. I've fallen for her. She took my heart right from my chest.

I know how hard it is for her to trust. I see how much she needs to be in control. I've watched her slowly allow me to take care of her and I don't think she's been aware of me doing it.

Our first round was a reward for her trust. However, what I did to Sidney and her body after that round on the swing, I'll admit—I might be ashamed. I took her everywhere, in every way, without mercy.

Her body was a playground I refused to leave. I spilled my seed in her, on her, anywhere I could to mark her as mine. I pulled toy after toy to aid in the destruction and recreation of Sidney's sexual DNA. She's a new woman, I made sure of it.

Now, I'm not proud of what I did. I released a darker shade of myself. The punishment I placed on her body was to feed my demons as much as it was to show her her Olympus of pleasure.

God, did her body sing like a goddess. I was the god of her desires and indulged her in a way that I know no other man has been or will ever be outside of me. Still, I fear it was too much.

I don't know how she feels about what I unleashed on her last night. Once she passed out, she remained asleep in my arms for the rest of the night. She didn't even stir when I carried her up to our bedroom in the wee hours of the morning.

I got up for a run when I couldn't take lying there listening to my own thoughts any longer. My worst fears came to life last night. I've always been cautious with the women I bed, never wanting to take things too far. Never wanting to push beyond their boundaries.

Now that I'm willing to admit to myself that I love Sid, I don't want my bullshit to send her running from me. I know what the contract says, but if she truly wanted to leave, I wouldn't stop her.

I pound the pavement harder. Sweat drenches my face, but I ignore it. I welcome the agony my body is starting to feel. It's the least I deserve.

I grunt when my phone rings. Looking, I see it's Gregor. His ass has been gone long enough. Whatever is going on with him, he's dragged my mother out of the country for it. I need my mother here to put a leash on my meddling father. Something about last night has been chafing me.

"Hello," I say into the phone after I tap my Bluetooth.

"Why do you sound so pissed off? It's too early in the morning," my brother greets.

"I went too far," I state simply.

Gregor sighs, remaining silent on the other end for a few moments. I know he understands what I'm saying to him. My brother knows me better than anyone.

"Did you hurt her?"

"No, not in any way that didn't bring her pleasure." I frown at my reply.

"Then what's the problem?"

"I pushed her, and I mean, hard. I was unyielding. She had no choice but to submit in the end," I huff.

"But did she willingly do so?" Gregor asks cautiously.

"Yes," I say tightly.

"She's a big girl. She made a choice," he responds.

"You know the problem," I bite out.

"Which is why I say again. She's a big girl, she consented to it. You were both consenting adults. As your conquests have always been." He tries to reassure me but only pisses me off further.

"She's not a conquest," I snap.

"So I'm gathering. Tell me this, what's the real problem?"

"I...I didn't know I would fall for her," I admit aloud. "Everything has changed. She's been sleeping in my bed since the first night."

My brother releases a long, low whistle. "Damn, I don't know what to say to that. It sounds like you've made up your mind about what you want from her."

"I want more time. I want her," I let out, stopping in my tracks.

I run a hand through my hair, letting my own words sink in. Subconsciously, I don't think I was ever willing to let Sid go once I made her mine. From the moment the ink hit the paper, I knew I wanted her in my life for as long as I could keep her.

"Then, take it from someone who has lost too much time and so much that meant the world to him." Gregor's voice draws me out of my revelation. "Stop treating her like the others. Tell her what makes you tick. You're a better man than you give yourself credit for. It's why people gravitate to you. Don't let your past rob you of your future. Especially not a past filled with lies."

I close my eyes, allowing his words to wash over me. They hit their mark. My frustration isn't with Sid and her reaction. It's with my past and what it will do to my future.

"Thank you," I breathe.

"Anytime, I just wanted you to know I'm on my way home," he replies before ending the call.

My mind made up, I head back for the apartment. I need a hot shower and then I need to talk to Sidney. It's time I reveal some things.

****

Sid slept right through my shower. Although, I could tell she got up sometime during my run. When I left, she was still wearing the wig from last night. Now, her natural hair is spilling across her pillow top and her face.

I smile at the untamed waves. They're just like her. Sidney isn't meant to be tamed. Even in her submission to me, she showed fire and passion that tempted me, challenged me, dared me to push her harder.

I grow hard just thinking about the depths I took her to last night. The look of awe of her face when she came from nothing more than the tease of a feather, the way she looked back at me as I claimed her forbidden place.

Her eyes continued to reveal she could take more, she wanted more. I didn't disappoint. Only stopping short of the whips and canes. With Sidney, I don't need that type of dark release.

All of that numbs the mind, it allows you and your submissive to release in a mental way through the pain and the infliction of it. For me, Sidney is that release. To mar her beautiful skin would be like hurting myself. I wouldn't be able to enjoy that or disappear into the act.

Just as I would never be able to go through with breaking her. Last night, I gave more than I received, which brought me all the pleasure in the world. It was something I didn't know I was capable of.

Sidney thought she gave me control, but she had every bit of it. Watching her open up, exploring what makes her bloom most, showing her that even silence can offer an intense lovemaking experience.

Yet, this current silence is killing me. I need to know where we stand. I need to know what my next move will be. My need for control has taken on a new face. I need to control the outcome of this. I need her to stay with me.

"You're watching me," she inhales, slowly opening her eyes.

I'm struck right through the heart by her beautiful eyes. I know I need to get her into a warm bath and pamper her for the day, but my mind and body are telling me to make love to her. To plead with my body for her to return the feelings I have for her.

I reach to brush the hair from her face. A soft smile touches her lips, she lifts her hand to cup my face. I turn to place a kiss against her palm.

When I look into her eyes again, concern wrinkles her brows, and her eyes are filled with worry. I lean in to kiss her lips, my own anxiety rattling inside me. I feel like that helpless teenage boy all over again.

"When I was seventeen, someone I trusted accused me of rape." I blurt out. "Fran was right, she and I do have history."

Her brows draw deeper. She moves her hand to the sheet to pull it to her chest as she sits up a little. I look away in shame. I don't want to see the look of doubt or mistrust in her eyes.

"Leeann and I were best friends." I shake my head.

"We were just starting to date here and there at the time. I'd gotten into a huge fight with my cousin, Wade," I say bitterly. "To calm me down, Leeann took me to one of my favorite restaurants and we hung out and laughed all night. The next day, I had the worse food poisoning. I was so fucking sick, I thought I was going to die," I snort.

"I could hardly stay awake or focus on the room without it spinning. I remember what I thought to be Leeann coming over. It wasn't out of the ordinary for her to climb into my bed just to hang out. I was too weak to protest if I wanted to.

"The next morning, my father and Leeann's dad stormed my room. I was groggy and confused. I had no idea what was going on. When I took in my surroundings, Fran was half naked and trembling in a curled-up ball next to me.

"I couldn't understand what was going on. She started to cry, saying that I had raped her. I spent the entire fucking day before shitting and puking my brains out. I was too weak to move, and she was accusing me of rape," I bite out.

"Wait, what?"

"I was so confused, I was fully clothed in the basketball shorts and T-shirt I'd worn all day the day before." I shake my head. "I thought my father would side with me. I thought he would make the bullshit go away, but he didn't. He knew how sick I'd been, but he did nothing. I was cuffed and taken to jail. Gregor was the one who stepped in to help.

"Our ties with some powerful people stemmed from that one disaster in my life. Never once did my father get involved. He had a deal with Fran and Leeann's dad that he was more interested in saving," I say in disgust. "I lost everything I cared about. I wasn't allowed to play any sports my senior year. My friends wouldn't talk to me.

"Leeann had this look in her eyes every time she came around. I felt like she didn't trust me anymore. It took so long for us to get back to normal. I was so embarrassed over something I never did."

"Oh, my God. That's insane," Sid whispers.

I nod. "You're the only woman I've allowed in my bed since. I've slept with my door locked behind me for years. I've never had a relationship or sex without a contract, something stating prior consent. When Leeann betrayed me, things got worse. I needed control. I needed a release for all the bullshit."

"How did Leeann betray you?"

"You heard what I said last night," I begin to explain. "I shut down at some point. Instead of my father being a dad, he had Leeann spy on my life. I'd just started to figure out how to have a social life with women. A friend mentioned the contracts and arrangements and I took things from there.

"Leeann told Dad and then she used my personal guard against me by sleeping with him, so he'd do her bidding. They tried to blackmail me with pictures and videos of the girls I'd been with and the types of things I'm into. I was violated all over again. This time with cameras in my room."

"Are you fucking kidding me?"

"No, I'm not. It's why I had to get to know you before I approached you. I needed to know they couldn't get to me through you...that my father couldn't use you against me.

"I'm sorry for last night. I...I know I pushed you to your limits—"

"Wait, why are you telling me all of this?"

The hurt in her voice causes me to look at her. I study her face. For a moment, I'm at a loss for words. I swallow hard and blink rapidly.

"I know I have a dark side. I should've been more gentle with you. I...think I pushed too much."

Sidney's face breaks into a huge smile. She scoots closer to me, curling up under my warmth. She reaches her small hand down to grope me over my sweats.

"I didn't complain once. I was with you the whole time. If I trust you with nothing else, I trust you with my body, Clay," she purrs up at me. "If that was your dark side, I welcome it to come out anytime you need."

She kisses my jaw, squeezing the hand wrapped around my length. When we lock eyes, hers twinkle up at me. I cup her face and run my finger over her lips.

"You're beautiful," I whisper.

She beams back at me. "I've seen you sexy, I've seen you pissed off, I've seen you confident, but this…this is adorable. It makes you human. I needed that after last night." She laughs.

"Is that so?" I join her.

"Yes, you were a combination of a pussy warrior and a sex god." She grins. "A girl could get lost in all that."

I brush my fingers over her soft cheek. The words almost slip from my lips, but I stop them. To Sidney, this is still a contract arrangement. I know most of her reluctance has been because she has an expiration date in mind.

I want to erase that date. I begin to form the words to tell her just that. As I open my mouth to start, her phone rings. Her brows knit while I take note that it's not her usual ring tone.

"Hold on a sec." She holds a finger up at me.

Sid reaches for her phone and answers it. I watch her face as she listens. My body starts to coil, I don't like the feeling I'm getting. My phone dings, pulling my attention.

"Shit."

I curse under my breath at the text David just sent. He could have sent this shit sooner. Sid is being ambushed. This is exactly the shit I don't need right now.

Sidney

I'm totally confused, but Marnita's voice is so excited coming through the phone. I don't have the heart to interrupt and tell her I have no idea what the hell she's talking about. I look over at Clayton and he looks pissed off.

The softness and vulnerability he displayed only moments ago is gone. I get the feeling this call has something to do with his change in mood.

I honestly haven't wrapped my mind around all of what he has told me. I can't believe Clooney would do that to him. Not the loving father I've gotten to know.

I didn't want to upset Clay by telling him that. I wasn't there. I don't know what happened firsthand.

However, I know one thing, he'd never be able to use me against Clayton. Not after the way I've fallen for this man.

"I still can't believe you're getting married. This is such an honor that you want me to come in and remodel the place for you. The pictures your fiancé sent with his assistant are amazing. I don't know what you need me for," she bubbles through the line, pulling me from my thoughts.

"Thank you so much for thinking of me as a bridesmaid. Between the wedding and the remodel, I'll get so much time to catch up with you. How's Chloe? You know we're going to throw you an amazing bachelorette party, right?"

"Oh, I looked up your fiancé. Girl, where did you find him? There are pictures of you two all over the net, funny I couldn't find much before you, but—"

"Marnita," I call, finally interrupting her.

"Oh, shit, I'm sorry. I'm just so excited. I'm on his jet," she squeals. She lowers her voice to whisper, "Oh, and David is fine as hell."

I burst into laughter. I love this girl. When she's excited, it shows. If she's pissed, she's silent as a lamb. I don't know what the hell is going on, but I'll admit I'm excited just from listening to her.

However, I dip my brows as her words sink in. David isn't Clay's assistant. His executive assistant's name is Levi. David is his head of security. The last time I saw David was sometime last night before we left the gala. I had wondered where he was when we left.

Clayton stands, leaning over to kiss my forehead. I purse my lips, watching as he leaves the room. This isn't over, he's going to explain what this is all about.

"Honey, we'll get into details when you get here. I have to get a few things done before you arrive," I say into the phone.

"Love you, honey. Thanks so much for all of this," she replies.

I toss the covers off, throwing my legs over the edge of the bed. When I go to stand, my legs buckle. I fall right into the nightstand, knocking the vase of flowers Clay had placed there yesterday to the floor.

Clay thunders back up the stairs as I sit, stunned. I can't help it, I burst into laughter. My legs giving out, my bewildered reaction, the wild look on Clayton's face, I can't hold it in. I laugh so hard tears stream down my face.

Clayton folds his arms across his chest, shaking his head at me, a small smile on the corners of his lips. That's until I go to move, and he sees the glass at my feet. He's in motion, moving to me to scoop me up into his arms.

"You need to soak. I'll clean this up and make your lunch," he murmurs.

"Lunch." I whip my head back. "What time is it?"

"A little past noon."

"I really slept that long?" I say in disbelief.

"Mm, you had a very vigorous night." His smile returns.

"What's going on?" I cut through the small talk, wanting answers.

He sighs, placing me on the side of the tub. He doesn't reply as he starts the water and retrieves my favorite bubble bath. I shift a little, the soreness in my ass biting a bit.

"The night you moved in, I had my guys go to your apartment. I told you before, your place was bugged. They were listening in on your conversations. I had your friend watched as a precaution.

"Anyone you mentioned or talked to became a target. Chloe has been away. Ally has been here in New York under my watch and security, like you. I've had eyes on Marnita's situation. She's become a target since they haven't been able to get to you," he sighs, reaching to shut off the water.

"Are you kidding me?"

"No, I'm bringing her here to keep her close," he replies.

"What happened? How have they targeted her?"

"She's been losing clients for no good reason and a few major contracts were reassigned in the last few weeks. She was more than willing to take our job." He stands, plucking me up and placing me into the warm water.

"But that's not enough to bring her here. What are you leaving out?"

He sighs. "I had Tristan, a friend of a friend, watching her place. Some guys started to come around and he called it in. I thought it best to extract her now."

I cover my face with my hands and groan. Why is all of this happening? Who the hell did I piss off?

Clayton peels my hands away and kisses my nose before nodding for me to lower into the water. I place my hands on my hips, glaring at him. He places his hands over mine, tugging me forward to the edge of the tub now between us.

"She doesn't know where all this is coming from. The wedding and the job were my way of keeping it that way. A little more time, Sid. I'll make this go away soon," he says, promise written thickly in his words.

CHAPTER TWENTY-NINE

Old Friends

Sidney

"Seriously, this place is gorgeous already, I don't see what you need me for," Marnita gushes as we get her settled and give her a quick tour.

We all take a seat in the living room. Clay takes a seat next to me on the sofa and Marnita takes the accent chair across from us. I hate the stress I see on her face, it's not like her.

I'll admit Clayton was right to bring her here. Something has definitely been going on with her. I knew it the moment she hugged me. She held on to me like I was a lifeline.

"I want Sid to start to feel at home. As a wedding gift, I want her to be able to put her stamp on the place," Clay replies.

I look at him and narrow my eyes. I get that he wants to protect my friend, but here we are, telling more lies and spending more money on things that aren't going to remain.

"I like everything the way it is, there's no need to change a thing. I guess we have similar tastes."

He waves me off. "I'll show you the room I was thinking of for Sid's new office. We can talk about other rooms later. I appreciate you doing this for us."

"It's not a problem. I'd do anything for Sid. Um...does David live here?" she asks shyly.

"On the lowest level. Those are his rooms."

"Does that mean he's single?" I want to burst into laughter as her cheeks turn red.

Marnita is very pretty. I'm sure David didn't miss that fact. However, now I'm curious as well as to whether or not he's single.

"He is."

I look to Clay, and he has an amused smile on his face. Turning back to Marnita, I catch the little smile on hers. Oh, David better watch out. I think my friend plans to pounce.

In all honesty, David is a nice guy. Marnita deserves someone nice like him. If Chloe were here, I'm sure she would try to play matchmaker between them.

"He'll be joining us for dinner tonight. Well, he'll be working, but I'm sure one of the guys can step in so he can join us," Clay offers.

"I mean, if he wants." Marnita shrugs her shoulders. She then gets a confused look on her face. "So wait, I think I got things all wrong. He's not your assistant, is he?"

"No, he's the head of my security. However, Levi, my assistant, was the one who contacted you initially." Marnita nods. Clay takes his phone out while placing an arm across the sofa behind me. "I'll text David. He stepped out with Ally for a bit. I'm sure they'll be back soon."

"Cane isn't around?"

"No," he says firmly. I lift a brow as I look at him.

He softens his tone and explains. "He's not around and Royce is with him. David will look after Ally until they get in. He should still be free for dinner."

Royce is Cane's head of security. Also, a nice guy. It's Royce who makes me relax when it comes to Ally's safety. I'm still not a fan of Cane's.

If Clay is the responsible brother, Cane is the bad boy. I don't know how I feel about Ally hanging around him.

Seeming to feel the shift in my demeanor, Clay leans in and kisses my lips. He reaches for my shoulder and starts to massage it, all while texting on his phone.

"I'm so excited to be in New York again. We absolutely have to do some shopping, Sid."

Now this gets my attention. I turn to her with a big smile. My pocketbook must groan in the distance.

I have so many plans for the shops we have to hit. I've been missing Chloe. I can do damage alone, but I love having someone to shop with.

"On that note, I'm going to make a few phone calls. We'll leave for dinner around seven. David says he's in."

"Awesome," Marnita squeals before she tries to play off her excitement—clearing her throat and running a hand over her hair.

I chuckle to myself. Clay laughs as he leans in and kisses me one last time before he disappears.

"Want to have a drink before we freshen up to go out?"

"Sure, you can tell me all about Clay and how you met."

I don't reply because I don't know how to tell her I knew him for less than thirty minutes before he proposed. Hearing it in my head sounds crazy. I don't know how it will sound to her.

Clayton

Dinner was interesting. I think David may be interested in Marnita as much as she is in him. However, I know David. What's obvious to me may not be so to others.

Unfortunately, Sid's friend may have missed it and it showed as we rode up to the apartment tonight. The shy glances and slumped shoulders said a whole lot. Knowing my friend the way I do, I'm going to stay out of it.

"Clay, they would make such a cute couple. I don't understand what happened," Sid says, her adorable face scrunched up as we enter our bedroom.

"I believe you both misread the situation. I suggest you mind your own business and allow things to play out."

Sid jerks her head back and places her hands on her hips. "Excuse me?"

I move to crowd her space. "Oh, no. We're not fighting over this. I've known David for years. This is the way he is. He's into her.

"He'll make things happen in his own time, in his own way. We're staying out of it. That's all. We mind our business and let him work." I kiss her lips, wrapping my arms around her as she frowns at me. "Trust me, we can find plenty of things of our own to be concerned with."

"I'm not in the mood." She pouts and crosses her arms over her chest.

"Do you want me to list all the ways I know that to be a lie?"

She continues to frown up at me, working her jaw. I brush my thumb across her protruding nipple. "This says you want my mouth here."

I take a step back and start to strip from my clothes while keeping my eyes on her. Her chest heaves as she takes in my body.

Once completely naked, I move closer to her and reach to touch her pretty face, I brush my thumb under her eye. "Your pupils are blown out. They tell me you want me inside you."

I reach to tug her lip from between her teeth and place my other hand over her rising chest. "Your heart is pounding, I bet you're soaked and ready for me."

Gliding my hand down her body, I tug up the hem of her dress and reach between her legs, chuckling darkly. "What do we have here, Sid? Is this a weeping pussy? Is it weeping for me? For my tongue?"

As I stroke her hot pussy, a look comes across her face. I can't help wondering what she has going on in her head, I know she's about to find a way to defy me and it only turns me on.

"Two can play this game," she hisses at me.

She then spits in her palm and wraps both her hands around my length. I push my fingers in and out of her faster as she works her hands up and down while circling her palms.

"Fuck, baby," I groan.

She drops to her knees and takes me in her mouth. I roll my eyes in my head and toss my head back, staring at the ceiling. She's sucking me so good my toes curl. Working her hands and adding more moisture as she goes.

"Sid," I groan.

I let her deep throat me until my spine starts to tingle. I'm not coming in her mouth. I want to watch her ride me. I pull away from her mouth and she looks up at me through her lashes. I grab her underneath her arms and move to the bed, tossing her onto it. She bounces with a wicked smile on her face.

I place a knee on the bed, and she starts to back away from me. I grin and reach for her ankle.

"Clay," she squeals.

I turn onto my back and guide her to straddle me. Slowly, she sinks down on me. I sit up, so we're nose to nose. She throws her head back as she moans. I capture one of her nipples in my mouth and groan around it.

Not able to hold back, I take over and thrust up into her. She begins to scream my name as she gushes all over me. I love the way her body quakes in my arms.

I don't stop bringing her body pleasure. We lock eyes and I know she's getting close to another orgasm. I love watching her fall apart like this.

"Haven't you learned yet? I always win, baby," I croon as she quivers and comes again. I could do this all night.

"Whatever, Clay," she says sleepily.

I kiss her head and fall back, taking her with me. I can't help smiling up at the ceiling as she relaxes against my chest.

CHAPTER THIRTY

The Gang is Here

Clayton

With Gregor and Chloe back, my parents have requested everyone's presence at their home. This day has been full of surprises. As I watch my father tonight, I get the feeling not all of them are surprises to him at all.

I think I might be underestimating him. Something I thought I learned better than. However, he gets more crafty with age. I look at my younger brother, who hasn't quite mastered being cunning, no matter how much he thinks he has.

I've been distracted, but with Gregor back, Cane is on my radar. I'm going to zone in on what he and Ally think they're getting over on everyone.

I saunter over to a nervous-looking Cane. To anyone who doesn't know him, he'd look as cool as a cucumber. However, from the years of watching him when he starts to spiral, I know better.

"I have enough on my plate. You want to tell me what's going on with you?" I question.

"Nothing's going on." He shrugs.

"You told me I could use your apartment for Ally. The apartment you said you wouldn't have any use for," I tilt my head. "Why are you still here in New York?"

"Last time I checked, it was my apartment. There's plenty of room for her and me to coexist," Cane says dryly. "Besides, Royce has been helpful to you guys. If I go, he goes."

I roll my eyes. We'll make do without Royce, and he knows it. It's a bullshit excuse. "What are you hiding?"

"Not everyone's hiding something, Clay," he huffs.

"You're not everyone," I retort.

"I like hanging out with her. I thought you guys wanted me around more," he mumbles.

"I always want you around, but I'm warning you. Ally is important to Sid and Chloe. Gregor will kill your ass and I will help him," I say pointedly. "Don't get her into any of that shit you like landing yourself into."

He snorts. "Are you forgetting? She knows how to get into her own trouble."

I run a hand through my hair. I don't need the reminder. That's one more issue I need to silence. I'm starting to feel like everything is caving in around me.

"Don't worry about it, bro. I'm not good enough for her. I know I'm not," he hisses before storming off.

"What's all that about?" Gregor asks as we both watch Cane rush out of the house.

I turn my head and narrow my eyes, taking note that Ally is watching him. She looks as if she may go after him. Her gaze turns back to her sister, a frown creases her face and her shoulders sag.

"He's using," I bite out.

"You're fucking bullshitting me, right?" Gregor grinds out.

"Nope, he owes, and he owes big. Those two think everyone around them to be idiots. She's into some shit that's taking a shitload of favors to try to get her out of." I nod my head toward Ally.

Gregor pulls a hand down his face. "How much time do we have to fix this one?" he grunts.

"Ally's out of time. I've been keeping her hidden. I'll tell you about that later. As for Cane, I think it's time we fall back and let him figure shit out," I reply.

Gregor turns hard eyes on me. I already know what he's thinking. However, this isn't the same thing.

"You sound like Dad," he growls. "I didn't leave you to figure it out."

"I wasn't stuffing white powder up my nose either. He has a problem, gambling debts and crazy-ass girlfriends, fine. We can get him out of that shit any time. This other bullshit will have us digging a grave for him, not keeping him from one. It has to stop," I hiss back.

"Fuck," Gregor blows out. "This is the last thing I need."

"Tell me about it. I'm still trying to wrap my head around all of this shit you brought to our door." I shake my head.

"You?" he snorts.

I pat him on his shoulder. "I'm here. Whatever you need. You did the right thing. She loves you." I squeeze his shoulder.

He nods. "She's mine. I didn't plan any of this, but they're both mine," he sighs.

"Clay," I turn to look at David rushing toward me.

I groan internally. I guess things are about to get louder around here. I know that look on his face.

"What now?" I grit out.

"You're going to want to see this, boss," he says, handing over a printed email.

I take the page and scan it quickly. I read it again to make sure I read it right the first time. I feel the vein in my head begin to throb.

"Fuck me."

CHAPTER THIRTY-ONE

Shopping!

Sidney

"You guys are so lucky. Back home, you can't find guys like you have. I mean, come on. They send their personal security to shop with you," Marnita prattles.

I look back at David, Royce, and Ethan. All three brothers insisted we take their security with us. Way to make four Black women stand out. Send three huge white men with them to follow them around. We've gotten so many stares. I don't blame Ally for being a bit jumpy.

"Trust me, it's not as romantic as it seems. It's just another form of control," Chloe says.

I want to laugh because it's true, but Chloe's tone keeps me from laughing. I've been wanting to ask her what's going on with her, but I never get a chance to.

Since she's been back, she's been down Ally's throat, which is understandable. I'm still angry with her for dropping out of school. The relationship or friendship or whatever it is she's taken up with Cane is just one more thing we're both fuming about.

Then there're all the other things I'm still wrapping my head around with Chloe and Gregor. This time I think I'll follow Clayton's advice and mind my business. Ally has become a young woman.

Chloe and I have to let go sometime. Although, I still wouldn't mind me and Chloe cornering Cane to kick his little ass. Clay has run interference every time I've tried.

"Can we go in this store?" Marnita asks, pointing to a posh boutique.

"Please," Ally groans, fanning her face.

"You wouldn't be so hot if you didn't have on that ridiculous wig," Chloe mutters.

I look Ally over and again want to laugh. She's wearing a waist length gray wig and these huge shades. You wouldn't recognize her at all if you didn't already know it was her. I was a bit taken aback when she came out of the apartment this morning.

Ally takes off her shades and rolls her eyes. I gasp at the gray contacts she has in. I hadn't seen them earlier.

"Okay, what's with the X-Men convention look?" I tease.

"I wanted to try something new. It's not like you guys haven't changed your hair or something in the past. Why is everything I do a problem?"

"Because you're making a bunch of poor choices and I don't like it," Chloe hisses as we enter the store.

"Right, says the sister who runs off to Dubai for what? Four months and comes back engaged. Setting awesome examples, sis," Ally retorts.

Chloe lunges for Ally, but Ethan catches her around the waist.

"Thanks," I say to him as I get between Chloe and Ally.

Tears fill Chloe's eyes. "You have no idea the things I've sacrificed for you. No idea."

"I didn't ask you to," Ally tosses back and pouts.

"Gah, you're so fucking ungrateful. I've never put a man before you, Ally. I'm only asking for the same respect. Talk to me. Tell me what's going on. Because if I have to beat that shit out of you, I promise we're going to have a long trip back to being sisters."

"Maybe we should all take a step back," I offer as everyone's attention is on us. I think they're about to ask us to leave.

Honestly, this shopping trip is over for me. Like Chloe, I want to know what's going on with Ally. She's been avoiding me as much as she can. This is the most I've seen of her since David brought her home. Yet, I know she spends most of her time with Cane.

Chloe rolls her eyes as tears fall and she works her jaw.

"Not everything is about you, Chloe," Ally fumes.

I groan as Chloe tries to lunge at her again. Clearly, Ally has struck a nerve. Ethan has to carry Chloe out of the store. Marnita rushes over with concern on her face.

"Is everything okay?"

"Sister drama. We're going to head back."

"Oh, okay. No problem."

Clayton

"Hey, Diggs. What you got for me?"

It grinds my gears that I have to go outside for this. However, I'm too close. My little brother has put my back against the wall, and I know if I handle this, I'm not going to have the type of focus I need. Calling in help from the Lost Souls was my next best option.

"It's drugs all right, but I'm not sure he's using. I need some more time to verify what we think is going on. The one thing we can tell you for sure is a million has been blown and he's headed for another million or two on this path he's on. Gutter wants to know how close you want us to get in on this," he replies.

"I told myself I wasn't going to get into this until that email showed up. I want you to get all up in their face. Tell King he has an all-access pass to anything he wants for this one.

"I want to know what my brother has been up to and with who. I know the girl is connected, but how? Once you have those answers, I'll handle the rest. Have Brick call me."

I end the call and sit back in my seat. I could strangle Ally and Cane. My mind goes to Sid. She's the only one who can calm me down at this point.

I text David to see where they are. A smile comes to my face when he texts back that they're in the lobby. "I hope you're up for my dark side," I murmur to myself as I get up to meet Sid at the elevator.

CHAPTER THIRTY-TWO

My Loss

Sidney

Eileen and Clooney outdid themselves with this engagement party and I thought the four hundred people they invited to the wedding were a bit much. My stomach hurts just thinking about all the money these people have spent on my fake engagement.

At least this party is for both Clay and me as well as Chloe and Gregor. My friend looks like she's in love. Although, at times, I see a melancholy expression come over her face.

I plan to corner her tomorrow at some point to finally get some answers. I know something is different about her, no matter how much Gregor dotes on her, it doesn't mean she's truly happy. I've watched Clayton put on the same act.

"You look stunning," a woman coming out of one of the stalls says.

I know we were introduced, but I can't remember her name or who she is. To be honest, I've been overwhelmed. This venue is breathtaking and the number of people we have as guests is mind blowing.

"Thank you," I reply.

"You're going to make such a lovely bride. You two look so in love."

I reach to tug at one of the earrings Clayton gave me. His father's face lit up when he saw me wearing them. It made me wonder if that's why Clayton gave them to me and insisted I wear them tonight—to give his father the sense that I mean something to him.

"I care deeply about Clay," I reply, not knowing what else to say.

"Dear, I can tell he cares deeply for you. He looks so happy. There was a time that couldn't be said for Clayton. Such a lovely couple."

I smile, not having much else to say. She moves for the door, patting my arm as she passes. I turn my attention back to the mirror.

I love this black sheer-overlay handkerchief-hem dress. The red heels were my idea of spicing things up. The look on Clay's face when I came downstairs said a million words.

I give myself a sad smile. If only that look was a look of love and not lust. I didn't think this party would cut so deep. I take a cleansing breath and exit the bathroom, heading back to the party.

As I walk the hall, the sound of someone hacking up a lung catches my attention. I slow down as I get near the room the sound is coming from, wondering if I should call for help.

The coughing stops but the voices in the room hold my attention. I move a little closer.

"Are you all right?"

"I'm fine."

The coughing starts again. Damn, that's a bad cough. He should have that checked out.

"Maybe you should tell them."

"I'm not going anywhere. Death isn't ready for an old bastard like me. I plan to beat this. I don't need to worry anyone with this nonsense." That's Clooney's voice.

I gasp and listen closer. Chewing my lip, I place a hand over my chest. I furrow my brows as I try to place the other voice.

"If you think they hate you now, if you don't say anything and something happens, they're going to hold that resentment forever."

"You let me worry about that, you work on what I asked you to. I promise you, I'm not going anywhere. Especially not now that Chloe is in the picture."

"Fine, I'm working on it. I'll see you back inside the ballroom."

I look around to see if anyone else is in the hall to catch me spying. I rush from the door back to the ballroom. I know that voice. I can't help trying to place it. Who would know Clooney better than the guys? Who would he share his secret with?

I catch sight of Eileen as she's beaming with a smile on her face as Clay, Cane, and Gregor surround her. This will devastate them all, no matter how much they all seem to resent their father, I can tell deep down they still love him.

I shake my head to clear it. There's way too much going on tonight. I need some fresh air to clear my thoughts.

I turn and head outside. Once out front, I stand at the portico where the valet is. I'm lost in thought when a black Maserati pulls up.

A woman jumps out and rounds the car. She's dressed in all black—jeans and a leather jacket. I take notice of her as she's not dressed for the venue. It's not until she's up on me that I place her face. It's Fran.

"I had to see this for myself," she hisses at me. "He's really going through with this. I hate that fucking family. Your fiancé ruined our lives and he gets to live happily ever after. It's fucking disgusting."

"The only thing around here that's disgusting is you. You're the one trying to ruin lives. You lied about him and have the audacity to stand here like you're innocent."

"You know nothing about me."

"I know if you don't jump back in your car and leave, you're going to wish you never left your home tonight. Don't make me come up out of my heels. I'll beat the brakes off you like someone should have done when Clay was seventeen.

"Try me, honey. I have a ton of pent-up anger waiting to unleash on your ass," I snarl.

She looks me over as if she smells something that stinks. I drop my left hip and place my hands on both. Narrowing my eyes at her, I dare her to try me.

"I'll have the last laugh. I promise you that," she says before she turns and storms back to the driver's side of her car.

I roll my eyes and shake my head. That woman and her sister have some serious problems.

Clayton

I look around the room for Sid. She's been gone for too long. My heart starts to race.

I can't place my eyes on her. She said she had to go to the restroom, but she should be back by now.

I find Chloe and Ally sitting at a table together. Marnita is at the bar, but still no Sid. I can't breathe.

I turn to wave David over and that's when I catch Sidney returning to the ballroom. I reach to rub my forehead.

"Fuck me," I murmur.

I don't know how I'm supposed to let her go. I've even thought of moving the wedding up so that when the contract is up, she's already my wife. I'm not ready for her to walk away.

Maybe moving the wedding up isn't a bad idea. She can't leave.

CHAPTER THIRTY-THREE

Celebrate

Sidney

It's been a week since the engagement party, and this all still feels so wrong. So many gifts, more congratulations, all things I'm forced to smile through. This is making me sick to my stomach.

Not only do I feel guilty. My heart aches because I wish it were all real. The pretty lingerie, his and her robes. I want to be able to share it all with Clay.

I've come to trust and care for him so much. I down my glass of champagne and wipe at my tears. I stepped out on the balcony to have a breather from all the fake smiles and happy talk of a wedding that's not going to happen.

"Oh, there you are. Everything okay, dear?"

I turn and force a smile for Eileen. She really doesn't deserve this. I wish there was a way to back out of this without hurting her or Clooney, especially after what I overheard.

Surprisingly, Clay hasn't stopped me from bonding with either of his parents. I would have thought he would have wanted to place distance between me and his mother. I was also sure his hate for his father would have caused issues with Clooney's weekly lunches he now requests my presence for.

"Everything is fine. I'm just thinking about my mother. You know, I wish she was a part of all of this."

"Oh, honey," she coos and wraps me in a hug. "I know it's not the same, but I've always wanted a girl and I would be honored if you'd allow me to step up in any way I can."

Pulling away, I swipe at the tears that break free. I can't hold them back any longer. I feel terrible.

I almost come clean with the truth. This is all too much. My heart isn't the only one that will be broken.

"Oh, Sidney. This is supposed to be a happy occasion. Life can throw us lemons, but we make lemonade and sell it to the highest bidder while smiling the entire time."

I start to laugh through my tears. Eileen's humor has grown on me. I think I'm falling for the whole family, with the exception of Cane. I didn't know that would happen.

I didn't have time to think this all through that night. Everything happened so fast. What I thought to be a boss move has backfired on me. I've lost more than money. I've lost my heart and I still don't know who's behind all this.

I need to talk to Clayton. We have to stop this. I need to leave before I hurt someone or my heart is broken.

Clayton

Standing from my seat in the living room, I walk over to the floor-to-ceiling windows and look out over the view of New York City. The brightly lit city does little to calm this uneasy feeling in my gut. I know Sid is safe, she's on the lower level of Gregor's place having her bridal party.

I've checked in with David a number of times. The ladies seem to be fine and having a good time.

Still, this feeling is coming from somewhere. I open my phone and look at the reply from Delta. I sent her a text this morning asking how hard it would be to move the wedding up. I'm willing to pay the cost no matter what it is.

"I think I should move up the wedding," I say aloud.

"Really? Why?" Gregor replies from his seat in the accent chair. He has a cigar in one hand and a glass of brandy in the other. He's been hanging out here while the ladies have their fun.

"I want to marry her. I don't want to let her go when this is over."

"So, you're ready to admit you love her." It's a statement, not a question.

"I do."

"Then tell her. This is crossing the line into playing games. That's not you. Talk to her and let her know how you feel."

I grunt and bare my teeth. There's truth in his words, but at this point, I don't know how Sid would feel and I can't have her run away from me.

"If I reveal my hand and she doesn't want this, then what? If I move the wedding up under the pretense of Dad forcing my hand, I have a better chance."

"You're going to do what you want. I can hear in your voice your mind is already made up," he says.

I look down at the text from Delta again. According to her reply, the venue will be the biggest issue. If I can square that away she can pull strings on everything else. Sid's gown is already ahead of schedule.

The thought of losing Sid makes me sick. I didn't know I was missing or craving the intimacy she has brought into my life. I have someone I can let my guard down with and that has made life better as a whole.

I hit send on my reply to Delta. Levi was able to get the venue secured for an earlier date earlier this afternoon. My mind is made up. Once Sid and I are married, she'll see how good we are together, and she'll stay.

"I'm heading out," Gregor says, pulling my attention.

"I'll talk to you in the morning."

"Yeah, I'll join you for your run."

I nod and focus outside the window. That feeling only easing a bit after expressing my thoughts and sending that text. What I really need is some time with Sid. Her in my arms and her scent surrounding me.

I widen my stance as I stare out the window and fold my arms over my chest. The moment she enters the room, my body is aware. A grin comes to my lips as she wraps her arms around my waist and places her face against my back.

"Clay, can we talk?"

I close my eyes. The sound of her voice tells me this is the reason for the tightness in my chest. I knew something was wrong.

I cover her hands with mine. "What about?"

"The closer we get to this wedding, the guiltier I feel. At what point are we going to call this off? Have you found a way out of this thing with your father?"

I turn to face her. "My lawyers are trying to find loopholes and haven't come up with anything. At this point, I'm being advised to give him what he wants."

This isn't a lie. I just haven't been focused on my father and his tactics to get us all married and have us take over the business. For me, this wedding is a win-win.

She looks into my eyes with tears. "This isn't right. We shouldn't be lying to all these people. There has to be another way."

I cup her face and take her lips. I know the kiss is all-consuming, but I need her. I've come too close to lose her now.

She moans into my mouth and laces her fingers into my hair. I only break the kiss to let her up for air. The dazed look in her eyes causes me to power through my decision.

"There is another way. I was going to talk to you about it. I think we should move the wedding up. Dad will back off and maybe I can force your problem to show its hand.

"I've narrowed it down to two players, but they don't make complete sense. Maybe going through with the wedding will get them to come out of the shadows."

I'm totally pulling this out of my ass. It's all true, but it's not how I thought I'd do this. Gregor is right, I'm too close to playing games. It's not in my character, but I'm so gone for Sid, I'm willing to work all my options.

"Tell me who they are. Maybe I can help."

I shake my head. If I'm wrong, these are some serious allegations and because I can't prove any of it, I'm not going to throw anyone under the bus. That asshole doesn't deserve my loyalty, but I'm not going to ruin him...yet.

"Trust me, Sid. You feel guilty about the wedding and all the money I've spent, right?"

"Yes."

"My father is still breathing down my neck and he seems to love you. We marry, that's one step closer to me getting around all this. It will buy me all the time I need to release his grasp on my companies."

She rolls her eyes up as they fill with tears. This is a big ask. I know she has trust issues. I'm asking for the ultimate trust with this.

I take her lips again and start to back her out of the room toward the stairs. A little time in my playroom will help with this trust issue. I'm ready to take Sid to a new high and gain more of her trust.

"Clay," she whimpers when I move my lips to her neck.

"Shh, it's all going to work out."

I lift her onto my waist and head down the stairs to the second level. I never take my lips away from her skin. Once at the door of the playroom, I take the keys from my pocket and unlock the door.

I step inside and allow her body to slide down my front. As I look down into her eyes, I question myself for only a moment. I love this woman and I'd rather have her in my life than live without her.

Selfish, yes, but I want to give Sid the world. I'm only doing what I think is best for her. I don't think there's a man better for her than me. If I did, I'd let her go.

I grasp her face and get within a breath from her lips. "I'll give you the world, Sid. I'll support all your dreams. For as long as you're with me, I've got you." She closes her eyes and nods her head. "All I ask is for your trust."

"Shelby," she whispers.

"What?"

"It's my safe word."

I chuckle and shake my head. She looks up at me in confusion. She's fucking adorable.

"You don't need one of those with me." I tap the tip of my nose. "Trust me." I tap it again. "Trust, I know you." I tap it again. "Trust me and where I'll take you."

She nods. "I'm scared, Clay. What if this all blows up in my face?"

I tap my nose again before leaning in and taking her lips. Passion surges between us. Marrying this woman before the contract is up is the right thing to do. Subconsciously, I think it was my plan all along.

I spend the rest of the night teaching her how to trust me. Every time she looks at me as if she isn't sure about where I'm taking her body, I tap my nose. With each tap, she relaxes more and more.

Made for me. I could never hurt her.

CHAPTER THIRTY-FOUR

Another Piece

Sidney

Rinsing out my mouth, I then place my hands on the sink and take a look at myself.

"What are you doing, Sid?" I breathe.

I want to help Clayton, I do, but at what cost to my sanity? Moving the wedding up may absolve me of my guilt about the wedding and all the money spent, but my heart is still on the line.

I'm only digging a deeper hole. When will it stop? I'm so confused.

I've handed him all my trust. Last night in the playroom tore me open for the world to see how much I love and trust him. However, I don't think he gets that. The words were on the tip of my tongue, but if this is truly only about his father and that contract, I don't want to embarrass myself.

My past is riding me, telling me I'm not enough and Clayton will abandon me like all the rest. The Sidney I've worked so hard to become is gone. I hate to believe I've become silly over some dick, but at this point, I may just have.

However, I know it's more than that. He's become my friend. He knows as much about me as Chloe does, if not more.

"Hey, baby," Clayton croons and kisses the top of my head as he places his hands on my hips. "You didn't get to tell me how the party was last night."

"It was nice. I think everyone enjoyed themselves. The girls loved their gifts."

"Good, my mother is having another freak-out. I told her we're moving things up this morning."

I gasp. "The invitations just came in. We were going to send them out this weekend."

"We'll have them reprinted. I'll make sure they're rushed. Listen, I'm taking the day off. Delta will be by to go over all the updates for the wedding. I was thinking once she's gone, we could go for a stroll on Rockaway Beach. Maybe have dinner or something."

"That sounds nice," I reply.

It truly does, but it's only going to cause me to lose another piece of my heart. I can't say I'm excited about that.

"Everything okay?"

"Yes, I have a bit of a headache. It's probably from all the champagne last night."

He kisses the top of my head. "Um, maybe we can take a rain check on the date. I'll make you some soup and we can spend the day in."

"I don't want to ruin your plans."

He turns my face up and pecks my lips. "Go back to bed, I'll handle Delta. You rest and we'll decide from there. Sound good?"

He searches my face, waiting for an answer. If I wanted a man like this in my real life, I'd never be able to find him. Now, I have the perfect man and it's all a ruse.

Story of my life.

CHAPTER THIRTY-FIVE

Going too Far

Sidney

I look in the mirror, trying to figure out who I'm staring at. I've found myself doing this a lot lately. I thought I knew who I was, but now I'm not so sure. Is love supposed to do this?

I blink at my tears. I should be happy, right? I'm getting married, there's an actual wedding license involved. I went to apply for it myself, along with my fiancé.

A fiancé I love. A man who I've fallen so deeply in love with, I don't know how I intend to live without him. Yet, this wedding is a joke.

I'm still trying to figure out how it all became real. There was an engagement party two weeks ago once Chloe and Gregor returned. A bridal shower followed that a week later and then Clayton decided the wedding needed to move up.

My head is still spinning. I never thought we'd go through with it. All wasted money as far as I was concerned because the day would never happen.

Now, my heart aches because I want it to be real. Every morning when I wake to those intense eyes, I think of what it would be like to do this for the rest of my life. Sometimes, when he kisses me, I allow myself to believe he wants the same thing.

"I've lost control," I whisper.

"No, you haven't." I jump when Chloe's voice startles me.

I turn to find her standing on the threshold of my closet, watching me. A tear slips at the sight of her. My friend was going through so much and I had no idea. Another indication I've lost my way.

"Stop it, Sid." She moves into the closet and sits on the bench beside me, bumping me with her hip so I'll give her more room. "I can hear you thinking. What I had going on had nothing to do with you. If I wanted to involve you, I would have. It was something I needed to handle by myself."

"What are we doing?" I choke out. "What have they done to help our situations? Why should I go through with this?"

She looks down at her lap, I can feel her sadness even through mine. We've shared so much pain and heartache over the years. I once believed we were beyond days like this.

"Sid, I've always seen you as the stronger one. When I had to make hard decisions, I made them with you in mind. How you would handle it, how you would survive it all.

"I teased you all the time for not needing a man, but I know why I never sought out a relationship. In my mind, I was still circling the one that got away.

"However, you, you were content in being by yourself. You weren't hung up on some guy and you didn't need to be. You know what I see when I look at you now?" She pauses to look up at me.

"A pathetic excuse of the old me," I scoff.

"No." She shakes her head. "I know you're the stronger one. I see my friend in love. You've fallen for him. With all our fucked-up shit that should have us scared to reach for the stars, you've reached past all that shit and grabbed hold of them."

"What good is any of that if he doesn't love me back?"

"I said you were the stronger one, not the smarter one." She chuckles. "Have you not seen the way that man looks at you?"

"He's playing the role," I huff.

"Okay, you believe that if you want." She twists her lips at me.

"I think I'm going to call things off," I blurt out.

Chloe places her head on my shoulder. "Love is patient, love is kind." I close my eyes as she recites the scripture.

I finish it with her, understanding fully what she's trying to say. "It always protects, always trusts, always hopes, always perseveres." We finish in unison.

"Be patient, Sid. The Hennessy men have a way of making everything right again. Even when it looks so wrong and impossible," she says softly.

"Has he made it right?" I ask.

"I'm letting patience have her perfect way. It's all my heart can take," she whispers back.

"Once I marry him, there's no turning back," I murmur.

"He's a Hennessy, there was never any turning back, hun."

CHAPTER THIRTY-SIX

Game Changer

Clayton

"These numbers don't make any sense. Someone explain to me what the fuck I'm looking at," I bite out into the phone.

"Sir, we stand to take a loss—"

"Are you really going to fucking tell me what I've already read and know? I want to know why. I want to know why the fuck the deal is suddenly bleeding money," I snap. "Don't talk to me like I'm a damn fool. Give me facts, not this bullshit data."

My shoulders relax the moment I feel Sid's small hands kneading the tension away. I almost forgot she was writing in the corner of my office. She seems to like it in here, despite me having a room designed just for her.

I turn my face to look at her and that smile stops my heart. She dips her face to kiss my lips. I want to get lost in her, but I need to focus on this conference call. I push my chair back and drag her into my lap. I grit my teeth and bury my face in her neck as the asshole on the other end stammers over his lame explanation.

"Excuse me," Sidney says. I look at her and lift a brow.

She looks at me with a sheepish grin but continues to speak. My chest swells right along with my cock. The authority which she uses to talk to my employees as if she's been by my side for years—it's a total turn-on.

She frowns as Dipshit answers her question. I know how she feels. It's the reaction I've had this entire call.

"No, not from what I'm looking at in front of me. It sounds like you've been over projecting on several aspects of the report and trying to compensate for losses with fluff," she replies, cutting Anderson off just as I had. "Mr. Hennessy and I are going to talk about this structuring and some changes. In the meantime, I suggest you clean up this mess. These numbers stink and if I get to digging, you're going to have a serious problem."

I lift my brow higher, earning me a wink and a little mischievous smile. She taps her nose, bringing a smile to my face.

The fact that she's carrying this outside the playroom makes my chest swell. It shows we're bonding the way I hoped for. I want Sid's trust as much as I want to give her mine. For me, safe words are signs of failure to learn my partner. Sid should never need one of those with me.

That tap is a part of an unspoken language we share in that space in our lives. It shows I know her, and she can rely on me.

"I want those fresh numbers tomorrow," I bark before ending the call.

"I see where the loss is coming from," she says excitedly. Reaching for a red pen from my desk, she begins to circle numbers all over the documents I have spread out. "There's a pattern. If you gave me a few hours, I could trace it to its source. This deal may be one you want to walk away from."

I reach for her face with my fingertips, turning it to me. My eyes bounce over her gorgeous features, but I see so much more beyond those. I know I've fallen in love with her mind as much as I have her body and looks.

When I look into her eyes, I see the woman I want for my wife, a business partner, the mother of my children, and the woman I want to spend the rest of my life with.

"What? Did I overstep?" she says, biting her lip nervously.

"No, not at all. You got all that in one glance?" I ask, truly impressed.

She shrugs. "Numbers speak to me. It's like they jump off the page. I saw the problem when I walked over to work out some of the tension I could see from across the room."

I bite my lip. She's so fucking sexy. To be able to write the way she does and the insane brain she has for numbers and business. I want to take her right here.

"I know that look. We don't have time for fucking. I have a dress fitting and you have another conference call in less than an hour." She laughs.

I feel a pang in my chest. Fucking. Is that the way she sees our lovemaking? The wheels turn in my head, and it occurs to me that she doesn't see that I've moved beyond the physical. I haven't wooed her.

I chuckle at my thoughts. I sound like my mother. Although, it's true. I haven't shown Sidney how I feel. I haven't removed the veil from the equation. I have to make it add up for her.

I moved the wedding up for selfish reasons. I don't plan to let her go, but it's time I show her what she truly means to me. It's time I court my future wife.

"Don't make any plans for tonight," I say as inspiration hits.

She gives me a side-glance and a smirk. I lean in, taking her lips to show her with my mouth that I'm completely wrapped around her finger. I will have Sidney, all of her, when I'm done.

CHAPTER THIRTY-SEVEN

Sweetest Thing

Sidney

When Clay said not to make plans, I didn't think that meant we were getting on a plane to travel. He won't tell me where we're going. He's been in such a good mood all day.

When he's like this, it makes it harder and harder not to get sucked into him and his world. Clayton is a force when he's still, when he turns on the charm and effort, he's lethal. Tonight, that smile is threatening to take my life.

I sit nervously in my seat on the jet, having no idea why I'm so nervous. I've been with this man for going on five months. As that thought hits me, my stomach tightens. All of this should be ending in a month. Instead, our wedding date has been moved up and we're getting married.

I still have reservations about moving forward with this. Clayton always treats the matter as if it's business as usual. When I tried to talk him out of all this, he moved the wedding up as if changing terms in a deal to make it work. All business.

I'm still in shock. That was almost a month ago. I look down in my lap, thinking of Chloe's words. Her situation is so much different from mine. Love may be patient, but you have to have love in order for it to be patient.

"A penny for your thoughts," Clayton breathes in my ear.

I turn to look up at him. My eyes searching his. The smile falters from his lips. I go to lower my head, but he brings his hand up, pinching my chin between his fingers.

"Talk to me," he commands gently.

"It's nothing. Just thinking," I reply.

"About?"

"My dress, the fitting, it's been a long day."

"Your dress has made you sad?" His brows draw in.

I shake my head, giving a weak smile. I don't reply because I don't know how to tell him my feelings. I don't know if he wants to truly hear them. I'd rather not go into all this carrying that rejection. It's best if I keep my mouth shut.

Clayton sighs, pecking my lips softly. He places his forehead to mine for a few moments. I take in his warmth and dream of a life where he returns the love I have for him.

"I have something for you," he says, pulling away.

He reaches into the bag the stewardess placed at his feet not too long ago. Pulling out a box, he places it on my lap. The silver paper and blue ribbon taunt me to tear into it, but I've already taken so much from him.

"Open it, Sid," he murmurs, dipping his head to kiss my neck.

Hesitantly, I unwrap the gift and open the lid. Once I have it open, I look into the box in confusion. Sitting in the box are two Kindle e-readers. Clayton reaches in, taking one out.

"One for you and one for me. I loaded the books from your wish list. We can read a few on the way and talk about them when we're done," he says with the biggest smile on his face.

He looks so proud of himself. It's the most adorable and thoughtful thing he has ever done. This is the sexiest he has ever been to me.

"You're going to read the books on my wish list?" I look down at the Kindle he's turned on and see the titles already loaded. "The romance books on my wish list."

"Why not?" He shrugs. "It's something you love. I want to do it with you."

"Who are you?" I blurt out.

He throws his head back and laughs. My heart squeezes. I didn't think I could love him any more. This has taken my love for him to new levels.

"Come on, we should get started." He winks at me.

I sit with my mouth open as he seriously begins to read the first book. I look over his shoulder to see which one he picked before I lift the other kindle out of the box and begin to read for myself.

I get so lost in the book, the flight zips by before I know it. Our descent is announced, and I'm filled with excitement instead of nerves. Clayton watches me with amusement in his eyes.

"What?" I laugh as his eyes twinkle at me.

"Nothing," he replies, dipping his head to steal a kiss and my breath away.

We disembark once the plane lands. An SUV is awaiting us. We hop in and I snuggle into Clay's side. He wraps an arm around me, kissing the top of my head.

"Did you finish?" he asks.

"Got to the end as the wheels touched down." I smile.

"Good, because I want to talk about that crazy-ass friend of hers. Did she really set all that shit up?" he says with all sincerity.

I look up at him and burst out laughing. "You really read the entire book?" I question in disbelief.

"Yeah, how else were we going to discuss it?"

"I seriously love that you did that for me," I say in a whisper.

He brushes my cheek with his fingertips. "You haven't a clue the things I'm willing to do for you," he breathes.

I lower my lashes, reminding myself that I've given this man steady sex for a little more than four months. He would be willing to do a lot to keep me in his bed. That has nothing to do with his heart. Men can fuck without their hearts getting involved. I know for a fact I can't.

Just look at me.

The truck pulls to a stop, but we're not at a hotel. I look out of the window, confused. I pretty much figured out that we're in California. It's after midnight here. I figured we'd be heading to a hotel for the night.

Instead, we're on Rodeo Drive. Only the stores aren't closed as they should be. No, they are well lit, as if they're open at this time of night. I scan the street again and notice David and a few others from Clay's security team. Each one standing guard outside one of the shops.

"What's going on?" I ask, turning to look up at Clay, who's watching me.

"Shopping is your next favorite thing, maybe even before reading and writing. Tonight, you will shop like a queen," he replies.

I bite down on my trembling lip, blinking rapidly, so the tears don't spill. I'm utterly gone for this man. If I was going to walk away, I should have done it already. The only thing I can think of now is how to get him to love me as much as I love him.

"Thank you," I choke out.

"Thank me later. Come, let's shop, baby." He kisses my temple before turning to get out of the car.

This is just sex for him. I'm not going to survive him breaking my heart. How did I get here?

CHAPTER THIRTY-EIGHT

Unfocused

Clayton

Things have been strained since we returned from LA. I thought the trip would bring us closer together, but Sid has that distant look in her eyes more often than not. I know I have the power to change that. In just three little words, I could make clear what I believe she questions.

I just don't know if I can say them. Sid is the most important thing in my life. I have this insane fear that once I declare my true feelings for her, the world will try to take her from me—or, should I be honest and say, my father.

Dad has been…different. I've been allowing Sid to spend time with him so I can watch him and see where his head is. I took him off my short list of enemies who could be behind all of this drama months ago. He had no prior connection to Sid, and he indeed stepped in to help stop the witch hunt.

"Let me out in the front of the club," I say to David as we near Dream.

"Got it."

We pull up to Dream and I step out of the car. My focus is on my phone. Sidney is having a girls' night with her friends tonight. I felt like she needed the space and I have some paperwork here I need to attend to.

Tonight is as good a time as any to get it done. I glance up for a moment and see we have a nice line waiting to get in this evening. This is the general public entrance.

Around back is the entrance for the elite and exclusive patrons. From inside, you wouldn't know the two different worlds exist exclusive of each other. My phone chimes, pulling my attention.

I smile as I open the text. I sent Sid a silly message and she's sent me a silly pic in response. My heart stops as I look at her pretty face, all screwed up with her eyes crossed. I come close to laughing out loud, but my attention is drawn.

I look up as a group of ladies walks toward the entrance. The blonde in the tight gold dress and high heels steps around her friend and her heel goes into a crack in the sidewalk.

I move into action to catch her before she falls. The last thing I need is a lawsuit. I tug her into my chest as she flails about, rolling my eyes as I steady her. The dramatics on this one.

I'm going to have to make sure she and her friends are taken care of. I can smell the bullshit ready to come from this. She looks up into my face, smiling.

"Thank you. Oh my God, that was so embarrassing," she says in this high-pitched voice.

"Are you all right?" I place a hand on her back as she stumbles a little.

"I am now."

"I'm Clayton and this is my club. Why don't you and your friends come in as my guests? I'll get you a table and a bottle."

"Seriously?" she says, batting her lashes at me.

"Sure, follow me." I beckon her and her friends forward with two fingers.

I turn my wrist to look at the time. I can't just rush off to my office. I need to make sure this girl and her friends have such a good night she doesn't think to sue, but I need to get to my office to make a call to have that damn crack filled.

The one who tripped wraps her arms around mine as I look at my watch. My first instinct is to throw her off, but I remind myself of my task. I roll my eyes and walk her into the club.

After getting the ladies a VIP table, I order them a bottle of champagne. I don't rush off. I own enough clubs to know how this one can come back to me. Yes, we have insurance, but the time spent on these lawsuits can be annoying and are better off prevented.

The one who tripped says something as she reaches to place a hand on my arm and looks up at me. However, I can't read her lips because she's placed a champagne glass in front of her mouth.

The music is pulsing, and I can barely hear her. I want to leave and get to my office, but the dreamy looks on her little group's faces tell me a moment more will get me the outcome I want.

I point up to let her know I'm not hearing her. She lifts and places a knee in the bench seat to get closer, I lean down to give her my ear. "This is so nice of you."

I nod and turn to the ear she offers me. "Oh. It's not a problem."

"It's my birthday," she squeals and turns her face to me quickly. I back away to keep her lips away from me.

I shout over the music toward the entire group. "Happy birthday. I'll have a cake sent over. You ladies have a good night. The tab is on me, enjoy."

"Thank you," they all holler over the music.

I nod and turn to make my way to my office. It takes me about ten minutes to call in a favor to have the sidewalk fixed.

My thoughts go back to Sidney. That silly picture gives me hope. Maybe she's just been stressed with the wedding moving up and becoming a real thing.

Shaking the thoughts off, I take my phone out to have one more glance at the picture before I get to work so I can get back home by the time her girls' night ends. I grin as I think of doing this for the rest of my life. I didn't know the woman in the purple dress would change my life. My grin grows as I think of the first time I saw Sid.

"You were more than worth the wait," I say as I brush a finger over the picture she sent me on my phone. "So worth the wait."

CHAPTER THIRTY-NINE

Setup

Sidney

The wine is flowing as we sit around Clay's living room. We've all made ourselves comfortable. Kicking off our shoes and curling up in our seats. It's like college all over again. Me, Chloe, and Marnita.

"Come on, Sid. You know I'm right," Chloe says.

I laugh so hard at Marnita and Chloe. This is exactly what I needed. A night to forget about everything and relax. I've been in such a funk since the trip to California.

It hit me how much I love Clay and how much I want him to love me back. His gestures are those of someone who cares, but I've been there, done that. I dated this guy who said and did all the right things.

However, I later found out he had an entire family. A wife and three kids. I was devastated. It took me so long to even think about dating after that. Talk about destroying my trust.

My mother's voice enters my head. It was something she said right before she abandoned me. It has always stuck with me.

This world ain't meant for us. We don't get to be happy.

I hate that her words still haunt me. It's not like Daddy left us on purpose, but you could never get her to see that. Her scars became mine and now I don't trust happiness. I know this feeling of bliss is only borrowed.

"Where are you?" Chloe asks.

Quickly, I shake off my thoughts. I hadn't realized I stopped laughing and zoned out.

"Nowhere. I'm here."

Marnita sits drinking her wine with a smile on her face, totally oblivious to my turmoil or Chloe's prying. It's a trait of hers I admire. She's always happy. It's infectious and something I welcome tonight.

"Remember that one guy in our study group? All the girls had a crush on him until that one time he took off his shoes and stunk up the place," she says as she laughs, and her cheeks turn red.

The atmosphere lightens again, thanks to her. It has to be a gift and I love her for it.

"Oh, I remember that. He was fine, but, *girl*, those feet." I double over in laughter from the memory. There had to be at least five of us girls in the study group and three other guys. We all wanted to kick his ass that night.

Chloe emptied two cans of air freshener and it hadn't helped one bit. The room still smelled horrible after he was gone. Like someone had hidden a bag of corn chips and a block of Muenster cheese under their bed.

"I thought someone ordered a pizza with extra parmesan cheese," Chloe laughs out.

"Yes, I almost gagged. The worst part was he sat there like nothing was going on." I frown as I'm taken back to that night.

"Wait, wait, I have a reason for bringing this up," Marnita says, laughing so hard she can barely get her words out. She wipes at her tears and takes another sip of wine. "Well, he works at a strip club now and, honey. From what I hear, the BO isn't just a feet thing.

"A friend of mine works with him at a gym where he's her manager, second job, I'm assuming. Turns out his personality stinks as much as his feet. Well, he had been giving her shit and she was about to quit. Her cousin came in to check the gym out and recognized him.

"Honey, she spent a good hour roasting him. My friend quit, but not before her cousin let him have it good."

"Now that you mention it, I do remember him having a funky-ass attitude," I muse and nod.

"Yeah, you're right. I think that's why I wasn't disappointed when he took off his shoes. I was already over his ass," Chloe snorts.

"I miss the laughs we used to have. New York is such a different vibe. You guys say what you think and let it be known what you want. No games are played. I love that energy," Marnita says, with a distant and longing look in her eyes.

"You're welcome to stick around as long as you want."

"I'll be here for both weddings and Chloe's showing, that much I know, but I need to figure out what I'm going to do about my business."

Guilt hits me in the gut. She wouldn't be having issues if it weren't for me. I have to talk to Clay to see what we can do for her. I feel terrible. My thoughts halt. When did I start to think of Clayton coming to the rescue?

"There's that look again," Chloe murmurs and taps her foot against my leg.

"What look?"

She takes a long sip of her wine. Marnita catches the exchange and tunes in, an expectant look on her face. I look down into my wine, gathering my thoughts.

"The other shoe is about to drop. I know it is. This feels too good to be true because it is."

Chloe groans. "Sid, we've beaten the odds. Look at this place. Three stories of opulence. Your man is worth trillions alone. Put him and his brothers together, you triple that. Then you can add on their father's wealth.

"But if you stripped all that away, you'd still have a fine-ass man who loves you and from the smile that's always on your face, I know he's giving you that good dick."

I roll my eyes and laugh. Leave it to Chloe. Yet I still can't shake the feeling that something is about to go wrong.

"I remember when I had to watch my mom decide if she was going to eat or feed us. That shit broke my heart. I never thought this would be our world.

"Now, I hold my head high as I go to work and get this money I was told I'd never have. I have a man who's trying his best to show me the love I deserve. Am I scared? Hell yeah, Sid, but as long as we look for the other shoe, we're not living in the presence of the good life has given us. And guess what happens?"

My phone pings with a text and I open the message. "The shoe drops," I sob.

Clayton

I'm still working through this paperwork at the club as my thoughts start to wander and I get this sinking feeling in the pit of my stomach. I look at my watch and not even an hour has passed. It's still too soon to go home and I have enough work here.

Yet, I can't help my nagging thoughts. The wedding is a week away and it feels like more of a sham now than it ever did in the beginning. The closer we get, the more I fear she's going to call it off. She's going to wake up one day and see she has all the power.

Nowhere in the contract did it state she had to marry me. I want to rush the days ahead before she realizes that. Once we say I do, I'll be able to breathe easier. She'll be mine and I'll spend the rest of my life worshipping the ground she walks on and showing her with me is where she's always belonged.

"We've got a problem," Vault's voice pulls me from my thoughts.

I look up from my desk and focus on him. He's been in New York a lot lately. I'm not complaining. He's been instrumental in helping me get all this drama under control.

I know it will come with a price. Vault isn't your usual Lost Soul. He's a Squad member, so you can say he's been on loan from King, the Lost Souls' prez.

"Tell me something I don't know," I huff, sitting back in my chair.

"Detective Garret has been receiving anonymous tips again," he says gruffly.

"Do I want to know how you know this?"

"Just doing my job," he says through a crooked grin.

"Mm," I grunt. "Why is this a problem for me?"

"This time, the warrant will be for you," he says as if he's tasting ash.

"Do we have enough on him yet? I'm tired of waiting," I snap.

"You seriously think he's the one behind all of this?" Vault's eyes cloud over.

"Of my two assumptions, he fits the best."

"Still, something feels off to me. Like we're painting half a picture. I have some of the brothers back at the New York chapter asking around for me and doing some digging. There's a lot of white space and gray areas," he muses aloud.

"Well, we need to fill in that space and areas. I'm a little tired of people trying to take a bite out of my ass," I snarl.

"Tell me about it. Making that little fed problem go away was a lot tougher than I hoped it would be," he mutters. "By the way, King wants to call in a favor for that one."

"Add it to my tab. Tell him to name it. If I can move enough to do it with all this bullshit, he's got it," I reply.

"He'll appreciate that." Vault nods. "Brick will bring you the terms and details."

"He's not too busy making babies?" I smile for the first time today.

"Why do you think I've been hiding out in New York? The clubhouse has turned into a baby registry." He chuckles.

"I wouldn't mind some of that luck." My smile broadens.

Vault looks down at his phone as it pings. His face clouds over as he swipes a few times. When he looks up at me, the floor feels like it drops right from under me. I know this isn't good.

He moves to my desk, shoving his phone in my face. My eyes nearly pop from my head when I look at the images before me. They're from tonight. The incident from earlier pops into my head clearly.

The blonde and her friends I comped. It was all innocent. I can't think of a moment when I wasn't thinking about the club and blocking a potential liability. However, the entire incident was captured at angles that changed the narrative of what truly happened.

From the pictures, every single part of that interaction looks like something totally different, from the fall outside the club to me escorting her and her friends inside to me checking on their table.

"What the fuck?" I hiss as I scroll through Vault's phone.

My phone pings, causing me to snatch it up to check it. My heart jumps in my throat when I see a mass text to Sid, Chloe, Gregor, Cane, and myself. It's the same fucking photos. I want to hurl my phone across the room.

I'm out of my chair, heading for the door before I can tell my feet to move. I have to get to Sid. This shit looks bad, very bad.

"You want me on this?"

"Find out where they came from," I bark over my shoulder as I storm from the room.

The trip to the apartment feels like it takes years. I can't stop flipping through these fucking pictures. I try to call Sid repeatedly, but she won't answer a single one of my calls.

I run a frustrated hand through my hair as we finally turn into my block. My heart nearly pounds through my chest when I see Sid exiting the building with a small travel bag in her hand. I jump from the back of the car before it can come to a stop.

My heart crumbles when I see her tear-soaked face. Sid is too gorgeous to ever look this hurt. I rush to block her from getting into the cab that seems to be waiting for her.

"Baby, we need to talk," I plead.

"There's nothing to talk about," she says, trying to step around me.

Her purse slips from her shoulder, causing her to reach for it. The sight is like a punch to the gut. Her engagement ring is no longer on her finger. I've grown so used to seeing my ring there. I never thought of it ever coming off.

"Sid, don't do this. There's an explanation," I rush out.

"An explanation for you humiliating me in front of the world?" She lowers her voice so that I'm the only one to hear. "If you wanted to sleep with someone else, fine. You could have told me and made private arrangements. You didn't have to make me look and feel like a fucking idiot."

"Do you listen to anything I say to you?" I snap.

"Get out of my way," she hisses back.

"Fuck this," I growl.

Doing what I know best when it comes to Sid, I grab her and toss her over my shoulder. She punches at my back with her small hands, but I keep moving until we're in the elevator. She continues to hurl curses at me as we ride up to the apartment. I allow it because I know she's hurt.

When we reach the top floor, I head for the apartment, still holding her over my shoulder. When I cross the threshold, I place her down on her feet. There's so much rage on her face, the hurt and embarrassment are so evident.

"I'm leaving," she yells at me.

"No, you're not," I sigh.

"This is over. I can't do this anymore," she sobs.

I close the distance, cupping her face. She tries to pull away, but I tighten my hold. I start to kiss at her tears as she reaches up to dig her nails into my hands.

"They're not real, Sid," I say. "The pictures aren't real. If you were there you would know their context was misconstrued. The incident was harmless."

"So they are real. That was you," she says stubbornly.

"Yes, it was me, but what's being insinuated is bullshit," I protest.

"I want out," she whispers, eyes closed, tears still running down her cheeks. "I have no reason to stay."

"I love you," I breathe. "That's your reason. I can't let you go. I'm in love with you.

"I would never look at another woman because all I want is you. I gave you my heart a long time ago, Sid. I just didn't know how to say it out loud. I can't lose you. I love you, baby."

She shakes her head, tugging away from me harder this time. I release her and she turns her back to me. Her little shoulders shake as she wraps her arms around her middle. The sight completely destroys me.

I move to her slowly, wrapping my arms around her from behind. I bury my face in her hair, willing her to feel my love. She feels so small and fragile in my embrace.

"I love you, Sid…I fall in love with you more and more each day…Those photos aren't what they look like…You're the only one for me…I love you, Sidney…I would never hurt you." I kiss her head in between each sentence.

Slowly, she turns in my arms. Her big brown eyes looking up at me. I see the hope in them, and it tugs at the hope in my chest.

"I love you so much."

I take her lips before she can say a word. I use my mouth to show her how much I love her. Relief begins to settle in when she melts into me and locks her fingers in my hair. She tugs me closer. I go willingly, tightening my hold on her.

Swiftly, I back her into the glass wall of the entryway. Reaching for her thighs, I lift her on my waist. The salt of her tears drives my need to make this right.

"I love you," I repeat against her kiss-swollen lips.

I look down into her eyes as I bunch up the tight folds of fabric from her skirt in my hands. She looks back at me with uncertainty I need to dismiss without question. Tugging the unwanted barrier between us up over her waist, I get my palms onto her smooth skin.

"I…I," she says softly.

I lift my hand to tap the tip of my nose. Pleading with her to trust me. Her eyes soften and she nods.

"I love you," she breathes slowly.

"Say it again," I plead, closing my eyes.

"Clay," she whispers. I open my eyes again to meet hers. "I love you."

I capture her lips again, delivering a kiss with the power to bring us both to our knees. I tug the jacket from her shoulders, pull it free from her body, and toss it aside. I anchor myself with a hand on her waist. Lifting one of her arms over her head, I then pin it to the glass with my other hand. Her heat sears me right through my slacks.

Reaching for her other arm, I then lift it to grasp both her wrists together in one of my palms. I allow my free hand to travel down her left arm to her face, down her throat, to her heaving breasts, over her belly, and between her thighs, where her heat awaits.

I grab a handful of fabric and yank the scrap from her body. Nothing and I do mean nothing, will stand between this woman and me ever again. Those words have placed the final nail in the coffin.

"I've allowed you to see inside me. I've given you access to all of me," I say huskily, working to free myself from my pants. "Everything I've done for you has been out of love, obsession, and devotion."

I thrust into her on the last word and groan, still locking eyes with her. I want it clear that this time we're making love. I start to move my hips in and out of her at a pace that creates a language of its own. The look of love in her eyes humbles and bares me.

I begin to alternate, grinding into her slowly, with long, deep strokes. I release her wrists to press my hands to the cool wall behind her. Sid reaches to push my coat from my shoulders.

It's then I register that the heat I feel isn't just from our burning love. I shrug my coat and suit jacket off, letting them fall to the floor. I'd snatched my tie off on the ride over, leaving just my shirt obstructing the skin Sid is trying to get to.

Using my thighs and hips to support her weight grinding against me, I grab the front of my shirt, tugging it apart. Buttons fly every which way. Sidney wastes no time getting to what she wants. She leans forward, kissing my chest, making a path up to my jaw and then my lips.

I angle my body, grinding into her harder, tearing a whimper from her lips. Her shirt is the next thing to fly through the air after I tug it up over her head. I wrap my arms around her back, holding her body to mine.

"Clay," she sobs.

"Take all of me, Sid. I don't exist without you. You're the silence to the rage inside me. You're everything I didn't know I needed," I croon into her ear.

"I love you," she sings as her sex soaks every inch of me.

"Show me," I command.

I love the saucy smile that takes over her full lips. Her fingers lock behind my neck, giving her the leverage she needs as she begins to ride me with everything she has. I move away from the wall, giving her body room to work me.

She rolls her entire body while still managing to isolate her hips. I can only watch in wonder. I roll my own body to match her movements.

"Clay?" she groans.

"Yeah, Baby?" I answer, licking my lips.

"Come with me," she begs.

I slam her back against the wall, taking her lips. I wrap my arms around her back. In a flash, I take all control, guiding us both where we need to go. She tightens around me as my own orgasm races to meet hers.

My head clouds with the fragrance of peaches and vanilla as her scent wafts up between us, filling my nostrils. I look down to watch as I move in and out of her. Her juices are creating a wet sucking sound as our bodies connect as one.

"Clay," her loud scream sends a shudder through me, snatching my climax and a growl from me.

I throw my head back and moan as my seed shoots into her by the load. I feel like I won't stop coming. When I shoot the last stream, my chest is heaving. I drop my sweaty forehead to hers, tightening my hold on her body.

"Where's your ring?" I question when I catch my breath.

"I left it upstairs on the bed," she pants back.

Still semihard and inside her body, I find my legs and move for our bedroom. I feel her staring at me, but I stay focused on getting us upstairs. I twitch inside her as aftershocks continue to ripple through her pussy.

I turn to kiss the side of her head when she tucks her face into my neck. I see the ring as soon as the bed comes into view. I move to the bed, sitting.

"Fuck."

"Ouch," we yelp the words in unison.

The zipper to the pants still fastened to my waist pinches my cock and I'm pretty sure my pull of the same zipper gets her in the ass. Sidney lifts and wiggles out of my lap. I miss her warmth the moment she's gone.

I trace her movements with my gaze as she tries to tug the fabric of her skirt back down her legs. I shake my head, clasping a hand around her ankle, tugging her back to me.

Placing my hand on the top of her thigh, I enjoy watching the jiggle of her big tits. Turning, I scoop up the ring and take her hand to slip it back in place. I lift my eyes to hers, catching her gaze.

"This never comes off again," I say firmly.

"Whatever you say, Mr. Hennessy," she says with a teasing smile, looking up through her lashes.

"Careful, soon-to-be Mrs. Hennessy," I tease, then pounce.

I remove both our clothes and move her to the center of the bed, where I sink into her welcoming sex and groan. She locks her legs around my waist. I take her lips and drink from her delicious mouth.

"I love you, Clay," she purrs as I rock into her smoothly.

I'm in no rush. I want to savor her and show her my love. The chase is over. I have the woman I want, and she'll be mine forever.

"I love you too, baby. I'm never letting you go."

CHAPTER FORTY

Wedding Bells

Clayton

"You're really going through with this?" Cane asks as he comes up behind me, fixing his tie.

"Of all days, today is not the day to test me, Cane. Yes, I'm going through with this."

"He's in love. Leave him," Gregor says.

Cane snorts. "You're giving him what he wants."

I spin from the mirror I'd been fixing my tie in. "It's not about him. I could give a shit about what he wants. This is about Sid and me. Nothing else."

Cane lifts his hands and takes a step back. "It was your idea to get out from under him. You said we'd be free. Now, you're bowing to his demands. I thought better of you, man. A whole lot better of you."

"I've done nothing but make moves to give us our freedom. We'll still have it. If you could get your selfish head out of your ass, you'd see this works out for everyone in the end."

"Whatever," he huffs and storms over to the bar.

Gregor comes over and fixes my tie. He gives me a smile and pats my cheek. "Ignore him. He's angry because you have what he's too afraid to admit he wants. This is your day. I didn't think it would happen, but you got the girl. Your way."

"And almost lost her," I grumble. "Maybe after this wedding, I'll be able to focus, pull all this back in close to home. What the fuck am I missing? Maybe I've allowed too many hands in the pot."

"You can't have your eyes on everything. You've taken on so much as it is. I'll step in and help out now that I'm back."

"You have a family of your own to worry about. This is my problem. Besides, I'm the man who knows it all. It's our business to know what's going on.

"If I didn't know better, I'd go back to thinking Dad was behind all of this," I say bitterly.

"No, I'm a hundred percent sure this isn't on him."

"Then who?"

"We can answer that tomorrow. Today, you have a gorgeous bride who loves you waiting to marry your ugly ass," he teases.

"You wish I were ugly so your fiancée would stop looking at me."

"That's my wife. Watch your mouth."

I narrow my eyes at my older brother. I knew he was keeping something else from me. I punch him in the shoulder when I see the truth in his eyes.

"Does Dad know?"

"I don't think so. Mom does, she was pissed, but you know how delicate the situation is. I had to make the move when it felt right. We'll still do all of this. She deserves it."

I nod and tug him into my embrace. "Congratulations."

"Thanks. Let's get you to the altar."

****

The golds and ivories all set the room off. This is a wedding to be remembered. There's a regal feeling about it. It's fit for a queen.

I stand with my brothers and my best friend at my side as I wait for the love of my life to come down the aisle. I look to David, and he gives me a knowing smile. I've come a long way.

My heart stops and my breath is taken away when Sidney comes into view. This venue pales in comparison to her beauty.

Her white dress, with its gold trim, fits her to perfection. It's classy and elegant while also enticing and flattering to her frame. Her skin is glowing as if covered in a sheen of gold.

"Wow," Gregor breathes beside me.

He has taken the word right out of my mouth. Sid is the perfect bride. Her hair is styled in large curls with a gold and diamond crown fixed into them. I know the diamonds are real because the crown was a gift from me.

Delta sent me an email about it during the planning. She told me Sid's face lit up when she saw the one-of-a-kind custom design, but she refused to get it. I approved the purchase without a second thought. It belongs on my bride.

I wish I could capture this very moment and play it over and over every day of my life. In this moment, I not only feel her love—it's as if I become it. It's like I'm watching this from outside of my body.

Time has slowed down, and my heart starts to beat a little more with each step she takes. The smile on her face is so bright, I can't help smiling back at her.

When she stops before me, I want to grasp the back of her neck and kiss her as breathless as she's made me. Instead, I take her hand and help her up the step.

"You look exquisite."

"Thank you. You look like a million bucks yourself."

We both laugh at her joke. "I don't regret a thing, I'd do it all again. Not a penny has been wasted," I murmur for only her to hear.

"Well, Mr. Hennessy, I think it's time we get you your money's worth."

I wink at her. "I've already tripled my investment."

"Ha, we'll see about that."

In less than an hour, I stand looking into the twinkling eyes of Mrs. Clayton Hennessy.

"You may now kiss the bride."

And that I do.

CHAPTER FORTY-ONE

Bliss

Sidney

"I love you," I purr up at Clayton.

The sound of the waves in the background is our soundtrack. This has been sheer bliss. A tropical getaway after an amazing wedding.

"I love you more." He kisses the tip of my nose.

Last year, I never would've thought this would be my life. I was too afraid I was on my way to jail for something I didn't even do.

Clay's eyes are glowing as he looks down at me. I can't believe I'm married. Our wedding was phenomenal. My wedding gown was perfect. When I came into view, the look on Clayton's face is something I will never forget.

From my diamond crown to the gold-and-white gown, it was all perfect. The white-and-gold light silk chiffon dress draped my body and flowed with me. I truly felt like a queen.

The location, the flowers, the food, all the planning that I thought was useless turned into the wedding of my dreams. I wish I could do it all over again.

This time knowing that I'd actually be getting married. I would have committed more of the planning experience to memory. Not for the first time over the last week, I wonder if this had always been my husband's plan.

As he would say, he's always a step ahead. Although, I don't think it's possible to be a step ahead of love. There was no way he could've known we would fall for each other. At least, he couldn't have known he'd fall for me. I, on the other hand, never stood a chance.

As I think back over everything, Clayton aimed for my heart and hasn't been so subtle about it. I've just been too dense to see it. Chloe was right, patience has paid off.

"You're overthinking again," he purrs, squeezing my waist.

"No, just wondering," I reply.

"Overthinking," he challenges with a teasing grin.

"You should smile like that more often," I change the subject.

"For you, maybe." He shrugs.

I twist my lips at him. "You like leaving everyone uncertain about you." I shake my head.

"Again, you're the only one who needs to be certain about me," he croons, tugging me closer.

He takes my lips in a tender kiss that shows his love for me. I feel it in my toes. I fall deeper into the moment, the more he kisses me as the ocean lulls me into a sense of comfort.

Clay breaks the kiss, turning to look out at the ocean. I watch him as he watches the crashing waves coming into shore. We came out onto the beach after an amazing lunch and drinks poolside.

Life is very different when your husband is one of the wealthiest men in the world. I forget that fact sometimes. All the Hennessys are so down to earth. Clay is hardworking and while stern, I see the compassion he has for those who work for him.

My father-in-law has even grown on me. I know Clay and his brothers see the old man as a jerk, but I see something else each time I get to interact with him. Not that I can ever forget what Clay told me about him abandoning him in his time of need.

I think they're like any other dysfunctional family, just with more commas in their bank accounts. Even now, as I look up at my husband, I can see the wheels turning in his head. He has a lot weighing on his shoulders.

Something is going on with Cane. Gregor is important to Clay. His situation is one Clay wishes he could do more about. Then there's me. Things still haven't been resolved. Just before the wedding, I was sent a summons to appear in court.

Someone is still out there trying their darndest to play with my life. Somehow, all of this has fallen on my man's shoulders. He tries to hide it, but I see the moments when he's plotting, planning, and scheming ways out of all of this. Clay takes care of everyone because everything always needs to be under control, his control.

"Now, who's overthinking?" I say, running my hands up his chest.

He turns to look down at me. His pensive look fades, warmth returning to his eyes. That simple warmth quickly turns into heat. A smile kicks up the right side of his mouth.

"I want you to stop your birth control," he says, shocking me.

I stare at him dumbly. I don't know what to say. I knit my brows as I try to remember when my next appointment is for my shot.

When Clayton replaced my laptop, my digital day planner didn't carry over many of my appointments, past or future. I've been so focused on my blog and book, I never got around to recovering the dates and updating them.

I should've asked my assistant, Nikki, to do it for me, but I'm still getting used to having her. I try not to overwork her. I frown when I seriously can't come up with an answer.

My mouth falls open when it dawns on me it's been well over three months. I haven't been in since around the time I moved in with Clayton. I face-palm myself, remembering the call I received a few days before we returned from Georgia.

I was supposed to call in to make an appointment. I forgot because my book came back from the editor and I was too excited and focused on getting through the feedback. I was supposed to schedule an appointment but never did. I haven't been on birth control in months.

"Would you like to explain what just happened?" He chuckles but has a hint of concern in his voice. "That's not the reaction I was expecting when asking my wife to have my baby."

I wince, looking up at him through my lashes. "Clay, um, we may have been taking a risk all along. I haven't had my shot in months. I never scheduled an appointment and I've been so bu—"

My words are cut off as he cups my face and crushes my lips with his. He groans into my mouth, causing my toes to curl into the sand. I cling to his forearms.

A yelp floats into his mouth from mine when he dips to scoop me up into his arms. I put my arms around his neck. Clayton starts for the back entrance of the beach house we've been calling our home for the last two weeks. It's been an oasis. All the problems back home seem light-years away while we hide in our bubble here.

We never make it into the house. Clayton deposits me onto one of the loungers by the pool. I'm panting as I watch him move down my body, kissing my heated skin on his way down.

He hooks his long fingers inside my bikini bottom, tugging it slowly down my leg. This man just loves to torture me. I need him, but he's taking his sweet time.

He reaches to splay his hand over my belly, drawing my attention to his wedding band. I suck in a breath and hold back tears.

I think it just hits me that I'm really married to this man. I'm Clayton Hennessy's wife. I want to pinch myself. However, his attention to my clit has the same effect.

My eyes roll back in my head. I twist my fingers in his hair. This will never cease to amaze me. His mouth is pure joy.

Every woman in the world deserves to know this type of pleasure at least once in their life. Just not from my husband. Clayton is mine and I don't plan on giving him up.

I rock my hips against his face with that thought in mind. Crying out when he hooks his fingers inside me to tap my spot, I go over in a blaze of glory.

I know he's not going to stop there and welcome the blessing he has planned for my body. Only the phone in the house rings.

Clayton lifts his head, his brows drawn. I have a sinking feeling in my belly.

"I'm not done, don't move," he commands.

I watch after his sexy bare back as he makes his way into the house. I'm curious, but I stay put just as he tells me to. I'm not ready for this bubble to burst just yet.

Clayton

I grumble to myself as I walk into the beach house. I'm pissed that we're being interrupted, but I know it must be important if someone is calling the landline.

I reach the phone and pick it up. "Hello."

"Clay, are you sitting, buddy?" Vault replies.

"No, I was about to make a baby. I can't sit. My dick is rock hard. What do you want?"

"Your dick won't be hard for long. Fran Baker was found dead…in your office."

"What?" I roar.

"Her body was found in your office at Dream. Everything about this stinks. The coroner said she was dead for two days before she was discovered."

"Two days? Cane is supposed to be acting as GM during my honeymoon. Where the fuck has he been?"

"According to the cameras, here doing his job. We have footage of workers coming in and out of here with no problem. Cane, the cleanup crew."

"I hear a but."

"But sometime last night, there was a gap in the video footage. It was long enough to drop a body off and be gone."

"So why are you calling me?"

"I'm sorry, man. It's your club, your office, your problematic past, a dead body in your office. They want you to come in for questioning."

"This is fucking ridiculous," I roar. "I've been here on my fucking honeymoon."

I'm not going back to New York until I'm good and damn ready. This bullshit has nothing to do with me. I don't care where the body was dropped.

I fold my arms across my chest and work my jaw, hoping Vault feels my energy through the phone. Then he speaks the words that will fuel me and the jet to get out of here.

"Yeah, but your wife is on some footage, in Fran's face, and there's an eyewitness who says Sid was threatening Fran in the video. Clay, come back before this gets out of hand. I'll have you guys in and out."

It feels like my head is about to explode. "Fuck." I hang up the phone, not even bothering to answer.

This shit can't be happening.

CHAPTER FORTY-TWO

Time to Talk

Clayton

I'm still in shock. I don't know how I feel about all of this. There was once a time when this news would have brought a smile to my face, or at least I thought it would have. Not today.

We cut the honeymoon short after receiving Vault's call. Once I was able to calm down, I called him back for more details. I'm still fuming.

I'd like to know how the fuck someone sneaks an entire body into my club undetected. Everything has changed. I'm about to get my hands involved directly. I'm tired of trying to connect the dots from a distance.

King personally offered to send help. Grim and Reap are on their way to New York. If I know Brick, he'll be right along with them. However, I'm not waiting for reinforcements. I want answers now.

The sound of glass smashing reaches me as I move toward the room where I know I will find the person I'm looking for. This has been a long time coming. It's time we settle the score.

I push the door to the office open to find just the person I'm looking for. I narrow my eyes to take in the sight. His hands are twisted in his hair, his back heaves as he stares into the fire in front of him. He looks a mess.

"What do you want?" he hisses.

"Hello to you too, cousin," I say dryly as I move to take a seat behind his desk. I sit smoothly, never taking my eyes off him.

"Not today, Clay," Wade replies.

"Yes, today."

He spins on me, revealing his bloodshot eyes. He looks like complete shit. I don't reveal my observation. Instead, I reach to open his cigar box and frown at the cheap-ass cigar inside. I won't even insult my lips with those.

"Why are you here?" he growls.

"You know why. I want answers. Why have you been trying to frame Sid? I know you have a hard-on for me, but why Sid? Is it because she wouldn't fuck you?"

"Fuck you," Wade snarls. "I had nothing to do with any of this shit with Sidney. What would I have to gain from any of that bullshit?"

"Let's see." I tilt my head. "All of this bullshit has affected Gregor and me financially. This all started when it spilled out that Gregor and I were considering running for a few offices. That would throw a wrench in your plans to kiss up to my father by securing the governor's seat.

"With both Gregor and I in politics, you'd go right back to being plain old Wade. Fucking with our money would put a stop to that. I just don't understand the hard-on for Sid." I lean back in his chair, folding my arms over my chest.

"You still don't get it, do you? You don't see what's right in your face, little brother," he says bitterly.

I freeze. My forehead wrinkling. I sit forward, replaying his words in my head to make sure I heard them right. Wade walks over to his couch and plops down on it.

"All my life, I knew I had three brothers, but they never knew about me. I was the mistake. Dad had an affair with my mother after Gregor was born.

"Your mom had postpartum depression. Things got bad and she filed for divorce. Dad met my mom during that time, and I happened. My mother didn't survive childbirth," Wade scoffs.

"Dad and your mom made up and I got to be raised by dear old auntie. For years, I carried that secret with me. It was why I was so pissed that night we fought. You called me a spoiled son of a bitch when I'm anything but.

"You never even gave me a chance to explain what you saw. You just flew off the handle." He laughs harshly. "I wasn't trying to hit on your girlfriend. That was Fran you saw. Leeann had just given her the jean jacket she was wearing because Fran was cold. Leeann went to get them fresh beers.

"Fran and I were a thing. I'd been fucking her all summer. I'd just told her that I wanted to break things off, that's why she slapped me when I pulled her in and tried to kiss her. That, Clay, is what you saw that night. Not me trying to kiss Leeann," he fumes.

"After we fought, for the first time in my life, I told someone who my father was. Fran sat and listened to me for hours. For years, she was the only one who knew how badly I wanted to be a part of my brothers' tight circle.

"I stepped up when Gregor disappeared so Dad would leave him alone and not chase after him. Not because I wanted to take his place. I fucking hate the bullshit and ass-kissing I have to do just to get a few donations and secure votes." He falls silent, his jaw ticcing.

I fall back in my seat. My mind blown. I wasn't expecting any of what he just said. I don't even know what to say to all of that.

"Fran was pregnant. When she refused to tell her father by who, that asshole told her to pin it on you," Wade huffs. "I found out a few weeks later and told Dad. He buried that son of a bitch. You were so angry, thinking he didn't do anything to help you. Our father has blood on his hands for you. Another secret I'd planned to take to my grave."

"What happened to the baby?" I ask.

Wade shrugs. "You're my brother. What Fran did was wrong. We had a fight about it and the baby. She fell down a flight of stairs running from me and lost it."

I pull a hand down my face. I don't know how I feel about any of this. My head is starting to hurt. I'm back at square one. I have no idea who's behind framing Sid and now murdering Fran.

"Clay, Fran has been plotting against our family for years. All that blackmail bullshit was Fran, not Leeann. She staged it all.

"Sid wasn't on her radar, you were. I don't know how Sidney got dragged into all of this. Dad wanted me to find out and shut it all down. I was just about to nail Fran for all this shit. I just needed to find out who she was working with. I think I'm the reason she was murdered. I was getting too close," Wade says in a strained voice.

"Dupont. I was trying to figure out how the two of you were connected. I thought he was working for you," I reply. "I thought he was your lackey."

Wade's head snaps in my direction. "Patrick Dupont from Steinway & Schwartz?"

"Yeah," I reply, getting an uneasy feeling from his tone.

"Clay, that guy loathed Sid. He hated her guts, was jealous of her and didn't hide that shit well at all." Wade's brows knit. He stands to come over to his desk, flipping open a file in front of me. "*Fuck*. How did I miss this?"

"What?"

"Fran was seeing some guy. The private eye I had on this mentioned the guy was married. I blew it off as just an affair. Nothing I needed to know or care about. Dupree Patricks was the name he used at the hotels they would meet at."

I have my phone in hand before Wade can finish his words. If this guy has it out for Sid and he's behind Fran's murder, I need to know where the fuck he is. Now.

"What's up?" Vault answers his phone.

"Dupont is our guy. Where is he?" I rush into the phone.

"Been MIA for the last twenty-four. I was just about to call you," he replies.

"Fuck." I hang up and start for the door.

I need to get to Sid.

CHAPTER FORTY-THREE

Adding Up

Sidney

I can't believe someone killed Fran. She wasn't the nicest person in the world, but I'm still in shock over her murder. I can't for the life of me figure out why someone would kill her and dump her body in Clay's office. Just the thought sends a shiver through me.

I pace the apartment, wishing Marnita or Chloe were here to help calm my nerves. Clay looked like a raging bull when he left the apartment after dropping me off. He ordered me not to leave the apartment.

I'm to wait for his friends to arrive. I have to say, when he said Grim and Reap were the ones I should wait for, I had to wonder what kind of friends my husband has. Those are not the names of your friends you invite over for a formal dinner party.

The doorbell rings and I feel a little relief. Hopefully, that's either Clay's friends or Chloe. Either would be better than me sitting in here going crazy by myself.

I'm not thinking straight when I open the door without looking out first. There were two guards out there earlier. I curse myself when I open the door to the barrel of a gun being pointed in my face. I'm even more surprised by the person holding the gun.

Patrick Dupont.

I'm in stunned confusion as he backs me into the apartment, closing the door behind him. I quickly look around for a weapon of my own but nothing useful is in reach.

"Hello, Sidney," Patrick purrs.

"Patrick," I breathe, licking my dry lips.

"Do you have any idea how close I was to walking away with fifty million dollars before you opened your fucking mouth? It took me years to figure out how to skim and funnel out all that cash. Then you went and started making all that money, drawing eyes and questions.

"Dear old Fran came into the picture with her plan to take down your boyfriend at the perfect time. I could kill two birds with one stone." He chuckles.

"What?" I whisper.

"That bitch thought she could use me. I was even going to leave my wife for her. How was I supposed to know she was obsessed with Wade Claremont? All this shit was to get back at him and Hennessy. That bitch was crazier than I am." He throws his head back and releases a crazy laugh.

"According to her, they took everything from her. I didn't give a fuck about your husband. It was you that I wanted to pay. You fucked everything up, you nosy-ass bougie bitch," he hisses.

I ball my fists at my sides, biting back my retort. The hood in me wakes all the way up. For one, I don't like that he's backing me up like he's trying to corner me. Two, he has one more time to call me out my name.

I want to swing and punch him right in the throat. I tamp down my anger. I need to make it out of here alive.

"Why are you here now?" I ask, trying to stall for time.

"Entitled bitch," he snarls and throws a punch at my face. I stumble back, catching myself on the accent chair. My first reaction is to go on the attack, but he shoves his gun in my face.

"Don't even think about it," he growls. "Fran was a lying bitch, there was nothing in her accounts. She had no fucking money. All her promises were bullshit. That bitch was going to get us both locked up or killed.

"I killed her first and planned to take what was mine, but the bitch had nothing. Can you believe that? Now your husband…he has a shit ton. Since you're the bitch who cost me everything I worked for, I figure he owes me," he replies with a sinister grin.

My stomach turns sour, this isn't going to end well. I think of screaming in hopes that Cane and Ally are home and might hear me. I just don't know if I can rely on either of them. They've been acting so fucking strange, I'm not willing to bank my life on them.

Patrick doesn't look like I can talk him down from this. From the snarl on his lips to the crazy eyes and sweat covering his face, I'd say that's a big no. I'm slim on options, but I'm not just going to let this fool kill me.

"Have you seriously thought this out?" I question, trying to buy more time.

"For the last five months. I knew things were going to go south the moment you walked into that club. Fran lost control the second you hooked up with Hennessy. She just couldn't see it. Her plan to pin it all on her love-struck twit of a sister and that pompous ass Claremont was weak at best.

"Hennessy is relentless when it comes to you. It's how I know I'll get a good price." He grins like a loon.

"Patrick, you d—"

I don't finish my words. The room goes completely dark. I don't think I just get low and run. I scream when I'm knocked forward and a hand wraps my ankle. I kick out with the other foot, trying to get free.

Oh God, please don't let this be my life. It can't end like this.

Clayton

Grim nods when the lights are cut. Reap is already in motion, leading the way with a gun almost as big as her. Brick is to my right, coiled to put this motherfucker down. We all have on heat-seeking goggles to navigate through the apartment.

I was so relieved to find them in front of the apartment building when we arrived. What I wasn't happy to find was my fifty-two-year-old doorman knocked unconscious behind the front desk with a goose egg on the left side of his head.

We all snapped into action. I was pissed to find the two guards I left with Sid knocked out on the top floor. It was then we decided to come in through the second level.

I've been losing my mind with each word this piece of shit Dupont has spoken while we prepared to move in. He's about to get the surprise of his life. Everyone has orders not to kill unless absolutely necessary. I have plans for this son of a bitch.

I look to my left quickly to find Wade. I still haven't processed everything he's told me. I'm not even sure I want to. Although in the back of my mind, him being here means something. It means a lot.

Sid's loud scream piercing the air hones in my focus. I move quickly in the direction of Sid's voice. I can make out Dupont's hand wrapped around Sid's ankle while she kicks out frantically.

That's my girl, always a fighter.

From the height of the heat print alone, I know it's Reap who slams the butt of her gun into the back of Dupont's head. He goes limp and Sid scrambles back away from him.

I rush to her side, wrapping my arms around her. She begins to thrash against me. I restrain her arms, pulling her in closer to my chest.

"Shh, precious, it's me," I coo. "I'm here, baby. You're safe."

"Clay?" she sobs, sagging into me.

"Yes, it's me. We got him, baby. I'm going to put an end to all of this now," I whisper, kissing the top of her head.

"Okay." She nods, clinging to me.

****

I can still feel the rage in my bones from seeing Sid's swollen face. It took me almost two hours to get her to calm down enough to go to sleep. Even then, it was because my father arrived, promising to stay with her while I was gone.

If I didn't have more important things to focus on, I would've wrapped my hands around his neck and thrown him out on his ass. That's some shit I'll have to deal with later. Though in the back of my mind, I keep wondering how much my mother knows about this.

The revving of motorcycle engines pulls my attention back to the warehouse we're in. I look at the piece of shit in the middle of the four bikes surrounding him. Vault, Brick, Grim, and Reap are mounted on their bikes.

Dupont's limbs are chained to the back wheel of each of their machines. They're just waiting for my signal. You fuck with my money, I'll kill you and make it quick and easy. Fuck with my family, I'll make you feel the pain. Fuck with my Sid, I'm going to send you to hell in the most painful and slow way I can.

"No, no, no," Patrick Dupont screams. "Don't do this. Please."

I take a drag from my cigar and blow it out slowly. "I wonder, did Fran get a chance to beg for her life?" I tilt my head, looking down at this filth.

"She was trying to destroy your life. I did you a favor," he bellows, spit flying from his mouth.

"A favor I never asked for," I scoff.

"Please, I'll disappear. You'll never hear from me again," he pleads.

I chuckle, taking another drag of my cigar and moving out of the way. I nod at Brick. He revs his bike three times to give the signal. Reap throws her head back and laughs as she takes off. The three men drive forward with cold looks in their eyes.

Dupont's screams fill the air as he's ripped apart limb by limb. He's still screaming as I walk over to his limbless body. I clamp my cigar between my teeth, lifting my .45, I don't pull the trigger right away. I let him scream and suffer.

I pull the trigger, putting a bullet in his kidney. It's not nearly enough to please me. None of this is. He put his hands on my fucking wife. He's been trying to get her locked up for almost two years. I don't even care about the shit he helped Fran try to do to my life.

I lift the gun, aiming for his head. "Tell Fran I said hello." I squeeze the trigger and silence him permanently.

CHAPTER FORTY-FIVE

One Wish

Sidney

Three months later...

"My boys are pissed at me," Clooney Hennessy walks up beside me to say.

I have my forehead pressed to the cool glass window in his study. I slipped in here to collect myself. I haven't told Clay that I'm pregnant. I don't know why I'm so afraid.

"Give them time," I say in a whisper.

He reaches to rub my back. "Becoming a father is one of the greatest gifts in the world. Have you told him yet?"

"No, he still has so much on his plate," I answer.

"The world could be on his shoulders, but this would be the one thing to make it all right in his world. Tell him, Sid," he croons gently.

I inhale and turn to him. My eyes search my father-in-law's face. I can see what I know written all over it.

"Will you tell him you're dying?" I ask softly.

Surprise crosses his face before he erases all emotions. He looks down into his glass. My heart aches for him.

"How do you know?"

"I sort of overheard you and Wade talking. They're only going to be angrier if you don't tell them," I respond. I hadn't known it was Wade at the time, I figured that out after Clay told me he found out Wade is his brother.

"I have grandchildren now, my sons are finding their way as men, and this new treatment is promising. I'm not going to lie down easily. This isn't over until I say so," he says firmly.

I smile. "You Hennessy men would defy death and succeed."

"You're damn right. I still have years in me. I've been through worse. I'm not going to let some snot-nosed, wet-behind-the-ears doctor tell me my time is up," he huffs.

I cup my father-in-law's face. "You better be around. You're the only grandpa our little one has."

"Still keeping secrets, old man?" Clay's voice startles me. "And now you have my wife doing the same."

I turn to find Clayton, Gregor, and Cane all standing with their arms across their chests and scowls on their faces. Clooney made some gorgeous boys, that asshole Wade included.

Clooney takes my hand and kisses the back of it. "I will not speak life into that bullshit those doctors are trying to sell me. And I was just telling my daughter here it's time she shares with my favorite son that he'll be a father," he says the last part with humor in his voice.

"I knew it," Cane huffs.

"He told me the same thing last week. We're all his favorite when it's time to save his ass," Gregor grumbles.

"Come," Clay says, ignoring everyone else.

I move to him, feeling his strength from across the room. He wraps his arms around me as soon as I get close to him. I place my forehead on his chest. He gently caresses my back with his warm hands.

"I've been waiting to see how long it would take you to tell me," he whispers.

I look up at him with wide eyes. I part my lips, but I don't know what to say. I had no idea he knew.

"I know your body better than I know myself. I noticed weeks ago." He flashes a sexy smile down at me.

"Oh," is all I push out, drawing laughs from everyone around us.

"Let's celebrate," my father-in-law croons out.

"We're still going to talk," Gregor says firmly.

Clooney just waves him off and strolls out of the room. I laugh and go to follow, but Clayton holds me back. He watches until his brothers and father are out of the room, before he crushes my lips in a heated kiss.

"I love you," he says when he breaks the kiss, his hand splayed on my just-growing belly.

"I love you too," I purr back at him.

His eyes light up. He takes a pass over my lips with his thumb. A loving silence passes through us.

"Come on, the chest board is ready. I want to win my pride back." He chuckles.

"Good luck with that," I tease and wink at him.

He throws his head back and laughs. It's such a gorgeous sight. It all hits me. It truly sets in.

I'm married to Clayton Hennessy. I'm happy and having my own little family. I'll never let them go.

Revealing Thoughts

Clayton

"Did you see this coming?" Gregor murmurs behind his drink, nodding out toward the bride and groom.

"Not at all," I reply.

"So he had a hand in it all?" Gregor shakes his head.

"Yup." I shake mine as we stand in the midst of another wedding.

"I didn't think the old bastard had it in him." He chuckles in disbelief. "Goes to show not everything is what it seems."

"You can say that again," I grunt. "It's the only reason I allowed Sid to talk me out of strangling him."

"Forgiveness is a gift. You never know the other side of the story until you see it firsthand or experience it yourself and even then, you only have your perception and what your feelings tell you to feel," Gregor sighs.

"I guess you're right." I nod, thinking over his words and the last year.

"Sid looks about ready to pop. How does it feel?" My brother turns to me with a sparkle in his eyes.

"Another reason I've forgiven the old man. I'd do anything to make sure that kid is safe and happy. It won't make all my choices right, but my heart will be in the right place," I answer. "I think I finally understand him."

"Chloe is my world. I'd turn it upside down for her. Again and again," he says while staring across the garden at the little girl sitting in the laughing woman's lap.

"Which one?" I chuckle.

"Need you even ask? It's the same reply no matter which," Gregor answers and starts across the garden without another word.

"Hello, brother."

I turn my head to find Wade with a smug smile on his lips. I roll my eyes at him and shake my head.

"Hello, asshole," I say with a small grin.

"Is that any way to talk to your big brother?" he taunts.

"You're really getting a kick out of this, aren't you?"

"I'm just waiting for the love to kick in." He shrugs.

"That will kick in as soon as you stop helping the old man meddle," I toss back.

"My job is done." He shrugs. "His golden boys are all happy. I can slink off into the shadows now."

I pop him upside the back of his head. "Cut the bullshit pity party. Besides, the old man hasn't finished playing his games. Payback is a bitch, big brother." I laugh and walk off.

"I love you too," Wade calls after me.

I stop and turn. "Yeah, Wade, I do. You don't have to question that. Breathe, bro. We know you're one of us."

I see the relief in his eyes and the sag of his shoulders. Because my wife has made me a better man, I move forward and tug him into a hug. Wade returns the embrace tightly.

"Now admit it. I'm the best-looking brother," he says in my ear.

"Fuck you, asshole." I laugh and push him away.

"Oh, my God," my wife gasps, causing me to turn sharply.

I find her standing near Chloe and Gregor, her hands out at her sides, her eyes cast down at her feet, and her legs wet beneath her dress. She snaps her head up, her gaze wildly searching for me.

When our eyes meet, we have a silent conversation. I can see she's scared. She's been telling me for weeks she's not ready to give birth, she's petrified.

I tap my nose and watch as her eyes soften. Her little head bobs her trust. My chest swells. I have Sid and I have her trust. Now, we're going to have a baby.

ABOUT THE AUTHOR

Blue Saffire, award-winning, bestselling author of over thirty contemporary romance novels and novellas, writes with the intention to touch the heart and the mind. Blue hooks, weaves, and loops multiple series, keeping you engaged in her worlds. Blue writes for her own publishing company Perceptive Illusions as Blue Saffire as well as Royal Blue.

Blue and her husband live in a house filled with laughter and creativity, in Long Island, NY. Both working hard to build the Blue brand and cultivate their love for the artists. Creative is their family affair.

Blue holds an MBA in Marketing and Project Management, as well as an MED in Instructional Technology and Curriculum Design. She is also an NLP Master Practitioner.

ACKNOWLEDGMENTS

Every time I work on this book, it challenges me, but I love this couple so much. I love the way Clay loves Sid and I love the way Sid finds her trust in someone other than herself.

I thank everyone for their patience as I expanded this book and set the frame for more from the Lost Souls world. I love the Hennessys and plan to build out their world and finish it as soon as I can. I think you're going to love them as much as I do when I'm done.

To all of my readers, you are the best. I appreciate you more than you know. Your understanding that books are birthed and not spit out means the world to me. I have to write what my heart wants, and it's not always a straight path to what you all want. Thank you for the encouragement and patience.

This book would not even be, if not for one person in particular. My husband started *A Million to Blow,* and I took it and finished it for him when he threw in the towel and said how much respect he had for us authors in the game. LOL. Writing books is not as easy as writing songs, he finds. ROTF.

No matter what book I publish, God is leading my hands. I'm blessed to see, hear, and feel these books the way I do. I give all the glory to the Source of who I am. This is just the beginning. I lay it on the pages, this is who I am. Thank you, Lord.

On to the Next!! Gregor, *Let the tears begin!*

Wait, there is more to come! You can stay updated with my latest releases, learn more about me, the author, and be a part of contests by subscribing to my newsletter at
www.BlueSaffire.com
If you enjoyed *A Million To Blow*, I'd love to hear your thoughts and please feel free to leave a review. And when you do, please let me know by emailing me TheBlueSaffire@gmail.com or leave a comment on Facebook https://www.facebook.com/BlueSaffireDiaries or Twitter @TheBlueSaffire

Other books by Blue Saffire
Placed in Best Reading Order
Also available....
Legally Bound

Legally Bound 2: Against the Law

Legally Bound 3: His Law

Perfect for Me

Hush 1: Family Secrets

Legally Bound 5.5: Legally Unbound

Brothers Black 4: Braxton the Charmer

My Funny Valentine

Broken Soldier

Remember Me

Brothers Black 5: Felix the Brain

A Home for Christmas

Be My Valentine

Coming Soon...
A Million to Stay Book 2
The Ones Left Behind Book 3: Work Husband Series
Ox Book 5: The A**hole Club
Kelex 6: The A**hole Club

Work Husband Series
Unexcepted Lovers
My Best Friend's Wish
The Ones Left Behind...Coming soon...

The Lost Souls MC Series
Forever
Never
Always

Check out Blue Saffire exclusive on the
BlueSaffire.com website
Dom
The Fixer
Lost

Other books from Evei Lattimore Collection
Books by Blue Saffire
Black Bella 1

Destiny 1: Life Decisions
Destiny 2: Decisions of the Next Generation
Destiny 3 coming soon...

Star

Other books from Royal Blue Gay Romance
Collection written by Blue Saffire
Kyle's Reveal

Beau's Redemption

Work Husband Series

Lost Souls Series

⭐Forever: Book 1-Brick
⭐Never: Book 2 -Gutter
⭐Always: Books 3-King
Again: Book 4-Cage
Before 4.5- Thor
Sometimes: Book 5-Jackie
Lifetime: Book 6-Grim
Still: Book 7-Kevlar
Once: Book 8-Diggs, Axle, and Sugar
Now: Book 9 -Tracks
When: Book 10-Holden

BLUESAFFIRE.COM

Made in the USA
Las Vegas, NV
01 August 2022

52473067R00181